FUNERAL ON ICE

FUNERAL ON ICE

Dieter Abt

BLAKE

Published by Blake Publishing Ltd,
3 Bramber Court, 2 Bramber Road, London W14 9PB,
England

First published in Great Britain 1997

ISBN 1 85782 179 3

British Library Cataloguing-in-Publication Data:
A catalogue record for this book is available
from the British Library.

Typeset by BCP

Printed in Finland by WSOY

1 3 5 7 9 10 8 6 4 2

**The one who knows,
will always know**

ACKNOWLEDGEMENTS

My family;

Johnny Gold, to whom I am eternally grateful;

Jan Gold, whom I love dearly, as well as Kilburn Kate;

Gynette Brown, whose jokey loyalty kept me
laughing come what may;

Knautschi von Meister, who has taught me a new
sporty, healthy and fun way of life;

My friends in Gstaad: the Billy Mattis, the Friis-
Wheatcrofts, the Mimrans, the Lowes and the Donns;

Red Bond, thanks for looking after my dogs,
and Gabriella Matti for the photographs;

Graham and Margaret Beere,
my surrogate Irish parents;

Oliver Caffrey, his generous ways have no boundaries,
as well as the Wildings and the Tiveys;

and for all the other people who have supported and
helped me over the last few years, especially Harry
Travers, Mara and Lorenzo Berni, Roland Christen,
André Hoffmann, Vinzenz and Michaela von
Tscharner, as well as Christina and Antoine Spillman.

PROLOGUE

Behind the opaque windows of a white stretch limo, shipping heiress Maria Gisikis was washing down the aftertaste from her line of cocaine with a huge fluted glass of Cristal Roederer. Her twin brother John was rolling a £50 note into a straw in order to inhale the line of white powder on the glass table in front of him. Their aunt, the formidable matriarch Helena Kokas, was preoccupied with her own reflection in the small hand-mirror in which she was making up her face, adding a fresh application of red lipstick to her half-open mouth, followed by a quick spray of breath freshener and a couple of Valium.

The stretch limo drew up outside the imposing neo-Classical offices of the Gisikis family's law firm, Bradley & Bennett. On the pavement outside his law practice, Charles Bradley could see Wren's master-piece of St Paul's Cathedral. The magnificent dome dominated the City skyline, rising several hundred feet into the mist that covered London that autumn morning. Wren's Classical vision was built with the aid of the finest craftsmen of his day, he reflected. It was spoilt for him today by the accompanying press of paparazzi.

A fierce wind helped to yank open the heavy door of the vast automobile and pull it back aggressively on its hinges. From the pale leather interior, Helena Kokas emerged, a petite, immaculately dressed woman in her early sixties. Her Chanel suit, tasteful beige with the trademark gold buttons, was matched with a Gucci handbag and shoes. Her make-up was pure Dior with a splash of Paloma red lipstick. Her jewellery understated but with a price tag that carried a huge insurance premium.

As she emerged from the inner plushness of the limousine, a chill wind ripped ominously around the tall buildings of the City. In the ensuing crush, her lawyer found himself vying for Helena's attention with the jostling group of paparazzi, intent on snapping the glamorous socialite, joint heir to the Gisikis shipping fortune now that the death of her brother-in-law, Costas Gisikis, had hit the international headlines.

Helena Kokas was reportedly racked by grief, her distress hidden behind huge, dark, 'Jackie O' sunglasses. She brushed at her face as if to wipe away a tear. Alone among the assembly on the busy City street, Charles knew that any tears Helena might shed were for herself. She was tough and could out-act the best on the Hollywood 'A' list when it came to getting her own way. If sorrow were the part she had to play, she knew its every contour. As she stepped from the car, she stumbled, falling with exquisite grace and timing into Charles' outstretched arms, availing herself of yet another photo-opportunity — this is what she lived for.

As they followed their aunt, John and Maria Gisikis, Costas' first-born children, paused just long enough to allow the paparazzi the shots they needed for the following day's papers. Not as classically groomed as Helena, theirs was rock-star glamour, better suited to the front row of the Versace show during Paris couture week.

In spite of the cold, Maria was dressed in an eye-catching ruby-red beaded shift with impossibly high-heeled tiger-print slingbacks. Her bare flesh glittered with jewellery, and the deep V of her cleavage left little to the imagination. Behind her, John levered himself out of the car, straightening the jacket of his gleaming Versace suit, high-lapelled and worn with a black shirt and shimmering tie. On the little finger of his left hand, he wore a ruby-studded signet ring, which he rotated constantly with his thumb.

Skilled at romancing the world's Press, the Gisikis twins posed briefly on the pavement, smiling thinly behind their dark glasses, their ears trained to the motor-wind of the Press cameras. Once assured of tabloid coverage the next day, they walked briskly through the grand porticoed entrance. Behind them, Charles dealt with the Press cross-fire, repeating his two-word response, 'No comment', like a mantra.

From the luxurious penthouse offices of Bradley & Bennett the views across the Thames were spectacular, and John remarked on it with uncustomary civility. Maria draped herself almost too casually over one of the vast red-leather Chesterfields. She chewed determinedly on her lip-gloss and picked at her talon-like nail extensions, flexing and tensing her fingers as she did so. Helena had immediately made her excuses and disappeared to the washroom. On her return, she'd added yet more powder and lipstick to a face that, for her age, was eerily free of lines. She stood gazing imperiously out of the window and watched a plane bound for Heathrow Airport circling overhead. She wished herself up there, away from all this.

Helena's confidence was normally immutable, but she couldn't stop a gnawing doubt as her mind raced here, there and everywhere. Costas' Will. Could any changes have been made to it without her knowledge? She'd kept a steely grip on his vast fortune so far, and had maintained her hold over him through thick and thin, but now? She felt a shiver of uncertainty as she contemplated the unthinkable.

The half-hearted small-talk in the room had petered out into an uneasy silence. John twisted his signet ring nervously, and Maria got up from the sofa and paced the room, her attention drawn to a photograph of her father with Charles Bradley outside the Reform Club in Pall Mall. It hung next to a small Matisse.

As they followed Charles into the chandeliered and mahogany board room, Helena could barely conceal her gasp of astonishment. Kimberley Gisikis and her brat, Oliver. What the hell were they doing here? Kimberley had just arrived that morning from New York, Charles announced by way of explanation, in a vain attempt to gloss over Helena's animosity.

Helena had not seen Kimberley since the funeral. Her hostility toward the younger woman was historic and histrionic. Kimberley knew her own mind too much for Helena's liking and held no sway over the spirited, articulate American, just as she had held no leverage over Kimberley's husband, George Gisikis, Helena's youngest nephew. He had always resisted Helena's dubious charms. Charles Bradley had never had much trouble seeing through George's aunt either. But his feelings towards her had changed from amused indifference to her gold-digging to fury at his exclusion by her from Costas' bedside during his time in hospital. Incarcerated in the intensive care unit at the Baltic, Athens' most expensive private hospital, the tycoon had been protected there by an array of armed security guards.

Charles could not forgive Helena for this. His dearest friend, his staunchest ally, the man alongside whom he had worked and played for more than 30 years, during all life's highs and lows, Costas had needed him most then. As Helena feigned interest in her great nephew and his mother, her composure now restored, she would soon discover that Charles Bradley had learnt patience in life, too clever and dignified for cheap stabs at revenge.

As he sat across the table from them, Charles focused for a moment on John and Maria. All cash and no class, he thought. Just a couple of rich kids, who knew the price of everything and the value of nothing. He watched them grow jumpy. Trained to observe such things, he saw John's foot tap incessantly under the table and his hand shake as he poured a coffee for his sister. It slopped into the saucer, and John swore under his breath with frustration. The foot tapping grew more frantic.

Then, when Charles had phoned through to invite his senior partners to the meeting, Maria had demanded to know why they needed to be present. Charles refused to be drawn; impassively, he told her the truth: this was the wish of her late father.

Subsequently, he had enjoyed the worried exchange of looks among the twins and the monstrous Helena that followed. As far as they knew, Costas had never mentioned any special conditions, but this only served to heighten their rising paranoia. After all,

Costas had always been meticulous in the handling of his affairs. There was always a reason for everything he did.

The tension in the room finally defeated John. Hot coffee splashed over the table-top as he banged his fist down on it hard. In a voice strangled by suppressed rage, he yelled, 'Just get on with it, will you? We haven't got all day!'

Helena Kokas turned pale with fury at her nephew's sudden loss of control. She lashed out at him fiercely reverting to her native Greek and then, trembling at her own outburst, reached down to retrieve her handbag from beneath her chair. Her hands shook as she swallowed a small blue pill. John excused himself at once and left the room, closely followed by Maria.

Charles Bradley watched the show with apparent indifference and continued to shuffle deliberately, carefully, slowly through the pile of papers in front of him. He had an innate ability to command most situations. His natural authority and gladiatorial prowess in the court room were legendary. Today was no different for him, except for the deep bond, almost a blood tie, and immutable loyalty he felt for Costas, who had entrusted him with this, his final act from beyond the grave. It had to be the performance of Charles Bradley's life.

In the bathroom where he had gone to restore himself, John sat on the floor of the toilet and chopped away with a razor blade at a line of the best cocaine that money could buy. He used the cream plastic toilet lid as a chopping board. As he snorted the snow-white powder up his nose, he rose to his feet and twirled around in the small cubicle. He was so close to the Gisikis billions. They were his by right — his birthright. No one would stand in his way.

Maria met her brother in the corridor. She was shaking like a leaf, perspiring yet shivering cold. He pulled an ampoule from his pocket and split it in two, giving one half to his twin. She swallowed it with a swig of Hine from a small, solid silver hip flask that John carried in his breast pocket. Then the Gisikis twins returned to the meeting together. That was how they had always worked best — as a team, as a unit — and Helena had nurtured this in them. Together, they believed themselves to be unbeatable.

Charles Bradley was aware as he began to speak that the moment belonged to Costas Gisikis. He even felt the presence of the spirit of his oldest friend beside him at the table — it was almost tangible. Costas was there with him now as he had always been in life. Rarely out of control, Charles began to feel overwhelmed by the strength of his emotions. But he knew he had to keep his feelings to himself. After all, like Costas, he believed revenge was best left in the hands of God, or destiny.

CHAPTER ONE

It was March, and the cherry trees that fringed Chester Road in London's Regent's Park Inner Circle would soon be in bloom. Costas Gisikis, a heavily built, characterful man in the last years of late middle age, looked around him at the world about to break into a glorious English spring. How could he be dying, he thought, when there was so much promise and vitality in the air?

He stood at the top of the steps of his heart specialist's large Georgian house on Harley Street, the late 18th-century street so popular a century and a half ago with successful doctors and specialists. It was a rich residential area then; 150 years later the doctors' practices had stayed and lent the street an air of calm unusual for central London. The street ran from Marylebone Road to New Cavendish Street, sandwiched between the tranquillity of Regent's Park and the mania of Oxford Street.

William Gladstone, that great British Liberal statesman of the 19th century, had lived here. Gladstone had died at Hawarden, north Wales, and was buried at Westminster Abbey in 1898. Born in Liverpool, the one-time Prime Minister had died just over the border from his native England. A century later, Costas Gisikis faced his own death thousands of miles from his own homeland of Greece. Rare blood group. Next to no chance of finding a suitable donor. High likelihood of rejection of donor organ. The consultant's words echoed incessantly, like a dull ache in his head.

He was one year past the threshold of his allotted three-score-years-and-ten and, as he'd crossed the decade from his sixties into his seventies, he'd known then that his health was failing. He suffered from all the classic symptoms of a person with heart problems — pains in the chest, frequent breathlessness — but he was too busy to go for a check-up. He had a shipping empire to run, for Christ's sake! What time did that give him to worry about his health?

Ever the fatalist, Costas had always known that he'd go when his time was up, called in like a rowing boat in summer on a suburban boating lake. There was nothing he could do about that; not even his enormous wealth could buy him out of that one. When the heart specialist broke the news to him, he'd already prepared himself. He had to accept that he had, at most, five years to live. He could go at any time.

Costas prided himself on being a realist. And he knew there was absolutely nothing he could do to save his own life. This was his toughest challenge, graciously to accept what could not be overcome.

His feelings churned and swirled like a whirlpool, threatening to drag him down. Yes, he'd accepted that he had to die, but that didn't mean he wasn't devastated by the reality of it. When he recalled what his specialist had said to him — 'I'm so sorry, Mr Gisikis, but your condition is untreatable' — he felt a hard knot of pain in his solar plexus. For the first time in years, he wanted to cry.

As he climbed into the Silver Cloud Rolls Royce waiting for him in Harley Street, Costas asked his chauffeur, Victor Aspinall, to drive him into Regent's Park. There he could gather his thoughts and attempt to salvage what was left of his life.

As one of the world's wealthiest individuals, Costas Gisikis had been ranked among them, the Onassis and Niarchos dynasties, the Guinnesses and the Goldsmiths, for longer than he could remember. He wore his immense fortune well.

And he had rightly earned his reputation as a compassionate and caring man, with a cool business sense, whose success hadn't changed him. His charitable foundation for the homeless was now a global operation that thrived alongside other offshoots of his shipping empire.

As they skirted the southern edge of the park, past the rows of Nash terraces, Costas asked Victor to drop him at York Gate. He'd walk over York Bridge and along the Broad Walk to reach the London Zoo exit near Prince Albert Road. Victor should meet him there, just the other side of the Regent's Canal. From there, they could drive straight up to Hampstead.

Costas usually enjoyed the rural charms of this most beautiful of London's royal parks, an oasis of calm in a frenzied city. It was an area of land that had become enclosed as a park in 1812. One of London's prime architects of the period, John Nash, had devised its master plan with the surrounding curved terraces, to be built in a variety of Classical styles. Although only part of Nash's overall scheme was executed, it was enough to escape the sprawling concrete.

But, today, Costas was oblivious to its beauty. Distracted, he walked for a while before sitting down to rest on a bench just off the Broad Walk. In the distance, across the swathes of close-cut grass that doubled in the summer as football and volleyball pitches, for games of cricket and rounders, his eye was caught by the glint of gold from the dome of the London Central Mosque, surrounded by trees on the edge of the park.

The Midas Touch. That was what he had. Everything he touched turned to gold. He had never planned to be a rich man. Perhaps that was why God had bestowed wealth upon him. On Myra, the island in the Dodecanese where he was born, a land of pine woods and fertile fields, he'd herded goats, with his sole ambition at the age of 15 to own a few animals himself. The island had become depopulated over the years, and a decade ago Costas had bought some land there. Now he owned most of it. As he sat staring across the green and pleasantness of the English parkland, he decided that he would like to return to Myra before he died.

He levered himself up stiffly from the park bench and continued along the Broad Walk, past the edge of the zoo. A pack of wolves paced behind double rows of wire netting, curved at the top to keep them in and the curious out. Notices warned against feeding, but there was always somebody throwing bread across the short, scrub-grass security strip and into the wolves' run. Thrown to the wolves. Is that what would happen to Gisikis Shipping when he died? He stood and watched the animals encircling the open-air cage. Ruthless, greedy, out for what they could get.

The scene wasn't too foreign to Costas. There were people in his family like that. All of those vices would no doubt come to the fore once they knew their inheritance was almost within reach.

Alone in the park, his mind raced. His affairs were in good order. He'd made provision for his family. His shipping empire could still be run profitably when he was no longer at the helm. He had made sure of it. Or had he? And he ran through his business affairs in his head, looking for loopholes, anything he might have missed. He'd built everything from scratch. The company was like a child to him, and concern about it now a welcome diversion from his fear of dying.

Costas' thoughts turned to his family: his twins, John and Maria, his firstborn children. Like Romulus and Remus, a she-wolf, Helena Kokas had come to feed them with her milk. His sister-in-law had taken over their care on the death of Costas' wife, Ariana, in a plane crash.

Costas had blamed himself for this for years. The twin-engined Piper was one of the smallest among his fleet of planes. It was he who had asked Ariana to fly to Athens to help him to entertain at an important business meeting.

On the way back to their rural retreat on Hydra, where she'd been spending the summer with the children, the plane had crashed. The black flight box was never found, and Costas was haunted by the belief that, had his aircraft been better serviced, had he not asked her to assist him at that meeting, had he not ... had he not ... his wife would still be alive.

Deranged by his loss, Costas became aware of what was happening to his family only when it was too late. The twins were indulged and spoilt by their aunt. Her own marriage had ended in divorce, shortly after she had suffered a miscarriage only a year before Ariana had died. And so Helena became obsessive about the twins. Physically, they were like their mother and bore more than a passing resemblance to their aunt. Looking at them, they could have passed as her own children.

In John and Maria, Helena had found the babies she had lost. And so she poured into them all her thwarted ambitions. She lived for them, manipulating Costas, too grief-stricken to care, to get her own way.

The beautiful, unusual Gisikis twins became Helena's showpiece. And as they grew up, Helena moulded them in her own image, weeding out friends she considered unsuitable. No one, she insisted, was good enough for the Gisikis family. They came to rely entirely on each other and upon Helena, whose control over them was despotic, albeit in the guise of benevolence.

The twins had to have the best of everything. When they were very young it was a full wardrobe of designer miniatures from Chanel or Dior, special foods flown in daily from exotic locations to indulge some health benefit that Helena had heard about. Later, there were the expensive, foreign tutors and endless travel to far-flung locations to improve their minds and assuage Helena's wanderlust.

Helena couldn't settle. Costas paid the bills for winter skiing at Klosters and Verbier; for Caribbean spring idylls; summer months on the French Riviera. Helena never knew what drove her, and she soon tired of wherever she was, of whatever company she kept.

As the twins grew older, they learnt to make their own demands. At the age of ten, John had his own scaled-down Ferrari, custom made for him. Maria had her clothes designed in Paris and Milan, where she flew for fittings each season from the age of 12.

They mixed with their aunt's friends, whose values were seasonal, whose morality was flexible, like the gold Diners and Visa cards they flashed everywhere they went.

George, John and Maria's brother, was just one year old when his mother died. He looked like his father, and even at so young an age he had inherited Costas' trait of not suffering fools gladly. His aunt had no time for him, nor he for her.

He was left in the care of his nanny, excluded from trips with the twins and Helena, always dismissed as too young to be allowed to join them. He was Helena's scapegoat for all of life's failings, while the twins were the jewel in her crown.

George was a serious child, no doubt affected by losing his mother when he was so young. He had about him a solemnity that belied his age. His habit of fixing people with a penetrating stare did nothing to endear him to his aunt, who disliked scrutiny of any kind. But George's was a thoughtful nature, and he had nothing to hide. Left to his own devices, George thrived, learning everything about those things that money can't buy.

Over time, as Costas recovered from the loss of his wife, he tried to spend more time with his children. But John and Maria were often away with Helena, tutors in tow, to yet another prestigious and glamorous engagement in London or New York, Milan or Monaco, or a smart party in Hydra or aboard a yacht.

And so Costas and George were thrown together. And the little boy became Costas' favourite child. He would be driven to the offices of Gisikis Shipping after school and sit around his father's offices, amusing himself for hours. He was sometimes accompanied by his best friend, Paul Mavros, from whom George had become inseparable since the age of seven. The children grew up together. Paul, the only child of a port policeman in Piraeus and George, effectively an only child by dint of circumstance, were like brothers.

In his teens, George would go to the docks at Piraeus with Costas to meet the men who worked the ships: stevedores and sailors, office shipping clerks and managers. And he and Paul Mavros often accompanied Costas to the ouzo bars and kebab restaurants there, amid the high grey buildings and dusty activity of one of the Mediterranean's busiest ports, drinking Metaxa and coffee on the waterfront at Mikrolimano.

Now George was married and living in New York. He was obviously in daily contact with Costas, but, more surprisingly, given his hectic work life and the separation of continents, he had made the effort to stay in touch with Mavros, who was now working for the port police like his father. Costas liked that quality of loyalty in his son, even though George saw his old friend only irregularly now, heavily preoccupied with running the North American arm of Gisikis Shipping from its headquarters in New York, as well as overseeing the Homelessness Project. But from time to time over the years, they met over an ouzo.

Both men had families. But this time it was the Gisikis clan that had only the one child. Costas' grandson, Oliver, was about to turn 17. And all Costas could think was that he might not be alive for that birthday.

Costas walked out of the park and over the Grand Union Canal. As he made his way towards the south-eastern corner of Primrose Hill and Regent's Park Road, where Victor had parked the Rolls, he didn't notice that his face was wet with tears.

His chauffeur knew better than to comment. He drove north-west between the smart inner-city suburbs of St John's Wood and Primrose Hill via the bizarrely named Swiss Cottage, so called because of the early Victorian construction of a Swiss chalet in its midst, to the aloofness of Hampstead on its high ridge to the north of the city. This was one of London's most desirable residential areas, in essence an unspoilt Georgian village, perched awkwardly on a hilltop, with its broad area of open heath to the north.

Victor manoeuvred the bulky Rolls through its familiar, narrow streets, heading up Heath Street to the cramped, triangular junction by the Underground Station that was backed up as usual with a queue of traffic. The roads squeezed tightly here between the buildings until opening out by Whitestone Pond.

By the old white milestone, he turned off towards the Gisikis mansion that bordered on to Hampstead Heath. The heath stretched out from its boundary in three square miles of uninterrupted hills and meadows, woods, ponds and lakes. It was, in effect, a magnificent extension to Costas' own considerable acreage.

Victor watched Costas discreetly in the rear-view mirror. He had never seen him so preoccupied, nor his face such a conflict of emotion. He wanted to reach out to help him. But he did not know how.

As Costas handed his coat to the maid in the entrance hall, he just didn't experience that surge of relief and elation he normally enjoyed when he got home. He felt detached from his surroundings, as if some inner mechanism had come into operation to shield him from the bad news.

He went straight to the library and shut the door, asking not to be disturbed. In the book-lined red room, he sat at his desk for a few moments, his head in his hands. Then slowly, deliberately, he dialled the telephone number of his old friend, confidant and lawyer, Charles Bradley.

He made a lot of calls that night, and it was midnight before he came off the phone. Around one in the morning, Charles was ushered into the library by one of the night staff. Costas spent the silent hours between then and dawn in conference with his friend. Most of all, they discussed the advice Costas had received from his tax consultants. He should re-establish his residency in Greece to avoid UK tax liabilities, and to ensure that his family and his homeland would benefit most from his demise.

For the past few years, Costas had used London as his operational base. The city had become his second home. He loved all that it had to offer: his friends, of course; the Heath, certainly; his club, the Reform; the *haute cuisine* of Le Gavroche; Centre Court at Wimbledon fortnight; Test Cricket at Lord's, where he often entertained business acquaintances; and his beloved Royal Opera House to enjoy Pavarotti or Domingo. Memories of his life in London unreeled in his mind's eye like a spool of film, reminding him of all he would relinquish.

But he'd let it go. All of it. He had no choice. And he would enjoy spending the remains of his days back on his native soil. He had paid his dues in Britain. But enough was enough.

His choices were these: he could stay in London, maintaining his British residency and leave the bulk of assets to the UK tax authorities — undesirable; he could settle his estate on his family before his death — unthinkable; he could move back to his vast estates near Athens, where after three years he would be free of any overseas tax obligations — tenable. He decided to fly south.

CHAPTER TWO

In London, Costas had always attended Moscow Road's Greek Orthodox Cathedral, Aghia Sophia, in Bayswater and gone on for late supper at his favourite Greek restaurant in London, Kalamaras in Inverness Mews. But not this year. In any case, the restaurant was under new management now, and he wasn't so committed to his usual routine, his nod at his Greek roots in an otherwise cosmopolitan life.

Costas stood in a white silk robe on the second-floor terrace balcony of his palatial Athenian mansion. Even in the height of summer, the climate could be chilly in Greece, especially when the wind was blowing. But there was no wind, and it was mid-morning in late March. The sun was bright, but not baking.

From where he stood, he could see the vast plane tree in the palace grounds. He would go down later and drink coffee in its majestic shade. For now, he could hardly believe he was home.

He'd flown into the West Terminal of Athens' Ellinikon Airport the previous night on an Olympic Airlines Boeing 747 from Heathrow. His secretary in London had organised his travel, as he'd wanted to return immediately, and none of his private jets was available.

Costas' London housekeeper had packed the few things he needed. His PA had notified the family to attend an urgent meeting in Athens. Helena, John and Maria would fly in from an unknown destination (why should they tell me what they're up to?' Costas wondered. 'After all, I'm only paying the bills ...') and George and Kimberley would arrive from new York. Charles was tying up a few critical ends for him. In his capacity as Costas' lawyer and friend, he had offered to join him in Athens.

Costas breathed a sigh of relief and thanked God for Charles. His life had changed so dramatically within the last 24 hours that it was important to know that there were some stars that remain fixed in the firmament.

And he'd always enjoyed Charles' company — a business lunch or an evening meeting at the Club, occasional family celebrations, which Charles attended in his honorary capacity as George's godfather. It was true to say that business matters had dominated their relationship over the past few years but, nevertheless, theirs was an enduring companionship founded on mutual respect and affection. As far as Costas was concerned, one thing was certain — when a person's wealth surpasses his own wildest dreams, there has to be someone on whom one can rely absolutely.

Which was how it was with Charles. Costas worried sometimes that he had would never be able to repay him for all the loyalty he had shown him over the years. Just now it was a time of reckoning.

As Costas gazed appreciatively over his palatial grounds, his thoughts wandered as he considered how strange it was that one could appreciate some people all of the time and other people none of the time. He was thinking in particular of Helena's chauffeur who had collected him from Ellinikon the previous night.

Frank Porter. From London's East End, not a true Cockney born within the sound of the church bells of Wren's St Mary-le-Bow in Cheapside. More Bethnal Green than Bow bells. Where had Helena found him? Now he remembered. Frank had worked as a bouncer in one of the West End clubs the twins liked to frequent. Yes, that's right. They'd introduced him to Helena.

Frank respected the moneyed classes. The middle classes and their moralising he could live without. Money mattered to Frank. He had a nose for it. And Helena had made it worth his while to fuss around her at all times, especially when she went out to face her public. Frank was a good-looking, muscular man, squarely built with broad shoulders and a thick, bullish neck. He looked the part.

It crossed Costas' mind that the chauffeur's duties sometimes took him out of the driving seat and into Helena's circular, satin-sheeted bed. But it was only a hunch. He had no hard evidence. Nor did it concern him anyway. He'd no moral hold over Helena. She'd helped him through a difficult phase of his life, and he'd regretted ever since allowing her so much power and influence over his family.

But Frank made Costas' skin crawl. He couldn't bear the man. His sycophancy, the smarmy solicitude, the incessantly inane small-talk. The over-elaborate, starched, stiff grey uniform with red braid trim, complete with a stiff-peaked hat, that Helena insisted he should wear when on duty.

Costas knew that it wasn't really fair of him to

dislike the man so intently, but it was the way Frank embodied Helena's pretentions, her appalling snobbery and hunger for material status that ate away at Costas' sensibilities. And Frank was not an honourable man. He had no scruples. But then neither was Helena honourable. And nor did she.

Costas chastised himself inwardly for harbouring uncharitable thoughts about Frank. After all, the chauffeur was unfailingly polite to him and certainly knew his job well enough. The car was always immaculate, polished like glass, and he knew his way around Athens, all the back streets and cut-throughs, as if he'd lived there all his life. This was essential in Athens, a hair-raising city in which to drive. Athenians had a singular disregard for any of the conventions of motoring. While horn-blowing was forbidden there, when the lights changed to green you'd never have believed hooting was illegal.

They'd driven along Amalia Avenue in the centre of town past Hadrian's Arch, an isolated marble gateway that once marked the limit of the ancient city and which was now part of one of the busiest traffic zones of modern Athens. Costas' thoughts drifted back to Helena. No, it was she who got to Costas through Frank. Needled him. Her pomposity, her ridiculous social climbing, her warped morality. What mattered to Helena was how things looked. She appeared never to want to see anything deeper than that.

When the stretch limo had driven through the electronic gates of Costas' mansion, set in five acres of grounds, there was the parade ground of servants to greet him. As if his peace hadn't been shattered enough.

It was first tested at the airport because of all the Press attention he'd received, presumably alerted by Frank's high-profile arrival, and then by the chauffeur's polite chit-chat. Did you have a good flight, Mr Gisikis? The weather here is so much better than London. Well, of course it damn well was.

But on his arrival at the house, when he just needed to be alone, there was the household circus out to meet him. As the car drew up outside the porticoed entrance, there they all stood, the scene lit up in the automatic security lights like a set from *Dynasty* or *Dallas*.

Who were all these people? This was his home for God's sake, not the ostentatious Ledra Marriott with its luxurious add-ons or the indisputable marble grandeur of the Grande Bretagne, where the crowned heads of Europe stayed when in Athens. What were they doing here?

The house was empty for large parts of the year, but Helena liked it to be ready, fully staffed, so she could impress some hapless new acquaintance at a moment's notice. Come and spend the weekend with us in Athens, darling, she'd suggest casually to someone she'd just happened to sit next to at a smart dinner party. Someone who might be of use to her, or might amuse and distract her for a while.

So a private jet would be wheeled out, the mansion shutters raised by the servants who resided in permanent quarters in the grounds, and favourite foods and wines would be flown in from around the world. The party would last a few days and then self-destruct in an orgy of sex and drugs and sensual excess. When no one got up until late afternoon, or slept until dawn or ever went to bed alone. And so Helena had instructed her twins.

The car door flew open as soon as the limo drew to a halt and a member of Helena's staff, someone he'd never seen before (wearing white gloves, for Christ's sake!) helped him out and welcomed him home. Did sir have any luggage he needed unpacking straight away?

Costas did not. He explained, almost apologetically, that he had only one small piece, albeit a monogrammed Louis Vuitton overnight bag, a birthday present from Helena. This he would carry himself. Thank you. And he strode off, dismissively, running up the steps of the neo-Classical mansion two at a time. He forgot how this made his heart race, and he sighed as he clutched at his chest. He'd always been so active.

Costas' arrival was in sharp contrast to the glamorous shows staged by Helena whenever she flew in for a few days. For a weekend stay she always travelled with luggage sufficient to sink the Titanic, much of it made up of her selection of shoes, her weakness.

Embarrassed by the line of household staff, Costas rushed past them and into the vast entrance hall, a construction resplendent in marble, grey and red and as hard as steel, from the Saronic islet of Dokos near Hydra. Costas had refurbished the house as much as possible using local materials. He always wanted to acknowledge his roots. Nothing and no one was ever taken for granted just because he was now as rich as Croesus.

With great wealth came responsibilities. And

Croesus was celebrated for the extravagance of the offerings he made at the Temple at Delphi, although they were given in a placatory spirit, as if to apologise for his greed in having accumulated so much at the expense of others.

Costas had packed very few items for his journey. His vital effects, both personal and professional, would arrive with Charles Bradley. What he did bring fitted easily into his one bag. Obviously he'd left in a hurry and, in his current state of mind, what he was going to wear had not been a priority. He'd never been overly attached to his material wealth, and now it had lost much of its scant appeal. Without wanting to appear in the least graceless, he wondered just how many bottles of cologne and towelling robes, Savile Row suits and John Lobb shoes did any one person need? His family were what really mattered, his friends, his acquaintances. But sometimes people failed you.

Costas left the terrace to bathe and dress before his guests started to arrive. When he'd finished this evening, when he'd told the family of his plans, he'd like to take off with George for the coast and Glyfada, to eat in a modest sea-front restaurant, just the two of them, just like old times. The holiday season was beginning, there'd be something open at the resort. At least you could breathe the air there, escape the gas bowl of Athens.

As he levered himself up out of the jacuzzi, Costas glanced at the ornate grandfather clock that stood at the entrance to his walk-in Molteni closet. It was one possession he treasured, a gift from his wife Ariana on their wedding anniversary, at the point when Gisikis Shipping had started to take off, when they'd begun to be able to afford to spend money on luxuries. It was of sentimental as much as symbolic value. If only Ariana had lived to enjoy it and all the other benefits life had brought him. He felt his life had been blessed in so many ways.

A rhythmic 'rat-at-at-tat' broke through his reflections. Before he had time to say 'Come in', the huge doors to his bedroom apartments burst open. It was his grandson Oliver. Who'd have believed it? Costas beamed with surprise as the young man rushed toward him, his arms outstretched. He hadn't expected the boy to be able to take time off from school. He was trying for a place at Harvard and the competition was fierce, requiring great attention to his studies.

But there he stood, all 6ft of him, a handsome, strapping 16-year-old, so like George at that age. And there, framed in the doorway behind him, was George, Costas' youngest son. He felt tears well up in his eyes as the three of them embraced warmly in the centre of his bedroom.

Eventually, George pulled away to give his father a long, questioning look.

'Not now,' Costas cautioned. 'We'll discuss everything later. In the library when you've had time to rest after your journey. Please make yourselves comfortable.'

With an excess of formality that hid his true feelings, he encouraged them gently towards the door. He wanted no one to have the advantage of prior warning. They would all have to face things together. Costas turned towards the huge French windows and thought how he'd suffered intolerable hardships in his life. He'd lost his wife who meant the world to him.

He'd come from a small island in the eastern Aegean to become one of the richest men on earth. But what of it? In the end, it was only earth to earth, ashes to ashes.

Through the huge windows of his bedroom he saw a flash of red and silver in the sky. The helicopter. Helena, Maria and John had arrived. A can of worms. It circled round and approached the helipad on the flat roof of the annex. Hell, he thought, was about to land on earth.

The library was out of bounds to Helena. Her decorative whims had stopped at the other side of the door, so it remained, as it had always been, a solemn, dignified room with no sign of the ostentation that predominated in the rest of the house. As well as Costas' rows and rows of books, neatly ordered on shelves that lined the walls from floor to ceiling, it housed his priceless red-and-black-figured pottery vases.

The remaining wall space was hung with Costas' fine collection of Italian baroque painting — Guercino, Poussin — work that was full of passion but which came, nevertheless, from a heart that was ruled by the head. The darkness of the paintings gave the impression that something was being held back, however brilliant the technique.

Helena was waiting for Costas in her usual seat with her back to the window. She was obsessive about everyone and everything being in its place. And this was her chair in the library whenever she was invited there by her brother-in-law. Perhaps she liked to know that she was set against the magnificence of the grounds outside and she certainly cherished the advantage of having the light behind her.

Costas had to look twice to realise what she'd done to herself. Her normally jet-black hair had been bleached to a dark, heavy blonde. Normally, Costas had grudgingly to concede that Helena's taste, though more extravagant than his own, was impeccable. But this latest transformation left him feeling uneasy; it just didn't suit her.

'Costas, darling, how lovely to see you,' Helena purred at him, holding out her arms slightly in greeting, as if any further effort might exhaust her, and making no attempt to stir from the depths of her red-leather chair, a reproduction Louis XIV, but nevertheless an expensive one.

Costas walked over to his sister-in-law and leaned down to accept her proffered kiss, made in the air on either side of his cheeks. Apart from the hair, Helena looked good in a simple, well-tailored red dress — Coco meets Jackie O — her lips, fingernails and shoes, on tiny, pointy heels, its exact colour match.

Around her neck she wore a diamond-and-ruby necklace. Her hair was swept back elegantly in a French twist and on each earlobe nestled a huge diamond set in a solid gold setting. On her finger was a diamond as big as the Ritz or, more accurately, one that would have given the Burtons a run for their money. Her wrist was encircled by an exquisitely narrow platinum-and-diamond watch. Helena reeked of Costas' money.

Helena's attention to detail paid dividends when it came to her appearance, enhanced by her obsession to keep her figure. If her face looked 20 years her junior, her body matched it. With her personal trainer, she spent each morning putting herself through a demanding exercise routine, a hybrid of the Pilates so beloved, she'd heard, by Madonna.

And then there was the bucket of vitamins and minerals that she took with the fervour of a religious convert every day before, after and during meals. Her latest find was Amla 49, made up of Indian gooseberry, or Amla, a sour-tasting berry packed with vitamin C, combined with a zillion other compounds. Everyone in Hollywood, Demi Moore included, was taking it. Ayurveda was an ancient Indian way of keeping healthy, and it seemed the more ancient, the more obscure the health system, the better. Full of eastern promise for Western despair.

Helena stirred in her chair and raised her arms again, more purposefully this time, and gestured towards the open French windows. As she did so, the sunlight caught her jewels, and she sparkled like one of the Christmas trees that line the designer boulevards in Paris in December.

'Costas, darling, come and say hello to your children.'

Outside on the patio, walking towards him from the direction of the swimming pool, John and Maria appeared, clad only in thick towelling robes over their swimwear.

'Hi,' they said in passing, as if they'd just seen him an hour ago at breakfast. 'We'll be with you shortly.' And they indicated their wet hair and general *déshabillé* as they trailed across the priceless Oriental rugs in their bare feet as if they had not a care, indeed all the time, in the world.

Costas had not, in fact, seen either John or Maria for several months. The last time they'd met had not been auspicious. He'd had to bail them out of some scheme they'd got themselves into, importing hand-made ornaments from India, reams of stuffed birds on beaded strings. But it turned out that the birds were filled with something more noxious than shredded rags and paper. Costas had had to put his reputation on the line to get them out of that one.

As the twins went up to change into dry clothes, George and Oliver appeared with Kimberley, who'd crept up behind Costas, blindfolding his eyes with her hands.

'Guess who?' she asked in her unmistakable New Jersey accent. Laughing, Costas replied, 'Well, Kimberley, I'd never have known it was you!?' And he pulled her round to rock her firmly in both his arms. Costas' voice was joyful as he said, 'Well, this is what I call a family gathering.'

They all sat talking for some time before Costas asked Helena if she could chase up John and Maria. 'I have something important to discuss, and I want you all here.' His tone was chastising, frustrated by the delay. It was well past mid-afternoon now. He wanted this over with. Suddenly irritated, he got up to pour himself a drink, a shot of rare old Macallan, his favourite malt whisky. He knew he shouldn't, but a little wouldn't do him any harm.

Helena prised herself out of her chair, muttering loudly about how Costas should have rung for the staff.

'Quicker to do it myself,' he countered, offering a general invitation for drinks and snacks. This time he buzzed the intercom and summoned the butler. They were all imbibing their drinks and enjoying seafood *mezedes* when John and Maria appeared.

'What kept you?' Costas asked. 'This meeting was

called for my convenience, not yours.'

For once, the twins looked suitably contrite. They knew better than to antagonise their father. Don't bite the hand that feeds you, Helena had always cautioned them never paying much attention to her own advice.

With his colour higher than it should have been, Costas walked over to his mahogany, roll-top secretaire and pressed the intercom button on the wall to the right of it, partially hidden by the folds of a Gobelins tapestry. He requested that Charles Bradley should be shown to the library as soon as he arrived. From one of the drawers of the escritoire he took out a roll of paper, encircled by a gold ribbon, which he placed on top of the writing desk.

Helena expressed surprise on hearing that Charles was to join them. There was no love lost between her and the lawyer. Too much murky water had flowed under the bridge for Charles to trust a word she said any more. They were constantly in communication about Helena's extravagances. She always wanted more money, an increase in her allowances.

'Oh, God,' she exhaled forcibly, 'then it's not a social occasion. Just tedious business?' Her question was rhetorical, and Costas left it hanging there unanswered in the air. Nobody said anything.

She went on regardless, 'You realise we're missing a party on the yacht, that we're hosting. It's so embarrassing.'

George felt himself shiver all of a sudden, as if someone had just opened a window in the room, and he was sitting in an unexpectedly cold through-draught. His thoughts began to race.

He'd known that to be summoned out of the blue to attend a family conference in Athens augured something ominous, but he'd pushed any speculation to the back of his mind and encouraged Kimberley to do likewise. His father could be whimsical. He'd left it at that. Now, fear churned him up. He felt sick in the pit of his stomach.

Costas must have sensed his youngest son's distress. He glanced over at him, concerned, then at the twins, who were glued to John's Gameboy, playing it with the sound turned off. At least that showed a token of respect. Usually it sounded like an amusement arcade around them. But they were too insensitive to notice.

Charles Bradley stretched out in the front seat of the red Porsche that had collected him from Ellinikon. The car was just another example of Helena's ability to spend Costas' money, and she couldn't even drive. It was cramped in there with Costas' papers and essential luggage as well as his own.

Charles saw the wrought-iron gates of the Gisikis mansion ahead, and he opened his briefcase to find his sunglasses. The Porsche's light-sensitive windows had absorbed all the glare, but he was about to step out into a bright, sunny afternoon. He reached into the pocket of his smart light-weight jacket for a handkerchief to wipe away the beads of perspiration that were threatening to break as soon as he left the air-conditioning of the car. Really, it wasn't that hot, but he was feeling anxious and nervous, too.

Charles made a mental note that he'd be expecting many more trips to Greece now that Costas had decided to move back there. But Charles loved — yes, that strongly did he feel about the place — Greece. So it would be no hardship. Although today he'd had to juggle to get away; his PA had rescheduled meetings, found a stand-in for a court appearance, informed Buckingham Palace that he would not be attending a state banquet that evening. Of course, he wouldn't tell Costas any of this. He wouldn't want to burden him.

'What do you mean, Costas? Are you not feeling well?' Costas ignored Helena and continued his conversation with Charles. She sent out warning signals to John, but he was too drunk to take any notice.

Like their aunt, the twins were not best pleased by Charles's presence in Athens. They had always thought that their father relied too much upon his lawyer, put too much trust in one man. As children, they had often heard Helena ranting about something that Charles had done to curb her ambition. She'd never had a good word to say about the lawyer and, as time passed, the twins also found themselves thwarted by Charles.

The fact was that he was the chief obstacle to them getting their hands on their father's fortune. Charles had control of their trusts and allowances from it. And he guarded Costas' billions as if they were his own. This did not suit the fast-living, high-spending Gisikis twins.

Maria was bitter about the number of times Charles had refused to advance what was, in effect, a paltry sum, sometimes just £10,000, to enable her to freshen up her wardrobe at the end of the season and her allowance period. And he'd refused to allow her to have another car. He quite reasonably pointed out that owning a BMW convertible and a Porsche was one car more than any one person needed. But she'd so much wanted to be seen in the new-style Jaguar.

The man would ruin her socially; didn't he know anything about how the world works? She had to keep the Gisikis profile high. She saw it as good for business.

The fine Puligny Montrachet 1959 travelling down John's throat tasted like vinegar when, during a pause in between courses, he looked over and noticed Charles deep in conversation with his father. Why should I have to answer to that mean bastard when it came to Gisikis finance? he thought.

Charles had even asked John to make an itemised list of his monthly expenses and, when John had refused, he'd stopped his monthly allowance. What about the embarrassment this caused when he went to pay for a meal one special evening, when he was trying to make a big impression on a woman he'd met at a party the night before in an attempt to seduce her, and his card was refused?

Christ! He'd felt mortified, but fortunately the Caprice was like his second home, and they were very discreet. They were content for him to settle up with them the next day. But what a potential loss of face that could have been. Never mind the steamy sexual seduction he'd planned.

Fortunately, he'd been deprived of neither. He'd kept his playboy reputation seamlessly intact. What a night that had been! He'd meant to phone her again. God knows she'd called him enough times. But there were so many busty, leggy blondes in the world who gave good head that he wanted to sample them all. One-night stands were much less complicated.

Helena was beside herself now. Not able to get any sense out of Costas or John, she exhausted herself further by thinking about the number of times she'd rowed with her brother-in-law in an attempt to ensure that he rid himself of the meddlesome lawyer. In her mind, she felt it would be best to keep things in the family. John should have been entrusted with financial control of their funds. After all, he was in his late thirties now.

When she'd suggested this, Costas had actually had the nerve to laugh in her face. He went to great pains to point out that the twins barely scraped through their exams at the frightfully expensive educational establishment she had demanded that he send them to. And from then on, neither of them had ever worked a day in their life. When Helena continued to nag away at Costas about the twins' position, or, rather, the lack of it, in the Gisikis empire, while George was MD in New York, Costas' usual reply was, 'Helena, while George was educated at Harvard, the twins are in possession of honours degrees from Versace, Gucci and Yves St Laurent.' And the subject would be closed until the next time.

'No, no, no, no.'

George's horrified repetition of the word echoed his shock and disbelief around the room. Costas felt that he'd felled his son in one blow. There'd been no way to soften the news, no way to make it easier to say. George sobbed as if his heart would break. When he'd calmed down a little, he became angry and started to argue with Charles, who was explaining the legal technicalities.

'Your father's priority is to regain his status as a British non-resident. As you are aware, he has UK residency status. Should he die as things stand, a large portion of the Gisikis estate will go to the UK tax authorities. If he were to die as a non-resident, then the bulk of the fortune will be able to be left to benefit the family, which is as your father wishes it to be.'

For the first time in his life, John showed a keen interest in the business affairs of Gisikis Shipping. He was perplexed about the difference between citizenship and residency and how it affected inheritance tax. But Charles, forsaking his Château Latour for a glass of the finest cognac, talked him through it, slowly and with more patience than John deserved. Costas needed to live away from the UK for a full three years before he was free of tax liabilities there. At this point, he would no longer be obliged to pay UK inheritance tax.

George, now frantic and fearful for his father and himself, interrupted his godfather. 'But the heat in Greece is too much for Costas. The temperatures here become intense in the summer. What effect will that have on my father's health? We already have more than enough money, even a quarter of my father's fortune is a staggering amount. My father must do nothing that might jeopardise his survival. It's simply not worth it.'

Kimberley drew Oliver close, comforting her son, clearly distressed about his grandfather and at seeing his own father so distraught. It was just as well that he was too overcome with emotion to hear his aunt Maria mutter *sotto voce* to George, 'Speak for yourself, you fool. How can you think of robbing our father of his final wishes.'

John, pulling himself out of his alcohol-induced haze, wanted to hear more of the intricacies of the UK inheritance tax structure that might salt away a large part of the Gisikis fortune he rightly considered his own.

'George, for God's sake, shut it. Let Charles finish what he has to say.'

Everyone turned to Charles, but it was Costas who spoke next.

'I have done enough for my adoptive country. I've never stolen in my life, and I don't wish to be robbed either.' Looking fondly at George, he continued, 'I've made my decision, and I believe the sunshine in Greece will do me good.

'Obviously, there's no need for you all to exile yourselves from the UK. Besides, I'm sure you would miss Bond Street too much,' he remarked, looking at Helena and Maria in particular. 'Well, I'm certain they would miss you.'

Surprisingly, for one so self-centred, Helena looked genuinely upset over Costas' announcement. Her voice seemed as unsteady as her legs as she got up to leave the room.

'Costas, let us talk more in the morning. I think we should leave you with your dear guest.' And she gestured towards Charles. 'Obviously, there are matters you need to discuss.' As she prepared to leave the room, her distress was palpable, the shock clear in her eyes.

'Charles, as always, there is a room prepared for you. I will see to it that it is kept in a state of readiness for your visits. I expect you will be gracing our home with your presence more often in future.' And with that she bade goodnight. Using only her eyes to command the twins to follow her, she turned on her heel and disappeared from the room without a backward glance.

As John and Maria prepared to take their aunt's lead, they took it in turn to hold Costas' hand and squeeze it gently before also saying their goodnights. Then it was Kimberley's turn. She kept her arm around her son and kissed Costas' cheek warmly as she whispered to him, 'I'm so, so sorry.'

Oliver was moved to throw his arms around his grandfather, and it affected Costas deeply as he felt the young man's tears on his neck.

'Now, Oliver, I'm not dead yet. I hope you will find the time to spend one summer with an old man on his yacht. Your parents, too?' And he knew from the look in Kimberley's eyes that he need ask no more.

'We'll be there, Costas. But I suspect you already knew that.'

George held his father in his arms for a long, long time before he could bear to let him go. Then he also left the room.

CHAPTER THREE

George ate little at breakfast and said even less. His face was fixed, his emotions restrained behind a tight social mask. He sensed his brother was high again — on what, God alone knew. On sex, possibly. On drugs, undoubtedly.

He'd heard him leave late that night, the soft purr of the new Mercedes SL 600, all £100,000 of the most luxurious convertible in the world. John liked to visit the bars and brothels of Piraeus when he was in Athens. His sexual palate was jaded, desensitised, and he enjoyed rough trade. The tougher the better. Like Marseilles and Naples, Piraeus was full of whores, women, transsexuals, young men. Any port in a storm.

Oliver sat close to his father, his face puffy with lack of sleep. Kimberley, normally a woman with inexhaustible reserves of energy, seemed unnaturally sluggish, as if held down by a great weight. She hugged her son to her from time to time, as much to reassure herself as to comfort him.

Helena was dealing with her emotions with a technique she had learned from the British — the stiff upper lip. It operated in tandem with golden rule number one: keep yourself busy. She flitted constantly around the table, not able to sit still, making sure everyone had what they wanted, sending out the servants for more coffee, ensuring the freshly baked sesame rolls were kept hot, ordering, organising, controlling. She appeared, on the surface, to have made a remarkable emotional recovery, restored to her normal self within 12 short hours.

Costas and Charles walked through the French windows around noon, sweating profusely. Their appearance caused something of a stir. Dressed in tennis whites, as if they'd just completed a match on the grass courts at Wimbledon, there was outrage at the idea that Costas, in his state of health, had been exerting himself during the hottest part of the day.

'Dad!' George exclaimed. 'What on earth do you think you're doing?'

Maria, conversely, found it impossible to hide her delight, attempting to disguise it with an acceptably *laissez faire* attitude.

'George, for God's sake, let father do what he wishes. I'm sure a light game of tennis is good exercise for the heart. You can't expect him to lie about all day doing nothing. Perhaps we could have a gentle jog together one morning, father, dearest,' she coaxed, uncharacteristically trying to sweet-talk her way into Costas' affections and endear herself to him.

George turned on Maria. 'You complete idiot,' he snapped. 'That could kill him!' Then he turned his anger once more in Costas' and Charles' direction.

'What do you think you're playing at?'

Suddenly, everyone was bickering. The room was ablaze with all the emotion so carefully concealed, carefully buried and now leaking into the sub-soil, like nuclear waste from Sellafield or Chernobyl.

Costas' voice boomed its way through the cross-fire. 'Just stop all this. CALM DOWN.' As the babble of voices died away, he explained how he had got up early that morning, eaten some fruit for breakfast, done a bit of office work, and then, as it neared noon, taken a walk in the garden.

'As you know, between the hours of eleven and one the sun is at its strongest. I could have stood on the balcony in the sun for a few minutes and I would still have walked in perspiring. Charles and I did not play tennis. Obviously, those days are over for me. But there's no harm in dreaming.'

The sense of relief among some of those present was palpable as he continued with what he had to say, this time to set the agenda for the next hour or so. 'We all need to sit down and agree on our strategy for the future. Let's move into the shade of the plane tree in the garden for drinks. Once we're through with that, we'll be free to get on with other things. Get back to normal, daily life. Let's try and co-operate with each other and get this over with as quickly as possible.'

But the wings of the bird of paradise lost had cast their shadow over the Gisikis family gathered in Athens. There was to be no escape from it and, at all times thereafter, their behaviour paid lip-service to the knowledge that the household of the billion-pound Gisikis empire had death nesting in his rafters.

It was Charles Bradley who conducted the meeting under the immense, soothing shelter of the plane tree and described their immediate plans for the future of the Gisikis empire and its massive financial assets.

'Now that Costas has changed his place of residence from London to Athens, he and the

executive board of Gisikis Shipping have asked me to
take over the Presidency of Gisikis UK.'

He looked around the assembly, expecting
comments. One came immediately and expectedly
from John.

'Why shouldn't it be a Gisikis who heads up the
London operation? We ought to direct our
international operations from within the family.
Frankly, I feel insulted. I want the chance to do
something for Gisikis Shipping. For you, father. I am
your son, and I should be given the opportunity to
take on that responsibility.'

Costas looked wearily at John, more with
disappointment than anger.

'Charles has been involved in the running of the
London office for years, since we bought our first
fleet of supertankers. He has masterminded our
expansion and knows as much about Gisikis Shipping
as I do, as well as all the fine legal tuning of such a
complex organisation.

'John, as much as I would like you to be given the
opportunity of heading up UK operations, can you
honestly tell me that you know one thing about the
way the shipping business works? Not just about how
to host a summit meeting for international financiers,
the glamorous social trips to the opera and the *haute
cuisine* dinners, but also the details of who supplies us
with the clips, nails and industrial staples that seal the
massive transportation crates?'

John looked uncomfortable, scrutinising his
fingernails in his embarrassment, unable to return his
father's level gaze. He said nothing, and Costas went
on to finish his point, one that he had made to his son
countless times before.

'You have a long way to go, John, before you can reach the top. And the climb there starts at the bottom. I will always provide for my own flesh and blood, but I shall never jeopardise the future of Gisikis Shipping on a whim to protect your feelings.'

It distressed the older man that he had reared such feckless progeny, not only John but also Maria. He acknowledged his own role in their stunted development. Whatever had made them the way they were, the fact was that they much preferred to burn the midnight oil drinking and dancing in a London, Paris or New York nightclub than in poring over an accounts ledger or attempting to understand the finer trade implications of some new point of international marine legislation. And who could blame them?

A heavy, uneasy silence followed in the wake of Costas' speech. Charles allowed time for the impact of what his friend had to say to sink in before he continued with his task of clarifying the new structure of the Gisikis business.

He addressed Helena. How, he wondered, did that woman always turn herself out so impeccably? Even for a low-key family occasion like this one, she had not one hair out of place. If only she could put as much time and energy into other things, like improving conditions in the developing world.

'You, Helena, have always proved yourself proficient at running Costas' private residences — in London and Athens, the Caribbean and the South of France. We should like you to continue to do so. Your support is vital to ensure the smooth running of the Gisikis households.' Helena nodded her assent. After all, it was in her interests to do so. Costas had always behaved generously towards her. He rarely denied her anything, be it fine clothes or jewels, all of which she received in addition to her generous personal allowance and household budgets.

Perhaps it was conscience money for all those years she had relieved him of the day-to-day burden of organising the care of his children. For a long time he could not bear to look at them, as they reminded him too much of his dead wife. Or, perhaps, Helena was simply being rewarded for the accident of birth that made her the sister of his beloved Ariana.

Or was it that Costas did not want to fight with his spendthrift sister-in-law because it didn't matter to him that she spent thousands of pounds in Knightsbridge or Manhattan? He could afford it, and he just couldn't be bothered to waste his time and energy. If Helena thought that shopping made her happy, then he didn't want to be the one to disillusion her.

'The US arm of Gisikis Shipping will remain under the direction of George Gisikis,' Charles continued. 'He will become President, with overall control of the American operations, including those in South America and Australasia, where there will be regional directors, answerable to George in New York.

'On the subject of our charitable investments, Kimberley will run the Homelessness Project, expanding it to open new shelters in New York this year. Oliver will join her when he can on the international committee that overlooks the refuges worldwide. He's asked for this himself.'

George and Kimberley looked proudly at their son. He muttered an embarrassed thanks, which was swallowed by a snort of resentment coming from

Maria's direction.

'Pleazzze,' she drawled out the word in an attempt at ironic emphasis. 'Please know that the poor will always be with us. Whatever we do. I really can't see why you want to waste millions on miserable shelters for worthless vagrants, too drunk or too lazy to earn their own living.'

Her voice reached a crescendo as she screeched, 'Look, I'm sorry, but I resent it. I really do. Remember, this is just as much our money as yours, father. Why throw it away on worthless low-lifes?'

Costas intervened. He knew how insecure his daughter had always been. Incredible, given the Gisikis billions. It was extraordinary how some people were never able to enjoy what they had, always worried that they might lose it. The more Maria had, the less she appreciated it; the less she appreciated what she had, the more she needed. It was a vicious circle. The final irony also escaped her. When it came to being drunk or lazy, Maria had no match.

'Our shelters help the homeless to repair their lives and souls, something they can't do on the street. We give them the chance to live again. Everyone is entitled to that courtesy.'

Maria swore quietly under her breath and then started to sob.

Her aunt tried to console her, but she brushed her off. She'd always had everything she wanted, but ultimately it left her dissatisfied. She was the original dog in the manger. The poor little rich girl who had everything and nothing.

Her self-pity mingled with the real sadness over her father's impending death. But Maria was not able to recognise that emotion, to allow it expression, to make it better. Love was something she had never really known. Only her aunt's feeble attempts at manipulation.

No, another shopping spree in Paris or Milan would distract her enough to forget. That and the amphetamines she took on prescription from her doctor in Harley Street. A cocktail of Valium and barbiturates rocked her off to sleep at night. The pep pills got her going in the morning. So it had been for as long as she could recall.

Charles Bradley returned to London. Together with the team of company accountants, he met up with the UK tax authorities to assess Costas' financial liabilities there. Charles and the tax accountants then flew back to Greece and went through each and every detail of Costas' business affairs with a fine tooth comb. They worked in the Gisikis Greek headquarters near Syntagma Square with its scents of orange trees, oleanders and cypresses that mingled with the carbon monoxide of the traffic fumes.

George remained in Greece. He worked with Costas seven days a week sifting through projects old and new, re-evaluating investments, informing shareholders, liaising with suppliers and clients. They were in close contact with New York and the directors based there. They held telephonic conferences, linked into Sydney, Buenos Aires, London, New York and Geneva at all times of the day and night.

Back in New York, Kimberley worked tirelessly on the plans for the new shelters. She missed her husband. Their relationship was still passionate after almost 20 years together. They'd been teenage sweethearts. Somehow, it still worked for them, when so many of their friends' marriages had fallen apart.

The absence of Helena, John and Maria in Paris for a fashion show was welcome. They were not missed. On the flight to the French capital, John seduced a young stewardess. He had to boost his own personal best with the Mile-High Club. His favourite trips were the ones on which first-class passengers were offered the luxury of a massage and fed grapes by obliging young women. From time to time, he struck lucky and met one of them later for sex at his hotel. Conveniently for him, they were never there the next day.

Their inheritance continued to preoccupy them, as well it might. They speculated about how much they would get. Who would be included in the division of the spoils? Maria became distressed at the prospect of her father's £2.5 bn fortune having to be split too many ways. Surely the bulk would go to Costas' three children, divided equally between them?

Ten years ago, Costas had informed the family that he had updated his Will and that the Gisikis billions would be shared equally among his family. But what about that bitch Kimberley and her ghastly, goody-goody kid? And then, of course, there was Helena. Even in her worst moments, Maria realised that her avaricious aunt did deserve some share of the loot.

Costas had lectured Maria and John then, a decade earlier, on how he expected them to start utilising their education by becoming more involved with the day-to-day running of the company as George had done, and to work actively towards learning about how the vast, complex empire functioned. The twins agreed. But somehow they never got around to it. Too busy socialising. Besides, George was doing such a splendid job that they didn't want to interfere. No, they saw their role more as social ambassadors for the Gisikis family name.

Whenever Costas complained that they were not pulling their weight, Maria would point out that they were constantly in the social columns in magazines and newspapers around the world, and each time their photographs appeared, Gisikis Shipping was given free publicity. This was not the kind of publicity he wanted for his empire, Costas said.

The twins certainly did not deserve the vast sums their inheritance promised them. Why Costas had not disinherited the twins was never clear, least of all to them. But their father was an honourable man, who bore no malice to anyone. He just could not find it in his heart to cast out his children. The twins and Helena were his Achilles' heel.

The two-month cruise around the Aegean aboard the sumptuous Ariana was planned for May and June. It passed without incident. The luxury yacht, a Bannenberg, had a crew of 32 plus the skipper. Costas loved every inch of the 280-foot mega-yacht, which he had called Ariana in memory of his wife.

To some people, a yacht was a status symbol on which to drink champagne in St Tropez, but for Costas it was a way of making his own world out there on the crystal-clear, sun-kissed ocean, at anchor in the blue with not a care in the world. But now, of course, he had his increasingly frequent angina attacks with which to contend. A shadow hung over the trip and his heart.

Costas had always needed to relax more, to take more time off from his hectic work schedule. He had always promised himself that he would put the Ariana to proper use and cruise the waters in her as much as he could. But now he was running out of time, and he regretted that he'd never managed to spend more than a long weekend aboard the sumptuous craft.

The Ariana was a Bannenberg special, magnificently equipped with a swimming pool and helicopter pad, a cinema room and sophisticated bridge or dining-room, plus a hangar that housed a turbo Rolls-Bentley station wagon. Everything had been taken care of down to the colour of the furnishings, the design of the fine porcelain china, the best Baccarat crystal and silverware. The boat had been overwintering in Palma for an extensive overhaul and redecoration.

Costas himself felt as if he could have done with a refit and refurbishment that winter. What he got instead was an early summer cruise around the Greek islands, skirting the edges of the Turkish coast in the turquoise eastern Aegean, sailing on to the delights of ancient Crete and the contrasting sights and smells of North Africa. The passage was smooth, the moorings magical, and he took the time to relax and enjoy himself. His family came and went and bickered incessantly behind his back. Oliver's 17th birthday was spent in the Dodecanese, anchored off the east coast of Rhodes, near Lindos and St Paul's Bay. The day itself passed in a hot haze of swimming, sunbathing and eating, the evening at the island's casino at the Grand Hotel Astir Palace.

John and Maria joined them for some of the trip, as well as their cousin, Stelios Gisikis, Chairman and Chief Consultant at the Baltic Hospital, who turned up briefly to enjoy a weekend on board. People came

and went, but the twins never stayed long, preferring
to be docked in some smart port attending elegant
parties rather than being part of the family. They saw
it as messing about on boats, albeit a £20m dream
boat, designed by Jon Bannenberg, the world's
premier yacht designer, whose clients also included
Khashoggi, Ronson and assorted international
business tycoons.

Some people were never satisfied. But those who
were included Oliver's college friend Graham
Sullivan, a serious-minded young man, and his sister
Deborah, an intelligent, attractive 15-year-old, whose
parents were both doctors at an exclusive, private
New York hospital.

Oliver had invited them to join the family party on
the Ariana. Their presence ensured that a degree of
courtesy, a pretence at least of civility, was
maintained within the family group. But its
discontents and the preoccupation with Costas' state
of health were never able to be pushed quite far
enough beneath the shimmering surface of the
Aegean.

July and August saw everyone back on dry land. For
Kimberley, there was a Homeless Project shelter to
inaugurate in New York and a lavish fundraising
celebrity dinner that generated enough money to get
the Los Angeles shelter rolling. George devoted most
of his time to Gisikis Shipping, in constant
communication with his father in Athens. Helena had
an emergency rejuvenation to attend at La Prairie
Clinic in Switzerland, and John and Maria were
summering in the French Riviera at a rock star's villa.

Kimberley and George decided one Saturday in

September to devote the rest of the weekend to themselves. They had barely spent a moment alone together in the past months. George decided to romance his wife by taking her to a fabulous dinner at Manhattan's Le Cirque restaurant. After an evening of seduction, of telling her how much he loved her over the best food and the finest wines in the capital, he whisked her home soon after midnight.

As the lift ascended to their penthouse apartment overlooking Central Park, George caressed Kimberley's bare shoulders, pressing the tip of his tongue into the hollow of her collar bone. Standing behind her, he pushed his hips forward so she could feel his erect penis through the flimsy gossamer of her dress. He rocked back and forth, holding her firmly by her hips, pushing hard against her buttocks.

Spasms of raw desire shot through Kimberley's entire body, and her hand shook as she tried to insert the key into the lock of their apartment. The instant the door yielded, George gently pushed her inside and against the wall, pressing on her, covering her with his entire body, licking the hardness of her nipples and cupping her swollen breasts.

George raised his lips up to his lover's face, and Kimberley's eager tongue found its way into every area of George's mouth. Their bodies, rubbing so closely, became heated with desire, and the urgent lust that rose within each of them rendered them uncontrollable with need, their hands travelling to regions of each other's bodies that hadn't been explored for far too long.

Groaning with urgency, George freed himself from the confines of his clothes, pushing Kimberley's silk dress high above her waist. He lifted her up and felt her long legs wrap instinctively around his hips, making it easy for him to find her willing, wet entrance.

Just as George had found what he was looking for, he steadied his legs to thrust his hardness into her. On and on he pumped, his penis thickening and glistening with her juices until Kimberley was moaning with excitement, pulsating to the rhythm of his plunging, swollen penis. She finally could stand it no more and climaxed with a cry of relief that released the floodgates of her hot, burning desire. And then it was George's turn. He orgasmed in a torrent that seemed to go on for ever, shooting his sperm into her abandonment, half-gasping, half-shouting, until, entangled with Kimberley, he collapsed, exhausted yet content, on the cool woodblock floor of the entrance hall.

It was only then that George recalled how he'd heard the phone ringing a little earlier. Somehow it had seemed so distant, in another country to the one they had just occupied. It had rung and rung and then stopped, shrill but not urgent enough to have disturbed their lovemaking.

When George walked through into his study that ran off their double-height living-room, he saw the red light flashing on the answerphone. A call in the early hours of a Sunday morning was something he'd anticipated with nothing less than dread. His heart was pounding again, this time in sheer panic, as he pressed the recall button on the Panasonic Easa Phone.

CHAPTER FOUR

The scent of pine filled Costas' nostrils. He was driving along the corniche route to the south-east of Athens, following the rocky coast road past conifer-covered slopes. The views were spectacular. Cape Sounion rose precipitously ahead, 60 metres up, up, out of the sea. He could see the Temple of Poseidon, there before him at the highest point of the headland, and its dazzling white marble columns. He felt himself mesmerised by the rows and rows of tall columns, interspersed with the bright, burning bright, fluorescent blue of the sky into which — or was it the sea? — he was now falling.

When Costas awoke with a start, all he heard was the sound of birds singing, all he saw was sunlight streaming into his room through the open curtains, and all he felt was a pain in his chest so excruciating that he thought he would rather die than endure it. It's killing me, he thought. Oh, please, God, no, he panicked. It hurt so much that he knew it was.

When Costas' personal maid brought him breakfast to his room as she'd done every morning for the past few months, she was looking forward to seeing him. She enjoyed the early-morning banter they shared, their exchange of pleasantries. Instead, she found him slumped over the side of his bed. He'd been trying to reach over to press the alarm button on the direct line to his nephew Stelios at the Baltic.

While awaiting the arrival of the paramedic team, the chambermaid and the pool attendant, on duty in the grounds outside Costas' apartments, gave him the kiss of life and massaged his chest in a desperate attempt to get his heart beating again.

Once the paramedics appeared on the scene, arriving in an efficient six minutes, they attached breathing apparatus to his nose and mouth and applied the two metal disks of a defibrillator to his chest. The medical team stood back as a huge jolt of electricity shot through the big man's motionless body like a bolt of lightning. And again. At the second attempt they succeeded in forcing Costas' unwilling organ to pump, while mechanically pushing air in and out of his lungs.

As the ambulance raced towards the hospital, the faces of the paramedics said it all — it wasn't going to work. He would never breathe on his own again. It was their duty, as medical practitioners, never to give up on a life, but they also knew when to give up hope.

Helena had been in a state of shock when she'd put through her call to George and Kimberley in New York. And when there was no one to talk to except the answerphone, even her voice had started to shake. She'd been in the sauna when her lady's maid had come to her. Her message began inconsequentially — would George please fly to Athens at once! — and then she got to the point: Costas had suffered a massive heart-attack. It was touch and go whether he would live or die.

A Gulfstream III from the Gisikis airfleet was on stand-by at the rock star's private airstrip near Cannes to take Maria and John directly to Greece. The twins were not quite ready to leave. They'd been on a massive drugs binge that had kept them up for three nights without sleep. Their host had called in his doctor, who was to give them a shot of one of the new designer drugs that guaranteed to get them back on their feet and in some kind of shape to fly to Costas' sick-bed, where his life, they were told, was slowly ebbing away.

Helena left for the Baltic an hour or so after Costas's departure by ambulance, and she was now carefully coiffured and dressed as befitted the ersatz grieving widow of one of the world's wealthiest men. She should have gone to the hospital with him, held his hand, supported him. But she had to compose herself. She was no use to anyone in the state she was in, neither emotionally or sartorially.

Helena had pondered over an assortment of clothes in her wardrobe before settling on an olive-green Versace trouser suit and matching it with a pale-cream silk blouse. She retrieved a long orange silk scarf from the depths of a drawer and wrapped the expensive fabric carefully around her neck.

It was just something she'd bought on a shopping expedition in London, from Liberty's, she remembered. Then she'd gone on to New Bond Street afterwards and spent a fortune in Asprey. She fixed the scarf in place with a gold brooch, one of several she had purchased during her spending spree that day. As she strode towards the waiting car, the scarf had the desired effect of trailing dramatically in a long flag behind her, Isadora Duncan-style.

Helena repaired her face in the back seat of the car. She touched up what, to most women, would have been recognisable as an already impeccable full make-up. She was much more interested in how she looked at that moment than in the welfare of anyone or anything else.

As the car drew up outside the hospital, Helena pulled a pair of Chanel sunglasses from her Gucci shoulder-bag. She put them on in a rush and pushed them back on to the bridge of her nose with her middle finger to ensure they were firmly in place. Frank had got out of the driver's seat to help her out of the car, a Mercedes-class saloon that she felt was more appropriate for a grief-stricken relative than the flamboyant smoked-glass, white stretch limousine in which she was normally driven.

A whirring and snapping of cameras filled the air as Helena rushed past the banks of reporters, photographers and camera units encamped outside the besieged hospital. Word had spread like a forest fire. One of the good sons of Greece was dying.

A reception committee was stationed inside the hospital entrance to take Helena straight to the intensive care unit in which her brother-in-law was receiving emergency treatment. Stelios emerged from there, dressed in a clinical green gown. As he yanked off his sterile face mask, he looked exhausted. Taking Helena's arm, he led her gently to his office and made sure that she was sitting down before he broke the news to her.

'I'm afraid it's not good,' he said sympathetically. 'The massive stroke has left Uncle Costas alive only with the aid of a life-support machine. He is in a coma. His brain is dead, so, therefore, effectively, is he. I am very sorry. Costas can not be revived enough to breathe on his own. His spirit has left him.'

Helena didn't move. She sat there, numb with disbelief. Stelios kept asking her questions, but she didn't hear what he said. Eventually, he leaned over her and shook her lightly by the shoulders to get her attention.

'Helena, Helena.' She looked at him blankly. 'Helena, the Press are waiting for information. What shall I tell them?'

The corner of Helena's bottom lip quivered slightly before she finally answered. 'Don't tell them anything. Say nothing for the moment. I feel it is only right that Costas' children get here before you announce anything to the rest of the world. Simply inform the Press that Costas Gisikis, President of Gisikis Shipping, is in intensive care following a stroke this morning. When the children arrive, we will release a full statement.'

Although she had known this day would come, Helena still found it upsetting to see her brother-in-law, such a great bear of a man, so vital, so dynamic, so driven, lying in a spartan metal bed wired up to assorted cables and drips.

It made her feel so useless, almost as helpless as poor Costas. Such an undignified end for a once-powerful man, his mouth wedged open by a large tube that passed down his throat and into his lungs, pumping air in and out of his otherwise lifeless body. Helena noticed the skin of his face, once glowing with health, now dehydrated and flaky, as if peeling off layer by layer to reveal the absence of the man beneath. Helena hid her face with her hands to block out the tragedy of the man who once been her sister's sweetheart.

Costas, like Helena and Ariana, had grown up on the same small Greek island of Myra in the eastern Aegean. It was sparsely inhabited with only ten families who all knew each other and each other's business intimately. They lived in tiny wooden cottages scattered all over the island. There was no running water or electricity. Their income came from the sea and the land. All there was, was what could be grown or produced there. And the water supply was a constant source of concern for them.

Most people dreamt of leaving to live on the mainland. At an early age, Helena was one of them. She liked what she'd heard about Greek's capital city, the wealthy Athenians with their beautiful clothes, smart cars and expensive restaurants. Their homes with bathrooms with toilets that flushed; showers that washed you clean in a stream of fresh water; and shops where you could buy whatever you wanted.

Costas enjoyed life on the island and had no ambition to leave. Where else could he enjoy the rural idyll that was his existence on Myra. His work as a goatherd suited him. He loved to wander the island all day, watching it change as the year progressed. He was happy, too, that he was engaged to be married to Ariana, Helena's older sister.

Helena had been surprised when her sister had accepted Costas' proposal of marriage. How could she give herself to a man who had nothing, who didn't even own the goats he herded? A local goatman was not her idea of marrying well. When a priest came over from the mainland to marry Ariana and Costas, everyone on Myra shared their joy except Helena. How could her sister have thrown her life away like that, when the riches of Athens beckoned from the other side of the Aegean?

But Ariana's happiness was interrupted by the War, when Greece was the first Allied country voluntarily to join Great Britain against the Axis. Costas was conscripted to fight. But he came back a hero and had learnt a great deal in the years he was away from home. Tales of his courage and strength in the face of adversity filtered back to Myra, but Costas always played them down. He went back to herding his goats but he could not settle.

Civil wars followed, and it was not until the early 1950s that a stranger from the mainland arrived in Myra, looking for Costas Gisikis. The Athenian was a lawyer who represented the father of a man with whom Costas had fought during skirmishes against the army of Occupation before Greek Liberation in 1944. Unbeknown to Costas, this man, whose life Costas had once saved with no thought for his own, was the son of an extremely wealthy Greek shipping magnate.

The father had died recently, but in his Will he had asked that Costas Gisikis should be rewarded for having saved the life of his son, one who would have been lost to him in armed combat had it not been for Costas' heroic actions.

Costas found himself the beneficiary of the man's gratitude with a small, subsidiary business within his shipping empire. A fleet of six passenger ferries, plus a cash inheritance of £10,000, in those days a small fortune. Costas vowed to use it well and to build on his good luck, respecting the memory of the man who had changed his life. Already unsettled by his wartime experiences, he left Myra, taking Ariana with him.

Helena came to visit her sister and brother-in-law on the mainland not long after they had moved into the smart house in the fashionable district of Kolonaki on the south slope of the highest of the hills of Athens, Mount Lykabettos. She never returned to Myra, which was the start of her making and her undoing.

It was in Athens that Helena began to live life as she'd always dreamt it. There were nightclubs, restaurants, smart cars, fast men, and before long she became involved with someone who quickly broke her heart. Her illusion of happiness ended shortly after her hasty marriage to the playboy gambler, whose child she was carrying on her wedding day. But the baby was stillborn, and her marriage quickly followed suit.

Helena had lost the man who had given her the luxury for which she yearned. But he'd been a trickster, a con man whose wealth was based on credit and fast talking. What she had not lost was her taste for the high life.

When Ariana died, it was only 12 months after Helena had lost both her own baby and her husband. Helena saw her chance and she took it, stepping into Ariana's shoes but never into her late sister's marriage bed. Well, only once, when Costas was weak with grief and desperate for comfort. But he regretted it almost at once, and she never allowed him to forget it. It was his downfall. His sister-in-law played on his guilt for the rest of his life.

'Madam! Madam! The jet has landed at Ellinikon.'
Helena snapped out of her reverie. Frank had arrived
to tell her that the twins were about to arrive at
Athens airport. On the six-mile drive south-east from
Athens to Ellinikon to meet their plane, Helena tried
to work out what she would do next. For the first time
in her life she had absolutely no idea.

'Is he still alive?' Maria asked.

'He's on a life-support machine. He's in a coma.
He can't breathe unaided. His heart is still pumping.'

Helena broke down and started to cry. After a
moment, she pulled herself together and said quietly,
in a whisper that was almost inaudible, 'I mean, what
I mean is that, yes, he is dead, in the sense that his
spirit's left his body. But his body's being kept alive
only through medical technology.'

Helena dabbed at her tears with a monogrammed
linen handkerchief, suddenly brisk again. 'The Press
are pressurising us for the latest news, but I told
Stelios to tell them nothing, apart from the fact that
your father's had a stroke. I wanted to wait for your
return before making any further announcements.

'George and Kimberley have been told about the
stroke, but only that. George is coming later today
from New York via a flight on Concorde to
Heathrow.'

John punched the air in victory. 'Yo!' Then, he
stopped, aware all of a sudden that he should appear
less ebullient, bearing in mind that his father lay
dying not many miles from where he stood. For once,
he almost seemed surprised at himself.

Helena and the twins had taken refuge in the VIP
lounge at Ellinikon, and now, at John's insistence,

they made their way to the Mercedes that was waiting to take them to the hospital.

Reclining in the back of the Merc, in the comfort of the Nappa leather seats, John asked Frank to operate the electronic rear roller blind to give them some respite from the interested stares of passers-by. Although all the car windows were made of tinted glass, they needed as much privacy as they could get from the prying eyes that seemed to follow them everywhere.

Perhaps if they had chosen to drive in a car with a cheaper price tag, to dress less flamboyantly, to behave less like travelling royalty, they would have been able to live more private lives. But, in truth, the only thing worse for them than too much attention was too little.

'Helena,' John's voice was purposeful, 'now let's go through it again.'

Helena was surprised at how attentive John was being for once. Usually, he didn't have the time to listen to anyone.

'What's got into you? Suddenly you're so concerned about your father's health. Have you begun to appreciate him now that it's too late?'

Maria rebuked her aunt instantly. 'If father had bothered with us more when we were younger, perhaps we'd care more for him now. Perhaps if he'd allowed us to be on the board of Gisikis Shipping instead of consigning us to an allowance and having to beg for that half the time. So frankly, my dear, I don't give a damn ...'

John interrupted his sister, finishing what she had to say. 'Because, my dear aunt, we haven't lost sight of why the old man's in Greece. You can't have forgotten the inconvenience of him dying before the time's up, which would lose us all the dosh.'

'Dear boy,' Helena interjected, 'not even you can arrange a convenient time for your father to die.'

John looked daggers at his aunt. All he said was, 'We will just see about that.'

And Helena, not one of life's hangers-back herself, had never before seen such determination in anyone, ever.

'I'm sorry that we meet again under such unhappy circumstances,' Stelios said, greeting both twins at once with a wide embrace. John pulled back from his cousin's affectionate greeting, a look of horror momentarily spreading across his face. 'You haven't switched off the life-support machine yet, have you, Stelios?'

Stelios was appalled at the possibility. He shook his head incredulously as he said, 'No! No doctor can ever do anything like that without speaking first to the family, without getting their permission in writing. But if you like, I can organise it all if ...'

Maria broke in to interrupt Stelios's deliberations. 'You'll do nothing of the sort.' She sounded frantic, beside herself with emotion. 'You must do everything possible to keep my father alive.'

'Maria,' Stelios replied gently, 'I'm sure Helena explained the situation. Your father is brain dead, only his physical body is alive, which is not enough in medical terms to say that someone lives. Once the machine is switched off, his body will cease to function. We can't keep him on the unit for ever.'

Stelios turned to include Helena and John in what he had to say next. 'I'm sorry. You'll all have to face the fact that, sooner rather than later, the life-support machine will have to be turned off.'

CHAPTER FIVE

Maria could see her inheritance draining away before her very eyes. She lowered her voice to a whisper as she informed her cousin, 'Lord in heaven, Stelios! You just don't understand, do you? You must keep my father alive. There's a fortune riding on this.'

John took over as his sister collapsed into a chair and dropped her head between her knees as if to stop herself from fainting.

'My dearest friend,' he addressed Stelios. They were, in fact, quite close, so for once John was being sincere. 'I think there are some things you should know about.' He sat his cousin down and started to enlighten him. It was a blatant attempt to persuade him to see things their way. John rarely failed when he set his mind to something.

Some time later, the cousins and their aunt sat locked in an uneasy silence in Stelios' office. John broke it when he suddenly said, 'Stelios, George will be here soon, we have to have something to tell him, not just any old whitewash for my saintly little brother. He could smell a rat in Australia.

'For God's sake, don't let him know that father is clinically dead. Dance around the truth a bit. Tell him what we've told the Press. The old man's in a coma. But tell him you think there's a chance, signs of brain activity, still hope. Where there's life there's ... something like that. Anything, Stelios, anything, but we've got to make it watertight.'

John babbled on, his words affecting Stelios like the surgeon's knife he used every day in the operating theatre. He felt himself being opened up, dissected, every bit of him calculated into the evil his cousin proposed.

Stelios broke into a heavy sweat as he realised how far the ripples of the lie would reach, and was horrified at the role John wanted him to play in it. Eventually, he found the strength to reply to his cousin's hectoring.

'I would be putting my career on the line for you if I do as you ask. I can't say a man is alive when he is dead. I could be struck off for much less than that. I've built up a good reputation for myself and the Baltic. I'm on my way to becoming a rich man. Why should I throw it all up just for your benefit?

'It doesn't matter to you what I've done here, the years I've put in, seven days a week, every week of the year, year in, year out. While you've been lotus-eating your way around the world, I've worked hard. You have a fortune at your fingertips. You've never wanted for anything in your life. But ...'

At this, Maria emerged from the trance she'd been in for the past half hour. She got out of her chair and walked towards her cousin, her face within an inch of his, menacing.

'Damn it, Stelios. Just tell George that father is alive, and that it serves no purpose for him to stay here. Tell him father could stay in the coma for weeks, months, years. Tell him any damned thing, but just get rid of him.'

She paced back and forth a few times, before continuing.

'I want the world to think, rather to know, that Costas Gisikis is still alive. For sure. Cast-iron certainty. We will leave the technicalities to you. Then that will give us the time we need to think this thing through properly.'

But Stelios was adamant in his refusal, undaunted by his cousins' bullying.

'I'm the Chairman of this whole damn hospital. I'm sure as hell not going to throw away my career for this obscene, warped idea of yours to clinch your inheritance.'

This was a red rag to Maria. She charged at Stelios, grabbing him forcibly by both arms, hanging on to him. He tried to pull away, but she held him in a vice-like grip. She stared at him as if possessed, transfixing him, her eyes almost piercing through him.

'What's your price, Stelios?' she hissed in fury. 'We can make it worth your while. Why don't we do just that and give you three million now, three million when the inheritance comes through. And one million meanwhile to any of your staff who need paying to keep their mouths shut. Now can we please postpone informing the world that Costas Gisikis is dead and thereby avoid putting our entire bloody fortune at risk?'

In the surgeon's washroom, Stelios splashed cold water over his burning face. If he could, he'd have plunged his whole body into it. He was sweating like a pig, shaking, out of control of his body. Sell his soul to the devil. That's what they were suggesting. What a horrendous idea! What a gamble on the rest of his life! He might just end up losing everything! But the worst of it all was that he was tempted.

Stelios Gisikis was not a wealthy man, but he was getting there. His father had died when he was three years into medical school, and Costas had stepped in to help him out. Stelios had never forgotten how his uncle had taken him aside at his father's funeral and what he had said to him that day.

'Stelios, my boy, you have shown that you are determined to become a doctor, and I want you to be the best there is. You have already achieved great honour for yourself by coming top of your year, and you show great promise for the future.

'I have no doubt that you have a great contribution to make to the world of medicine. You have chosen a hard road for yourself, and I would like to make it as smooth for you as I possibly can.'

Costas was as good as his word and, from then on, for his remaining four years at college, he paid for all Stelios' educational expenses. He bought him a two-bedroom flat in Kolonaki, near the Gisikis town house, and a new Volkswagen. A generous weekly allowance always meant there was money left over for fun. And he knew Costas had made him a beneficiary in his Will. But, most importantly, Stelios always had a home from home with his uncle's family. He'd never wanted for anything thereafter. And he liked it that way.

Stelios caught sight of his reflection in the frameless mirror on the wall above the washbasins. The fluorescent lighting didn't do him any favours, mind you, but, God, he looked as awful as he felt!

What on earth was he going to do?

All that stuff with Costas was in the past. His uncle was as good as dead now. Yes, he had been proud of his nephew and once confided how he wished his twins had taken their lead more from him and learnt to study harder and follow a more purposeful path in life. Costas' admiration was important to his nephew, the top surgeon in his league, highly respected in the medical profession, now the most powerful man in the hospital.

But it didn't really matter any more what Costas did or did not think of him. In any case, Costas had never sat in judgement over him. But Stelios was aware of the goodness of the man, of his morality. But he was not God. Now Stelios had to make his own choices and work out how best to invest in his own future. And he had also to confront his weaknesses.

At the age of 42, Stelios considered he had a great deal to lose. He had made a life for himself. He had built on firm foundations. Why jeopardise what he knew, what he'd made of himself for Cloud-cuckoo-land? But money had always been his driving force. He was motivated by it.

Perhaps it was a consequence of the poverty in his early childhood, when existence on the island had been hand to mouth. Once you've been in a famine, you never want to be hungry again. But he wasn't scarred by not having money in his youth. It was more than that.

The truth was that Stelios had always spent more than he earned, and had consistently lived beyond his means for years.

It was possibly the result of his billionaire uncle

mopping up after him whenever he got into debt as a medical student. But he enjoyed the prestige, the status that money brought him. He liked the standing it gave him among his peers, the edge it gave him when the others had less than him, when he was the only student in his year with a car, when he could wine and dine women in smart clubs while his classmates struggled to take a girl out for a pizza.

These days, a large chunk of his substantial income went on keeping up appearances. He'd done a bit of property speculation that hadn't quite worked out. Then he'd had his flat refurbished by John Pawson, one of the most fashionable interior architect/designers in Europe.

He had a weakness for all the good things in life and, although he was in his early 40s, he'd never married. Like his cousin John, he preferred to lure women in with his Jaguar XK8, his dark good looks and his sophisticated lifestyle; to wine, dine and bed them, then to lose interest in them. After a short game of cat-and-mouse, he'd leave them.

But pursuing this sort of life over the years hadn't come cheap. Stelios had begun to slide into debt and, although he could see his way out of it, wouldn't it be a relief to know that financially he'd never have to worry again if he were to accept Maria's offer? And so Stelios found himself back in the Garden of Eden, and about to accept a bite of Eve's apple.

CHAPTER SIX

On one of the fine sandy beaches of the fashionable Greek seaside resort of Vouliagmeni, UK tax inspector Anthony Burton lay dozing in the comfort of the hotel's sun-lounger, preparing himself for the day ahead. He'd planned for the three 'S's — sun, sex and sleep — punctuated by an occasional trip to the bar for a Metaxa and Coke or a cold beer and a swift read-through of the *Athens News*.

He surfaced from his nap and sat up, looking around for Margaret. Scanning the vast blue expanse of the Saronic Gulf, sparkling, dazzling in the morning sunshine, he guessed his wife was out there somewhere, swimming. The sea at Vougliameni was wonderfully warm, especially so because of the overspill from the nearby lake, its sulphurous green waters enclosed by the sheer limestone rocks of the east cape of Kaminia. The overflow from the lake ran underground and bubbled up into the sea bed like a special kind of marine under-floor heating.

Anthony couldn't decide what to do. Perhaps he'd join her. Perhaps he'd just stay right where he was. As a compromise, he sat up, swung his legs over the side of the lounger and, picking up a handful of sand, sat pouring the soft white grains from one hand to the other, aimlessly considering his options.

He couldn't believe his luck. They'd managed to get into the luxury hotel complex as a last-minute booking. September in Greece was magnificent. The high-season crowds were beginning to thin out, and the real Greece was beginning to emerge.

He'd had a busy year in his job at the Special Compliance Office of the Inland Revenue. One way or another, the changes in the UK tax system had proved an enormous headache. So an autumn break was a life-saver. And he liked Greece enormously. It never failed to enchant him. Its classicism, its paganism, its extraordinary energy, zest for life. Its *kafeneions* where Greek men played cards or backgammon endlessly. And its triple measures of spirits, standard in all the bars.

As Anthony mused on his good fortune, the front-page headline of the English-language newspaper on his wife's adjacent sun lounger caught his eye: TYCOON IN HOSPITAL FOLLOWING SEVERE STROKE. Hell, it couldn't be!

Stelios was lost in the sort of deep, dreamless sleep that results when the body finally stops running on adrenalin. He was completely exhausted. Physically so but, most of all, emotionally. Half-an-hour earlier, he'd finally give in and taken the opportunity to catch up on a few hours sleep in a hospital ante-room. After all, he deserved it. The strain of the past two days had been intolerable.

Stelios had had no practice in the art of deception. He'd decided it was best to remain at the Baltic just in case he were needed. Once, that is, he'd ensured that

Costas was comfortable and that no one had access to his private room except for the hand-picked few whose silence had been paid for. Later that day, he was expecting a torrent of distant relatives and wellwishers, who had to be kept at bay. It was vital that he kept up his strength and didn't allow himself to get worn down by his duplicity.

'Get up, Mr Stelios. Come quickly. Get up now. Something is happening with Mr Costas.'

Stelios' peace was shattered by the arrival of one of the nurses who had been keeping constant watch at Costas' bedside. At the mention of his uncle's name, Stelios sprang out of bed like a greyhound from a trap and was out of the door, along the corridor and into Costas' isolation chamber before the nurse had time to explain anything further.

One look at the heart monitor and Stelios' face drained of all its vestigial colour. 'Shit! Shit! SHIT!' he chanted as he whipped off his jacket and rolled up his shirt-sleeves ready for action. He rushed round the room like a whirlwind, ever watchful of the rapid rise and fall of the line that plotted the regularity of Costas' heartbeat on the machine's monitor.

'Quick, damn it,' he yelled at the nurse as she hurried into the room behind him. 'We've got to stabilise him. NOW. Where's the adrenalin? What are you waiting for?'

The nurse froze momentarily, paralysed by what she saw on the screen, watching Costas see-saw between life and death. When Stelios barked at her again, she shook herself into action.

The screen's fluorescent green line rose and fell wildly all the while, until, suddenly, it became long, flat and horizontal. The machine emitted a piercing monotone hum like a television set at the close of the day's programming. Stelios was beside himself, all his professionalism discarded, as he yelled obscenities at the nurse who was, he felt in his distress, too slow to remove the wrapping from a syringe. He screamed at anyone, at everyone who happened to be in earshot, at fate for getting him into this. When the nurse handed him the shot of adrenalin, he injected his uncle straight into his heart. If this didn't do it, then nothing would.

When Margaret returned from her swim she found her husband engrossed in the front page of the *Athens News*. Anthony was beside himself. He just couldn't believe it. Only a few months earlier, he'd been processing stacks and stacks of documents that related to the Greek billionaire's self-imposed exile.

He'd balked from the mountain of paperwork he'd had to plough through to sort it all out. He'd thought all the while about the hundreds of millions the British tax authorities stood to lose by Costas' return to Greece. Now, with Costas only resident in Athens for just a matter of months, his status not yet non-resident, the money might well be redeemable under UK tax laws if he were to die soon.

Christ! The Gisikis brood must be nervous as hell at the prospect of losing a large portion of their family fortune in inheritance tax. But the idea of so much wealth concentrated in one family was not one that appealed to Anthony. In truth, it stuck in his throat. Too bad! Anthony thought. They'll do well enough, whatever.

Anthony Burton had not himself benefited from an auspicious start in life, but he'd struggled through, he reasoned. He had been raised in south-east London, not far from the unfashionable satellite suburb of Croydon, the son of a mixed marriage — a Jewish mother and a non-practising Catholic father. He'd been brought up to be Jewish, though, and that had given him a lot of determination. He liked the Judaic disregard for the afterlife. What mattered was the here and now. No fuss about storing up points for when you died.

Anthony's childhood had been tough. His father worked hard just to make ends meet, but with his mother's brilliance at money management — that's where he'd got it from, he supposed — they didn't go without and always had an annual holiday. His father often didn't accompany them, just taking them to a boarding house or caravan site, returning to London to work for the week and then coming back to bring them home the following weekend.

Anthony was a bright child and shone academically. He was something of a changeling, because from somewhere in all that ordinariness he'd had, from birth, an ambition and drive to succeed in life. He'd walked at nine months, talked soon after and could read before he went to school. A child prodigy would be overstating it, but he was a clever boy who turned into an intelligent and determined man, who never lacked in compassion for those less fortunate than himself, however successful he became.

He won a scholarship to Oxford and thereafter studied accountancy with Arthur Andersen, one of the City's Big Six. He'd worked in the City and then decided to move into public service. His first government job had been with the Inland Revenue, and he worked his way up there to become an Inspector of Taxes.

It was while he was at Andersens that he had met Margaret, a brilliant and budding tax lawyer. Until then, Anthony had played the field. He liked women, and he had been out with a series of girlfriends, with no desire to settle.

Beauty with brains was a combination Anthony found irresistible, and, as a bonus, Margaret earned more than he did. They had been married for two years. For the moment, children did not figure in their plans. They just wanted to have fun together.

Anthony's reverie was interrupted by Margaret's return from her swim. Playfully, she flicked a few drops of seawater on to her husband's sun-baked chest. He howled with the shock of the cold water on his gently roasting flesh: 'Leave off, Mags! That's freezing. No, don't.'

Despite himself, Anthony felt a stirring in his groin as he watched his wife standing over him. The sight of her long, slim legs emerging from the tiny bikini that barely covered the triangle between her thighs aroused him. But he decided to ignore it. He had something else to consider for the moment.

'Sorry, love, I didn't mean to snap, but that water's ... I must tell you, something's just come up.' He grinned to himself as he realised what he'd said, but carried on regardless. 'Do you remember that Gisikis file I was working on for months?'

Margaret nodded.

'Well, the old boy's just had a serious stroke. I've just been reading about it in here.' He waved the *Athens News* at her. Margaret laughed incredulously. 'God, Ant, of course I remember. It was me who suggested that MI5 should assign an undercover agent to the case to bump off the poor old bastard to increase Britain's tax revenue at a stroke. But just now it's heatstroke that I'm going to get if I stand around here, discussing this any more. Listen, love, we're on holiday, remember? Let's not mix business with pleasure. I want to get out of the sun for a couple of hours. Care to join me?'

Margaret stood in front of her husband, stretching languorously in the noonday sun. Then she leaned forward and kissed him full on the mouth, trailing one hand over his muscular physique and cupping his bulging groin gently but firmly with the other. Anthony groaned with pain at being taken off the Gisikis case so abruptly and with pleasure at what was to come. Without another word, he found himself not able to resist his wife's invitation and allowed himself meekly to be led indoors. The Gisikis story would have to wait. On this occasion, it simply couldn't compete.

As he followed Margaret to their apartment, Anthony reflected on how, although their lovemaking was always passionate, there was something about the sun that made it even more so. He ached for the pleasures of the flesh that were in store for him. He could hardly restrain himself at the thought of it as he watched his wife walk ahead of him towards the privacy of their room, her shapely hips swaying, her taut buttocks exposed by the G-string that cut through her twin mounds, enhancing their uplift and leaving nothing to the imagination.

As Margaret reached the door of their apartment, Anthony's excitement grew as he saw her reach behind her back to undo the top of her bikini. As she turned to face him, her full breasts tumbled out and bounced invitingly, her normally large nipples small and hard with desire. As she completed her striptease and entered their apartment, Anthony went in behind her and closed the door.

Stelios made the sign of the cross when the heart monitor indicated that Costas had responded to treatment. The steady blipping sound that replaced the dreaded monotone hum was music to his ears. He dropped the long hypodermic back on to the sterilized metal tray and left the room, mumbling something incoherent to himself.

He went into his office and rubbed his eyes wearily several times before picking up the phone and punching in a number.

'Helena?'

Her personal maid transferred him to her. 'Thank Christ you're there, Helena. Costas has had a heart-attack. No, no, don't bother coming over. I stabilised him, and there is nothing to worry about yet. But I'm treating this as a warning that anything can happen. We'd better discuss the options sooner rather than later, though.'

Stelios paused for a moment before continuing. 'I hadn't wanted to consider the possibility of Costas' body joining his spirit ...'

When Helena finally put down the phone, she went straight to the Gisikis private chapel to pray. For Costas. For the family. For the evil there is in the world. But, most of all, for herself.

She promised God that if everything went smoothly, and she wasn't exposed as a liar and a thief or — heaven forbid! — as a self-serving, greedy, conniving bitch, that if she got the money from Costas' estate, then she would donate the bulk of it to charity, for the good of mankind.

Helena spilled out her intentions in a panic-stricken torrent of words that didn't make much sense, but her motives were, she insisted, nevertheless honourable. However, it was doubtful that Helena would ever recognise anything good or honourable were it to hit her full in the face.

Stelios had prepared a large room in the Baltic for Helena and the twins to receive concerned family and friends later that day. It was already brimming with bouquets, the air full of their heavy scent. Costas could have no flowers in his isolation ward. It was a sterile environment. In any case, Helena explained, he wouldn't have known they were there in his current condition.

For once, Maria and John, even Helena, had dressed soberly for the occasion, playing down their habitually flamboyant tendencies when it came to selecting what to wear from their wardrobes. No one wore anything bright, though all three were careful to avoid black widow's weeds, the colour of mourning.

During the course of the day, a large number of people tried to get through the security cordon surrounding the hospital, but only those whose names appeared on a selective list, some twenty people, were allowed in. For those privileged few, Helena, Maria and John put on a fantastic show of grief and grit in the face of adversity. None was allowed access to poor Costas in his lonely splendour.

Anthony lay on his back on the huge double bed, staring up at the whirring ceiling fan. Margaret slept lightly beside him, exhausted but satisfied by what had turned into an exhilaratingly steamy afternoon. God, there was no doubt about it, Anthony thought. She was an amazing lover. How she kept him hard for so long. And then when she rode him, sitting on top, her breasts swollen with lust, rising and falling, teasing his throbbing penis, pulling away at just the right moment to keep him stiff and ready to take her again. This time from behind. He loved to take her from behind.

He could feel himself stiffening again. And he turned her gently on to her side and took her breasts in his hands, encouraging her nipples into points of lust between his fingers. He stroked her back, the softness of her inner thighs, caressed her buttocks. Then as she slowly woke, he began to penetrate her, at first gently, seeking out her wetness, then, as she responded, more fiercely until they were making love again, their cries filling the room as they rose in a peak of excitement, climaxing together, this time in a pulsating frenzy of lust.

Towards early evening, Stelios' secretary appeared in the reception room and discreetly requested Helena's attention. Could she, John and Maria please come through at once to see Stelios?

'Dead?'

Maria's mouth hung open, the word almost visibly dragging it down. John went over to comfort his sister. She held on to him for support.

'He is dead,' Stelios continued. 'Your father was dead before, only we managed to get his heart going again through the wonders of modern medical science. But ...'

'Do something else, then!' John interrupted Stelios, imploring and angry at the same time. 'If your beloved medical science has made such bloody amazing progress,' he yelled, 'then damn well get it to do so again!'

Stelios walked over to John, equally angry and distressed. He stood with his face a hair's breadth from his cousin's.

'This time ...' he raged, '... this time your father is properly dead. There is nothing anyone or anything can do to bring him back to life. He is dead! Dead! Dead!' At this point, Stelios backed away from John, shocked by his outburst.

Still enraged but exhausted, he asked more calmly, 'Now, do I make myself completely clear?'

For a while, no one spoke. But the silence in Stelios' office was abruptly shattered by a curt knock at the door and the appearance in its frame of Athena, Stelios' elderly mother and Costas' sister-in-law. She looked all the world like an avenging angel.

Although stooped with age, Athena's spirit was indomitable. Pointing her walking stick at Stelios, she advanced on her son unaided and, like Stelios a minute or so earlier, she was wild with anger.

'Where is Costas? You don't even tell me he is ill. My nurse read it to me from the newspapers. Is that how you respect your mother? Consigning me to a home. Keeping me in the dark?'

'Mother,' Stelios said, relieving the old woman of her weapon and finding his professional bedside manner in spite of himself. 'Please sit down. You cannot see Costas.'

The tiny woman's frail body continued to shake with rage. 'Don't you tell me I can't see Costas!' And she grabbed back her walking stick, turned back to the door and marched out determinedly in the direction of Costas' isolation ward.

Maria, who had just washed down an aspirin with a glass of water, dropped the expensive Baccarat crystal goblet from Stelios' drinks cupboard to the floor, where it shattered into a hundred pieces. She bolted out after the old lady, screaming at the top of her voice, 'Stop, Aunt Athena. Stop! You can't. You just can't.' Athena struck out at her niece with her stick. 'What's it got to do with you, you stupid girl!' And she hit out at her again before heading off down the corridor. 'You always were a stupid girl,' she repeated furiously.

'She's mad,' Maria yelled. 'Bloody mad. Stop her, Stelios.'

Stelios was in the process of doing just that. There was an urgent need to restore some dignity to the area around his office that had turned into a war zone. He grabbed a wheelchair from a cupboard near by and sped after his mother, overpowering her gently and making her sit down. Then he summoned a nurse to help him as he wheeled her swiftly away, in the opposite direction to the one in which Costas lay.

Having made love for much of the late morning and lunchtime, Margaret dozed and read into the late afternoon. She was aware that Anthony had grown preoccupied and distant as the day wore on.

'Sorry, darling,' he said, 'it's just that I can't get my mind off this Costas Gisikis case. I've an odd feeling about it. My instincts are telling me something. I just don't know what.'

'It's probably because you did so much work on it.

The tax division won't benefit from it at all. It comes under the category of 'thankless task'. That's all.'

'I wish it were,' Anthony replied. 'Look, please indulge me this once, Mags. I've got to get this out of my system. Follow through my hunch.'

In her post-coital languor, Margaret was at her most giving. She could spare him for a while. She'd relax in the jacuzzi, finish her novel, take a nap or a walk along the beach. He'd be back for supper, he told her, as he changed into his slacks and a casual shirt and set off to hail a taxi to the Baltic. He wanted to check out the situation to his own satisfaction.

The drive to the hospital in the north of Athens was a long one and gave Anthony time for reflection. He had never been keen on the establishment and despised people with more money than they knew what to do with. He especially loathed people who came into possession of fat inheritances. The bulk of the money, he felt, should be ploughed back into the community.

Anthony was a confirmed socialist, with communist leanings, who was fanatical about making sure every penny of tax due was collected. This was one reason why he had risen so fast up the tax-office promotion ladder.

When the taxi pulled into the hospital entrance, the security guards on duty outside eyed Anthony with suspicion. When he got out, paid his fare and made his way towards the air-conditioned foyer of the élite establishment, he was faced with a wall of refusal.

'May I ask who you are?'

'Harry Travers of the *London Times*. I have been sent to report on Costas Gisikis' health and progress.'

Having consulted Helena's list and discovered no

Harry Travers among its names, he was dismissed with a curt response that reaffirmed his first impressions of hostility.

'Mr Gisikis is not permitted visitors. He is in a coma. Journalists are not permitted in the building. You must respect the fact that Costas Gisikis is seriously ill and needs to be left alone. Please leave immediately.'

As he was unceremoniously ushered towards the exit, behind him he heard raised voices. It was the beginning of what became a vehement argument. An old woman in a wheelchair was protesting fiercely about something. And, like him, she was being ejected from the hospital and its grounds. Anthony stood for a moment, waiting to see what would happen next, but when he spotted a burly security guard marching straight towards him, he thought better of it, turned on his heel and left. Outside, he was surprised how the afternoon temperatures had risen and now hit him in a wall of heat. Anthony observed the comings-and-goings at the hospital from a discreet distance across the road. A clutch of photographers and reporters were hanging about. But they had nothing to add to what Anthony already knew. Just as he was about to take a cab and move on, the hysterical old woman was wheeled in his direction and into a waiting ambulance. She was screaming something in Greek, which an English-speaking news reporter helpfully translated for Anthony.

'She's the mother of the chief surgeon at the Baltic, and Costas Gisikis' sister-in-law. But even she's not allowed to see him.'

And then he laughed and shrugged helplessly. 'If *she* can't get near him, then God help the rest of us!'

Anthony decided to complete his investigations with a trip to the Gisikis mansion, where he also tried to gain entrance, using the same alias as before. To no avail. There was a cordon of silence and secrecy around Costas Gisikis. But with his flight back to Heathrow booked for the following day, there was little more Anthony Burton could do in Athens to get to the heart of the matter. His tenacity, however, was legendary. He would pick up the trail in London.

No one, Helena had instructed, but no one, was to be allowed access to the Baltic in order to visit her ailing brother-in-law.

The bickering between Helena's contingent — herself, John and Maria — and Stelios had become surreal and bizarre as they had to deal with the reality that they had a corpse on their hands.

'You should respect the dead,' Stelios reminded them. 'Besides which, in the temperatures of Athens in early September — 25°C and rising — his body will start to decompose imminently if we don't take it soon to the hospital morgue for refrigeration.

'In my view, we have no choice but to tell the world that Costas is dead. I did what I agreed to do. Now the game is up. We can't carry on with this plan any longer. It no longer works.'

Aware that the first stage of his payment, £3m, was already his, Stelios was quite prepared to settle for what he made so far. And he was quite without scruples at having cheated his cousins and his aunt out of the money.

'You people are mad to think that you can get away with this. I wouldn't carry on, not if you tripled your offer to me.'

At this Maria totally lost it. She flew at Stelios and grabbed him by the throat, screaming.

'How dare you, you fucker? You're haggling over my father's death.'

With some difficulty, John dragged his twin off their cousin, though not before she had dug her nails into the flesh of his neck and drawn blood. Maria went down fighting, landing a good strong kick directly into Stelios' groin. As John pushed his sister into a chair out of the way, Stelios sank to the floor in agony, clutching his balls.

But despite helping his cousin to escape Maria's fury, John had no sympathy for him. With an edge of steel in his voice and a cold, hard look in his eye, he turned on Stelios.

'You're in this up to here,' he said, indicating the air above his head. 'You're implicated as much as we are. So you might as well stop trying to slide out of it, leaving us in the shit up to our necks, and begin to think up a plausible way out for all of us.

'You've already lied to George, issued a false Press statement, accepted bribes not only for yourself but also for your staff. You're in it as deep as we are. If you think we're mad, then clearly you're crazier than us for getting involved with us in the first place. So start thinking, and fast.'

As Stelios limped painfully over towards his office sofa to recover his composure and consider his next move, Maria just shook her head in disbelief. She couldn't get over how calm John could be in a crisis. So level headed and clear thinking for a junkie.

'There is one major problem,' Stelios announced finally, resigned at last to his predicament. 'I can't put Costas' corpse in the morgue without someone somehow coming across it. There is just too much traffic down there. And the police arrive from time to time to examine the dead.

'We've got to do something soon before he starts to rot. And we can't move him to another morgue. Someone will spot him. Everyone knows the face of Costas Gisikis. Oh God, I can't believe this. I was fond of the man. Now it's come to this.' Stelios closed his eyes and screwed up his face as if he were going to cry.

'Now's not the time for that,' said Helena, her first words for a very long time. She was sympathetic, but brusque. 'You can do your crying later, on your own, like the rest of us.'

Maria was less patient and more direct.

'Use your head, Stelios, for God's sake! That's what we paid you for. Keep my father here if necessary,' she stormed, fast getting out of control again, 'but make it impossible for anyone to see him. Find a way! You're just going to have to put any thoughts of decency and respect for the dead out of your head. For now, we've got to put our father's funeral on ice.'

Suddenly, unexpectedly, Stelios raised himself slowly and deliberately from the depths of the sofa, all his self-pity and regret apparently dismissed.

'That's it, Maria! Do you know that you're a fucking genius?' He was nevertheless grudging in his use of praise towards a woman whom he now recognised as being perilously unstable.

'Perhaps you might have read or heard of a machine that has been developed to put bodies in a state of suspended animation?' he asked, as if he were addressing a lecture hall of medical students. He received only blank looks.

'Well, yes, I know it all sounds a bit like science fiction but, the fact is, there's been research going on for years into the feasibility of freezing a person at death, with the view to defrosting them 15 or 150 years hence, whenever a cure becomes available for whatever killed them in the first place.'

Helena was sceptical. She wasn't certain that Stelios was all there now that he was faced with losing everything for which he had worked in his life. When she expressed her doubts, Stelios countered with his trump card.

'Helena, I realise this sounds bizarre, but in America a few very wealthy people have already put money up front to avail themselves of this service should the technology have developed sufficiently by the time they die for it to be of benefit to them. Some people are obsessed with control, even of their own mortality, and are able to pay for it.

'But the fact is that a prototype of the machine exists, and I'm storing it here at the Baltic. There was a medical convention held here in Athens some months ago. One of the exhibits was this special sort of human deep-freeze machine. There are several of them in existence, but it was here that doctors from around the world had a chance to assess its capabilities for the first time. It's still very much at the experimental stage, and the manufacturers are improving on it all the time.

'They left the prototype here because it's a delicate mechanism that doesn't travel well, and they'll come back to exhibit it again with any innovations in a year's time. But what have we got to lose, meanwhile, if we attempt to put Costas' corpse into a kind of suspended animation?'

Stelios poured himself a glass of water from the jug on his desk. 'The principle is very simple. The body is inserted into a tubular glass vessel, but the freezing process is done very carefully so that every part of the body is cooled down and uniformly frozen. This involves the removal of fluids and gases and a great deal of technical expertise.'

Then he stopped what he was saying and simply shook his head.

'This needn't concern you,' he continued, his voice now subdued. 'All I need to know is whether or not you're willing to give it a try. Of course, I don't expect you to say no. This is really our very last hope. Please think about it.'

And with that, he turned and left the room.

CHAPTER SEVEN

Costas Gisikis — or what was left of the man — lay suspended in icy gas high above the floor, at eye level, on a transparent shelf encased in a tube of clear crystal. His arms were neatly positioned by his sides, his hands spread palms upwards. He lay perfectly still, enveloped in the strangeness of his hi-tech coffin, lit from below by an arc of powerful lamps. His eyes were shut. His chest did not rise and fall with his breath. He had none.

The isolation ward in which he lay was soundless, except for a low chant that emanated from his sister-in-law Helena Kokas, who was praying quietly in a corner of the room to the count of her worry beads. Maria stood beside her, watching her father, then her aunt with increasing agitation. Suddenly, she snatched the amber string of beads from her aunt's fingers and threw them across the room.

'Get a life, Helena!' she stormed quietly. 'For God's sake, he's not going to help you now. Forget the paganism, we're approaching the new millennium. There's no room for ritualised superstition any more.'

Helena was too surprised at first to react, then she just burst into tears. As she sobbed, she recovered her spirit sufficiently to say, 'No good will come of that, Maria. No good will come of any of this. The gods are angry. We have the mark of Cain on us now. Remember my words.' And with that she fell into a faint on the floor of Costas' icy makeshift mausoleum.

Anthony Burton had gone straight from the airport to his office in London's East End, leaving his wife to return home alone. She knew there was no stopping him now, so she had resigned herself to being a widow to his obsession for however long it took to resolve. Margaret Burton was too intelligent to try to dissuade her husband once he'd got the bit between his teeth.

The headquarters of the Inland Revenue were housed in the Strand, beside the river in Somerset House, the imposing 18th-century Classical compound that contained the spectacular small art collection of textile magnate Samuel Courtauld alongside multifarious Revenue policy-making departments.

This was in sharp contrast to the distinctly unglamorous Borough High Street, where the Special Compliance Office, for which Burton had worked for the past three years, was based. There, they dealt with any cases that were especially complicated, such as those in which there was reason to believe some malpractice or those of the mega-rich.

It was the latter over whom Burton was especially vigilant. His socialist inclinations did not support the ownership of immense wealth. It verged on a crusade for him, seeing himself as a sort of Robin Hood figure, not stealing from the rich to give to the poor, but ensuring that any fiscal evasions were stamped on firmly.

There was no one else around at that hour of the night, so Burton could work on undisturbed by his colleagues and the inevitable office politics. His priority was to amass the facts on the Gisikis estate, and he called up the Gisikis Shipping file on his computer.

He already knew that the income tax due on earnings was immense, never mind the inheritance tax bill. From what he saw as he collated the facts and figures of the case, it was clear that if Costas Gisikis were to die a British resident, his heirs would be forced to auction off a considerable part of their global assets to finance the UK tax bill.

By the time his colleagues arrived for work at 8.30am the following morning, Anthony had gathered all the information he felt he needed on the billionaire tycoon. But he didn't make any attempt to relay any of this to his workmates or to relate to them at all. In any case, his ambition and single-mindedness went some way to ensuring that he was not popular within the department. All he could think of was coming first and rising as fast up the greasy pole as he could manage. He didn't have time to operate at half-cock.

The morning was no different from any other in his eyes, and he was unwilling to chat about his Greek trip or find out about what had been happening in the office in his absence. Nothing, frankly nothing, would have changed there. Just like any other day, he opted to ignore the inevitable snipes and jokes of office life and get stuck into his work. But not before he'd booked an appointment with his boss, Frank Argent.

Well, he had to go through the formalities. Though he doubted he'd get much change out of Argent, a job-for-life man who was two years short of retirement and concerned only that nothing should get in the way of his pension.

There had been a time when Argent had enjoyed taking risks, pursuing hunches, the thrill of the chase, but now all he wanted was a quiet life. He was not keen on any investigations, which made his inspectors' working lives tedious to say the least. But he didn't want to jeopardise his future. After all, there was always the chance that something might badly backfire. He was no longer a man who wanted to take chances. And this put him at odds with his younger colleague.

Because of this and other reasons not unconnected to Burton's stubborn personality and intransigent nature, there was no love lost between the two men. Argent bristled whenever Burton came into his orbit. Not surprisingly. It could not have been pleasant to be in the company of a man who was clearly after his job.

To Anthony's annoyance, when he turned up for his 11.00am meeting with Argent, his boss had cancelled the appointment, simply because he didn't want to face the younger man, didn't want him to ruin his day. He didn't know what Burton wanted of him, but he had a hunch that it wouldn't be to show him his holiday snaps.

Helena lay in her flotation tank, cut off from the world, attempting to relax and forget, just momentarily, how hazardous her life had become. The deception over Costas' death was all so complicated and wearing. She didn't mind telling lies to get what she wanted, but this was more than that.

There had been the endless phonecalls from assorted dignitaries and ambassadors, political allies and business acquaintances, friends, employees and distant relations. They, each and every one of them, had to be dealt with properly, tactfully dissuaded from visiting Costas. All she could say for sure was that Costas was too ill for visitors. He could receive no one. At least she could be unequivocal about that.

One person who could not be fobbed off was Stelios' mother, Athena. Despite her advanced years and failing health, she was singularly persistent. So much so that she'd turned up again at the Baltic and created another scene.

Fortunately, the Press had given up their vigil outside the hospital entrance, so there was no media uproar to placate. But it had been unpleasant to say the least. And they'd had to call in extra security. Stelios had insisted, and Maria had arranged it. No one in their right minds would meddle with the team of security consultants she engaged for the job. Barbara Meier and Jacques Schotsmans struck fear into the hearts of even the most hardened ex-cons. Maria knew that when she'd booked their services.

Maria was a paradoxical character, so weak and dependent in many ways, yet with a remarkable ruthless streak, an inner toughness that bordered on the cruel. When push came to shove, it was her twin who was the more vulnerable.

She had organised the security back-up with a surprising briskness and efficiency that she showed about anything to do with her own well-being. She was accustomed to calling on the Meier/Schotsmans partnership whenever she required a minder for a social engagement at one of the season's high points, when she most felt in need of a buffer between her and what she saw as the 'hoi polloi'.

Maybe she'd decided to wear an expensive piece of jewellery to a film première or first night, or she and John just felt like bolstering their image out on the town, doing a tour of the nightclubs with a brace of bodyguards beside them. Whatever the motive, Meier and Schotsmans were ideally cast for the part of putting the fear of God into most people.

Helena had met the team just once before. She shuddered at the memory. They offended what few sensibilities remained to her. Meier was a statuesque blonde with an hour-glass figure, who, at just over 6ft and oozing a fierce kind of sex appeal, either turned men on or scared them witless. Either way, she drove them wild. Her past was certainly shady, and she carried with her an aura of menace. Her partner was a muscle-bound hard man with a shaven scalp that bore a small tattoo at its base. Schotsmans was in thrall to Barbara Meier, but in his own right more than capable of inspiring terror in the hearts and minds of others. What they both possessed, and what most discomfited Helena, was attitude.

Helena lay in a blanket of dark; no chink of light could penetrate the tank, no sound could reach her ears. The warm, herbal infusion lapping around her held her gently in its watery embrace. No one, nothing, could reach her there, except her own thoughts. But her mind would not let her rest. For all the wickedness she'd sanctioned over the years, this time life had got to her. This was something that couldn't be overlooked. She could find no rest from it.

Unlike Helena, John and Maria were not victims of their own consciences. After deciding to consign their dead father to his icy limbo, they dismissed him from their minds and chose not to dwell too long on the morality of their decision and its possible repercussions. The only thorn in their collective flesh was their kid brother. George's phonecalls from New York were a daily irritant, but they made a supreme effort to remain unerringly polite and solicitous towards him. It was vital to keep him sweet — and in the dark.

In a rash display of spontaneity that was ill considered under the circumstances, the Gisikis twins threw a lavish dinner party for a few close friends, a motley selection of low-lifers and high fliers. Stelios was among them and turned up in some style in his new Porsche convertible. The ravishing woman who stood next to him in the vaulted marble porch as he rang the doorbell and waited for an answer would not have looked out of place in a Playboy centrefold.

He kissed his cousin John hello, twice on the cheeks. Stelios tilted his head in the direction of his date and, with a lascivious look on his face, muttered quietly, 'It's called Porsche power.'

Maria, standing nearby, overheard him and cut through his complacency with a loud stage whisper that was almost designed to be audible to the other woman. 'She's got something more important than that, Stelios. It's called pussy power.' Stelios smiled stiffly at her remark and left it unchallenged.

And so the evening progressed in a display of extravagant poor taste and flamboyant excess the like of which the Gisikis staff had not seen before. There was no attempt made to hide anything, no sign of restraint or decorum. Lines of coke were laid out on tabletops, next to the Veuve Clicquot, the caviare and the white truffles. No one tried to conceal anything from anyone.

During the course of the evening, one of the servants was shocked to discover that among the guests was a Parisian couturier, who had been specially flown in to design something suitable for Maria to wear at her father's funeral. It was incomprehensible to them that Costas Gisikis' children could desecrate his good name, almost to dance on his grave, while he lay helpless in a coma.

But when Stelios awoke the following morning, any misgivings he might have had vanished at the sight of his bedmate. He watched her as she slept, his penis stirring involuntarily, and he moved to wake her to satisfy his lust. He couldn't believe his luck. Life was perfect, he decided, now that he had the pulling power of money.

Anthony Burton's meeting with Fred Argent proved entirely fruitless. The older man rejected point blank any idea of an investigation into the powerful Gisikis empire. When Anthony presented him with the details of the case, he scanned the report in silence for a few minutes, before passing it back to him wearily.

'You have no real proof there, whatsoever, Anthony. This man Gisikis is immensely influential with friends in high places. He dines not irregularly at Downing Street and Buckingham Palace.'

Fred Argent took off his spectacles and placed them deliberately on the leather-topped desk in front of him. He sighed heavily and rubbed his eyes in a way that indicated he was suffering from the effect of too many disturbed nights, for which, it was implied, Anthony was to blame.

'If we open an investigation into the integrity of a corporate structure whose executive is so well connected, at the point when its Executive Chairman is critically ill in hospital, we could trigger a diplomatic incident with God knows what repercussions. Especially if our inquiry proved groundless. I'm not prepared to take the risk, so let's just forget that you brought the subject up, shall we?'

And with that, despite his strongest attempts to stand his ground and describe a more positive outcome, Anthony was dismissed.

Down but not out, he arranged a meeting at the Ritz with an acquaintance from the Serious Fraud Office. He spared no expense over lunch in the opulent Louis XVI Terrace restaurant, where voluminous swagged curtains hung at huge windows overlooking the Italian Garden in the tree-filled oasis of Green Park. But to no avail.

Not even the wonderful Arcadian painted ceiling, where gilded chandeliers hung from a fresco of clouds, was enough to distract Anthony's dining companion from the reality of life at the SFO, where their track record had been so dismal of late that they weren't keen to make another wrong move. Indeed, they were required to proceed with extreme caution with any potential prosecution.

Anthony took it on the chin and appeared to shrug it off as he parted from his lunch guest in the traffic roar of Piccadilly. But back home in bed that night, he took it out on his wife. For the first time since they had met, he could not get an erection despite her best attempts to arouse him. At 2.00am, he switched on the bedside lamp and they sat up in bed together, talking it over, and inevitably returning to Anthony's feelings about the Gisikis case.

Anthony held his wife tightly in his arms as he talked on and on, not able to reconcile himself to the inadequacies of a system that blocked him.

'That's what power does to people,' he said, thumping his fist down on to the mattress. 'Those who have it use it to intimidate, those who don't have it fear those who do. It's against everything I believe in, contrary to all my principles.'

And he poured out his frustrations about a system that left him feeling so impotent. Margaret knew her husband exceedingly well, almost better than he knew himself, and she realised how much he was suffering. It seemed as if he were trying to take on the whole world. And although she knew it was an impossible task, she loved him for it.

And so it was Margaret Burton who suggested that her husband should return to Greece under his own steam, taking what was left of his holiday entitlement and sorting out the business in his own mind as best he could, once and for all. In any case, it was the only practical solution that would save their marriage.

Argent couldn't deny him this. And he didn't. But the tax inspector washed his hands of him. Anthony was on his own, fighting a lone battle. Which, for him, was nothing new.

CHAPTER EIGHT

Costas had been negotiating with the People's Republic of China for a licence to run a ferry service in Shanghai for some time before his emergency admittance to the Baltic. Keen to build a bridge, to meet them half-way, he'd taken the trouble to learn some basic Mandarin and to visit the capital, Beijing, on two occasions. He was slowly discovering how best to deal with a culture that was totally different from that of the West, gradually moving on to first-name terms with influential Communist Party leaders and the Central Committee Secretariat, who had responded to his efforts and eased his way through the maze of Chinese bureaucracy.

George was not so lucky. Stepping into his father's shoes was much harder than it looked. And now the Chinese Government was insisting that if he were to pick up where his father had left off, then he must come personally to Beijing. But every minute of George's working day was spoken for, block-booked for meeting after meeting, and he just was not able to put in the time and effort required to smooth the path for Gisikis Shipping.

Then he'd had a less than enlightening telephone conversation with Maria. Whenever he called she was unfailingly polite, but what she said amounted effectively to nothing. He had no real idea of his father's condition, of whether or not he was progressing. And he realised that the only way to get things straight would be to fly to Athens and see for himself. It was only Monday, the beginning of his working week, and already he felt that he'd lost his grip.

Kimberley had been preoccupied, too, with a charity Cinderella Ball in New York to raise funds for the Homelessness Project. The guest-list was studded with stars and celebrities, and she'd had an extraordinarily generous response. Among the guests had been Jack and Karen Sullivan, the New York heart specialist and his doctor wife, parents of Oliver's schoolfriends who had spent time on board the Ariana that summer.

The Sullivans had asked about Costas and the kids' college plans, and Kimberley, not able to give them her full attention at the Ball, had later invited them to dinner. They were due later that week. She'd have to order something in; perhaps she'd get Daniel Boulud to cook for them. Yes, she would. She was so terribly busy. God knows they could do without supper guests right now, the strain was getting to her.

Maria and John were about to go out to dinner when Maria mentioned that she had spoken to George earlier in the day, and he was proving difficult. Asking too many questions. Making waves.

John dismissed her fears by saying that George had too many other things on his mind to prove any real threat to them. He poured his sister a large Hine and suggested that she should just relax before their friends arrived. He walked over to her with her drink, handed it to her and then stood behind his sister to massage her neck and shoulders and help her to unwind.

Although not to her liking, Helena knew that the twins led a double life. They mingled socially with international celebrities, society's richest, most highly esteemed and well connected, but there seemed sometimes to be a fine line between them and the world's dregs. A thin white line.

Their tendency was towards decadence, a sort of fiddle-while-Rome-burns, let-them-eat-cake approach to life. And while they were always seen in the company of the smart set, they were never seen out without each other. The twins were inseparable. And this was the focus of some gossip among the in-crowd. The word on the street, albeit Bond Street and Kolonaki, not Harlem or Canning Town, was incest.

This couldn't, in fact, have been further from the truth, which was that Maria was really only infatuated with one person — herself. She had affairs, but they never lasted. She was too insecure and narcissistic. And whenever a man showed any real interest in his sister, John would find a creative way to discourage it.

It suited her twin to continue the familiar pattern. To have Maria there on call, reliable, an undemanding, glamorous escort. John loved his freedom above everything, and he had no space for a woman in his life. He couldn't stand the idea of dealing with anyone else's needs. He was an indiscriminate womaniser, and when he'd wined, dined and slept his way through his friends and acquaintances, assorted gold-diggers and career-

shaggers, and exhausted the supply of one-night
stands he met in nightclubs and drinking clubs and
casinos, whenever he wanted sex he bought it.

With their father's fortune within their grasp, the
twins both knew they would soon be able to do and
have whatever they wanted. John had his eye on a
McLaren FI, and Maria on a shopping spree at the
Chanel Joaillerie Boutique in New Bond Street. And
that was just for starters. God knows down which
road to nowhere it would all take them. But they had
no such doubts and anticipated with a degree of
ruthlessness the day when no one would have any
control over them. No over-solitictous father, no over-
zealous accountants, no over-scrupulous Charles
Bradley and, especially, no wonder-boy brother.

George was relaxing with a large Macallan on ice. It
was Saturday, early evening, and his week had just
ended. He'd made it back in time to dine with the
Sullivans. Fortunately, he didn't feel the need to
change into one of his many Armani suits because
they were entertaining at home, in their magnificent
double-height dining-room with its stunning views
across Manhattan. He could dress more casually in
Chinos and an open-neck shirt, his Swiss-made Gucci
timepiece his only display of wealth, although the
apartment was hung with a selection of modern art
that made the Saatchi collection look tame.

'My children became very fond of your father
during the summer vacation. I understand that he's
not well?'

Over dinner, Jack Sullivan took advantage of a gap
in the conversation to talk about Costas. He'd heard
from his son Graham that the old man was in hospital

with a heart condition, and his professional interest had got the better of natural reserve and caution around people.

George stopped eating at the mention of his father's name. The Sullivans, of course, were in the game themselves. Perhaps he could take advantage of their presence at his supper table to pick their brains and get things straight in his own mind.

'Yes, yes,' George began hesitantly, trying to order his thoughts. 'My cousin Stelios Gisikis is a heart specialist in Athens. My father's under his care.'

Jack Sullivan's forkful of food hung in the air like an unanswered question. He appeared momentarily preoccupied.

'Ah, yes, Stelios Gisikis. Now that name rings a bell. I was out in Greece, attending a seminar in Athens a while ago. A fascinating conference with some amazing technological advances for medicine. I recall he was in charge at the host hospital, the Baltic.'

George nodded, 'That's right. He worked for a while in Harley Street, but moved his practice to Athens a few years ago. We're so out of touch with what's happening from day to day there, but my father's been in a coma for some time now. Stelios is keeping him in an isolation ward.'

'What!' Jack Sullivan couldn't believe what he was hearing. 'Isolation for a coma patient? Surely not!'

Kimberley took over from George, who seemed overpowered by the strength of the disbelief in Jack Sullivan's voice. She continued diffidently on his behalf. 'Yes, it's apparently because he's on a respirator and needs to be isolated from any external influences, which ...'

Jack Sullivan couldn't restrain himself from interrupting again. 'I've never heard of such a thing. Anyone in a coma needs someone there at all times, talking about everyday things. Just the sound of a familiar voice can bring someone round. It makes no difference that he's on a respirator.'

Jack realised he'd overstepped the mark and should have responded more tactfully. George was becoming visibly upset, and so he back-pedalled furiously.

'Listen, George,' he said, 'we in the States have our own ways of doing things. Nothing's set in stone. What is common medical practice in one country may well not be in another. I'd be quite happy to talk to Stelios if you'd like some medical input from this end to make more sense of it for you here.'

George pulled himself together enough to reply, thanking Jack for his offer of help. Once he'd spoken to Stelios to tell him about Jack, he'd put them in touch. But it took all Kimberley's not inconsiderable diplomatic talents to get the supper party flowing again.

On the road back to Long Island, Jack Sullivan finally let rip.

'Christ, Karen, that Stelios Gisikis must some kind of a quack to put a coma patient behind a fucking glass screen. Either that or he's completely deranged.' And Karen Sullivan could only agree with him.

George tried but failed to contact Stelios that night. It would have been the early hours of Sunday morning in Greece when he dialled his cousin's home number and left a message on his answerphone.

He lay awake most of the night, Jack Sullivan's words reverberating around his head. As the night dragged on without sleep, he became increasingly paranoid. Did Stelios have his father's best interests at heart? And the twins, even they couldn't stoop so low as to put his welfare at risk. But money could sometimes be what they always said about it, at the root of all evil. And he feared the worst — and worse — as the sun rose palely over Central Park.

When Kimberley woke later that morning, he talked to her about it. Having someone else to discuss it with made him feel more positive.

'Perhaps Sullivan will get a better explanation out of Stelios if I put them in touch. He might be able to clarify it for us in laymen's terms that we can understand. Maybe Stelios and I have got our wires crossed.'

But, in the back of his mind, he was all the time thinking that he must return to Greece to find out what was going on. And when he finally succeeded in getting through to Stelios, he was even more convinced of it. Although it was just ten o'clock in the morning in New York, the time in Athens was around six in the evening. Stelios sounded drunk and wrong-footed.

'How are you, George?' he asked warily.

'I could be better, thank you, Stelios,' George replied coolly. 'But let me get straight to the point.' And he reported his conversation with Jack Sullivan to his cousin. The time it took him to reply made George think that he'd been cut off.

Eventually, Stelios' voice came down the line loud and clear and very angry. 'Perhaps your friend should check out all the facts before making rash judgements from thousands of miles away about a case of which he knows nothing.'

George tried to reply, but Stelios talked over him, saying, 'As a matter of fact, your father's condition has improved. We have taken him off the respirator for periods when he is able to breathe unaided. He is under constant supervision, and occasionally we have to put him back on the machine. His heart is stronger, though, and he is showing good signs of recovery.'

'More than that,' he continued, unstoppable now, 'you ask about the isolation. Well, that was Helena's idea. She was worried that Greek natural demonstrativeness, too much touching and kissing, would put him at risk of infection. In the event, I had to agree with her.'

There was silence now at the New York end of the phone, and after a moment or two of it, Stelios sensed his victory.

'So, George,' he continued, triumphant at the way he had so cleverly disentangled himself on the spot with no time to rehearse his deception, 'perhaps your friend would like to think carefully before trashing a colleague's diagnosis and treatment. At least he should have placed a courtesy call to me before alarming you as much as he obviously has done already.'

And, as George began hesitantly to explain and apologise, Stelios knew he had succeeded in his cover-up. But if George had been talking to Stelios face to face rather than over the thousands of miles of telecommunications equipment, he would not have been so reassured. Stelios' feigned annoyance over the phone had done a good job of hiding the fact that his voice was trembling and his body profusely sweating and smelling rank with fear.

CHAPTER NINE

Helena's face turned pale at the thought of her contribution to Stelios's pay-off — £2m. And then the Baltic personnel. Probably another £2m. At least she had the cash. Over the years she'd creamed off thousands of pounds here and there from Costas' accounts — for her own peace of mind, she always told herself. After all, she could never be sure whether or not her hold over Costas would last, whether one day he might just throw her off the gravy train.

Helena had never invested her own money in anything in her life, but this would certainly be money well spent. Well, when you got down to it, hit bottom, you had no choice.

'I want to see my father,' George said, trying hard to stifle his emotions. Stelios had just turned his world upside down with the news about his father. While he'd been travelling to Athens, he'd felt as if he were doing something, making a difference. Now he'd arrived and discovered the truth, or, at least, Stelios' economy with it, he felt at a loss, angry and sad at the same time. Stelios had performed his part well in the Greek tragedy that had been scripted for him by

Helena and the twins.

George had been up all night. He hadn't managed to sleep, not even for five minutes, on the long flight across the Atlantic. His mind raced constantly, round and round in circles, always bringing him back to the same point. Will he be alive when I get there? Will I have a chance to say goodbye? And he remembered a million things he still wanted to say to his father. Most important of all, how much he loved him.

George changed planes at Heathrow as if in a dream. But once he touched down in Athens, the nightmare really started.

Stelios led George through an eternal maze of corridors, swing doors and ante-chambers, past rooms where, through porthole windows, he glimpsed the sick and the dying, the terminally ill cancer patient next to a fracture; the very old, the infant, the middle-aged, the adolescent; the sick tinkers, tailors, soldiers, sailors, rich men, poor men, beggar men, thieves. Illness was no respecter of age or social status.

They also walked past the nearest and dearest, the grieving, the anxious and the silently waiting who kept their vigil dredged up against the walls of the hospital in waiting rooms and corridors like so much flotsam washed up on the early morning tide. Cigarette smoke hung in the air like the white spiralling trails from a funeral pyre. And, from time to time, there was someone with a spring in their step, relieved, this time, that they or their loved one had escaped the Grim Reaper for the moment.

When, finally, they reached intensive care, Costas was not there.

Stelios had moved him to a special care unit, he

explained. George could see his father only at a distance, through a large reinforced pane of glass. No one, apart from Costas' hospital carers, could enter the room where the sick tycoon — George's father, Oliver's grandfather, sugar daddy to Helena, John and Maria — lay alone in the uncomfortable, narrow-looking hospital bed.

Costas was too at risk of infection for visitors, Stelios explained. If Costas were to catch anything, even to be exposed to the common cold virus, there was every chance his respiratory system just wouldn't be able to cope. It would kill him. They couldn't be too careful.

But Stelios had been very careful. He'd learnt his lines as if his life depended on it. Practised his deception, worked on his delivery, the right degree of sincerity, of sympathy, of empathy. No actor on a first night could have done more. He knew with a certainty that was adamantine that he couldn't afford to make one false move, not one slip of the tongue, not sound a single discordant note. His future wealth and happiness depended on it. And now, having taken this one small step, negotiated this minute bend in the truth, Stelios was committed to perpetuate his lie for however long it took, probably for ever. It had to be their secret — Helena's, Maria's, John's and his own — that would never be told, that would go with them to the grave. Stelios could not bring himself to think of what might happen thereafter.

He did not consider himself a religious man. Pilgrimage to the Cycladic island of Tinos twice a year to kiss the gold, diamonds and pearls of the icon at the chapel of Our Lady of Good Tidings was not for him. But he had a healthy respect for Orthodoxy and would often attend the midnight Easter service in Athens Cathedral. He liked all the pomp and circumstance, the candles, the incense, the shimmering lights, the red carpet, the gold and silver *ex votos* and lamps.

For all his urban sophistication, Stelios remained at heart the young Greek fisherman from Myra, who prided himself on his blunt, straightforward approach to life. And he'd learnt integrity and a sense of moral responsibility from his uncle, who had always encouraged him to be honest above all things. But Stelios knew now that he had fallen from grace. He wasn't sure he liked it, but he knew he had no option now but to put up and shut up. He'd burnt his bridges.

George turned slowly from the window of his father's hospital room. It was more like a prison than a sick-bay. He couldn't bear to look any longer.

Costas was a larger-than-life person. The man who lay there was not like that. Grey and still, almost corpse-like, shrouded under a white cotton hospital sheet, with a spaghetti junction of tubes attached to his body, to his nose, his mouth, his arms. His head thrown back by the nursing staff to maximise the flow of air into his body. Lost in a world that no one could reach. Unconscious. Comatose. This man had turned his face to the wall. This was not his father.

George began to walk away. Before he could make it along the corridor and through the revolving doors that swung him out into the warren of the main hospital, Stelios watched his cousin lean against the wall at the end of the corridor and slide to the floor. He saw him break down and weep, overcome by it all — his father on the edge of life or death, his own self-pity for the loss that was imminent. He found himself not able to hold back the avalanche of emotion that was triggered by grief. And his shoulders started to tremble, then shake, as he sobbed out his heart.

Stelios left his cousin on his own for a few minutes, barking out orders in every direction to his staff to chivvy them along and perpetuate the illusion that something could be done, that miracles can happen. Indeed, Stelios prayed for a miracle. At that moment, he would have walked on his knees to the chapel in Tinos to effect a cure for what he knew was not able to be healed — not by faith, hope or charity, and certainly not by any recent advances in medical science.

Stelios found himself more affected by George's distress than he'd ever imagined possible. He called on all his own considerable experience as a doctor, all those years of shutting off when patients were diagnosed or died. And when they did die, you let it run off you like water off a duck's back. It was your personal duty to your professional self to do this. But this time, it was different.

Stelios the doctor walked the length of the corridor towards George like a condemned man. He'd landed himself in the shit. Now he had to swim through it. 'George,' he said, putting his arm gently around his cousin. 'Listen to me now. You came all this way to see Costas. He knows you're here, even from the depths of his coma, even through the other side of the glass. He'll feel your support, and it will give him strength.

'But for now, the best thing you can do for Costas — and for yourself and the family — is to go home. There is absolutely nothing you can do here. Staying will only upset you, and that won't help anyone, neither you nor your father. Besides, we have no idea how long he might remain in the coma. It could be weeks, months, even years. You can't stay here just in case, putting your life on hold.'

George raised his head towards his cousin and regarded him with a despair that was discomfiting in its rawness. Stelios the man felt suddenly afraid. But his other self took over. Squatting down beside George, Stelios faced him squarely, looking steadily into his eyes.

'George. Your father really needs you now. He is depending on you to keep the Gisikis empire afloat, the shipping and the shelters. It will do you good to keep busy and take care of all that Costas has achieved, that he worked so hard for. Please try not to worry. Modern science is progressing all the time. Something might come along to help him. He might just pull through. His indomitable spirit might surprise us yet.'

George didn't reply for a long, long time. When he finally spoke, it was to thank his cousin for all he was doing for Costas, and to agree with him that, yes, he was right in what he said. It was best for him to protect the interests of Gisikis Shipping. He would return to New York the very next day, and keep linked with the Baltic on a daily, even hourly, basis. He could always fly back at a moment's notice. The world couldn't stop. Not while Costas still had the chance of a stab at life.

Stelios sensed a new resolve in his cousin that surprised him. But perhaps it shouldn't have done so. He was Costas' son, after all.

In the peace and tranquillity of the garden of Costas' Athenian home, Charles, who'd just arrived that morning, sat talking intensely to George beneath the spreading branches of Costas' favourite plane tree. Greek superstition had it that its shade was beneficial, good for your health and your spirit.

With that in mind, they talked fondly of Costas and made a deliberate pact to channel their energies into keeping Gisikis Shipping on track. It was what Costas would have done. It was what Costas would have wanted them to do. They would do it for Costas. They would do it for themselves. They would do it because it was the only thing to do.

That night, George went to bed early because he could not bear to share any part of the evening with either John, Maria or his aunt, for that matter. God knows what made them tick. Nothing natural, that was for sure.

But he need not have worried, at least not about the twins. He heard them return some time in the early hours of the morning. The crunch of the car tyres on the gravel of the driveway must have roused George. He was sleeping only lightly that night.

Soon, headlights beamed through the open blinds of his room, followed by the slamming of car doors and the choking sound of suppressed laughter. They had been out celebrating something, as usual. And with Costas at death's door, George shuddered to think what.

The next day, Costas' photograph was on the front page of all the international newspapers, attached to the Gisikis family Press release. Its closing paragraph described the Greek billionaire's condition as stable.

Which was how George felt after a reasonably

good night's sleep. At least he'd rested. It didn't take the pain away, but he felt calmer.

Over the breakfast table, Helena put on a magnificent show for George. She ate nothing, despite constant attempts to entice her to do so from the attentive team of staff on duty in the dining-room. She sat edgily in her chair, wringing the white damask napkin on her lap.

'It was horrible to see him like that,' she whimpered. Then she stopped dramatically for a few moments, her eyes blinking rapidly as if to hold back her tears. Recovering her composure, she went on.

'I just couldn't bear it yesterday. I had to leave the hospital. Then the guilt took over, and I thought to myself, I should — I must — be brave. So I went back, Frank took me, to sit on the other side of the glass, believing I was doing something useful for Costas.'

She choked back her tears once more and, after another dramatic pause to compose herself, she said, 'Then, I realised I wasn't doing him any good at all. I was better off getting on with the things I normally do for Costas. After all, he might wake up some day soon, and he wouldn't want to know that I'd let his home, all this ...' she indicated the room in all its finery, from its sparkling chandeliered ceiling to the glorious oriental carpets on the polished wood-block floor '... to fall apart. He would be very disappointed.'

George responded just as Helena had hoped he would. He leant over across the table and took his aunt's hand, stroking it gently.

'At first,' he said, 'I didn't understand why you weren't there at his side in the hospital, sitting near him, willing him well. But I understand now, and I think you're doing the right thing.'

As the Merc taking George and Charles to the Baltic en route to the airport disappeared through the gates of the Gisikis mansion, Helena returned to the task that interested her most in life — studying the social columns of the assorted newspapers and magazines they'd ordered to view the media coverage of Costas' sudden ill health.

But, for once, John rebuked both her and Maria, who was gloating already about their victory in successfully seeing off George and Charles Bradley, dismissing them as suckers. 'They think they're so clever and so virtuous. They're nothing but ...'

'For God's sake,' John interjected, 'just shut up. Both of you. Don't you realise we've only succeeded in getting over the first hurdle. We've got a long way to go before we can pull this off. So let's just keep our heads screwed on and see this thing through to the end.'

The two women exchanged looks of fake annoyance. But they knew he was right. When Stelios phoned a few hours later to say that George and Charles had just left for Ellinikon, they all heaved a sigh of relief. Stelios would come by later that week to work out a feasible game plan. They all knew that they had to win not only the game, but also set and match.

CHAPTER TEN

Anthony Burton's attention was firmly focused on his wife. On the roundness of her full breasts, and on her nipples that he felt hardening beneath her flimsy, black satin slip. Her sweet, natural body perfume filled his senses and drove him wild with desire. He tugged at the thin straps of her gown and slipped it off impatiently, throwing it carelessly to the floor.

He felt his penis rising as her heavy breasts fell free, and he took one in his open mouth and cradled the other in his hand. His hard tongue teasingly rimmed her nipples before sucking hard on them, each one in turn.

Anthony's remaining item of clothing, his Calvin Klein boxer shorts, had only reached half-way down his strong, muscular legs when Margaret took hold of his hand to stop him. He gave up on undressing himself to let her finish stripping him, but she took no notice of whether or not he was fully naked and instead took his hard, throbbing cock greedily into her mouth. Excitement rushed through his body as she sucked and sucked, occasionally stopping to work skilfully at the eye of his cock with the tip of her tongue. She enveloped his testicles, one by one, in her wet mouth, caressing them with her tongue, sucking and encircling them. In and out, tantalising. Anthony grabbed the headboard of the bed and tried desperately to stifle his wild groans of unabashed, unabated pleasure.

Her tongue, still so wet, traced the contours of his scrotum gently, yet, at times, unbearably, excruciatingly, probing, licking, until his body tingled and burned. Once more she took his penis back into her mouth. At this he found he could no longer control himself and lifted his hips to push his massive cock ever more deeply between her thick, sensual lips. He released his grip on the bed and took hold of his wife, holding her tight as he plunged in and out of her mouth, steadily pumping and pushing his swollen penis harder and deeper into her throat.

As lust overcame him, it weakened his ability to slow down or stop his orgasm. He started to pant rapidly as he launched into a series of short thrusts, finally exploding in her mouth with an animalistic scream of surrender that arose from somewhere deep inside him.

Before falling asleep that night, he took his wife and made love to her, raising her to heights of pleasure that she had never thought possible. Fulfilled but exhausted, he slept better that night than he had for some time, and left the following morning to catch a flight back to Greece, the memory of their lovemaking fresh in his mind. As the Olympic Airways jet from London taxied towards the terminal building at Ellinikon, he stared blankly outside at the concrete runway. The pollution hung thickly in the afternoon air, and he realised that he had no idea of where to start to look for the corruption that he was convinced had taken over the soul of the Gisikis empire.

It was commonly said that New York's Central Park was like a valve letting the steam escape from the pressure-cooker city. And George could relate to that description today. But he had no way at all of letting off steam himself. So he'd tried walking around its 750 acres, past the roller-bladers and the cyclists, the joggers and the dog walkers, the strollers and the watchers. Past the Central Park West folly of the German Renaissance mansion, the giant Dakota Building, where John Lennon was shot. Through the Ramble, up to Vista Rock and Belvedere Tower.

Here he took stock. His body ached, not from the walk but from a lack of sleep and the endless interruption of nightmares that wouldn't let him rest. He'd become obsessively concerned about his father. Something inside him would not let go of it. Back at the apartment, he'd made his decision and picked up the phone to book a Concorde flight to Heathrow. He knew Kimberley would support him, and he put in a call to Charles Bradley to see if they could meet at the Heathrow Sheraton Skyline for cocktails.

Charles was in town and willing to make the journey to Heathrow to see George. In fact, he met him straight off the plane from New York's JFK, and the lawyer was shocked to see how tired and drawn the younger man looked. Next to the indoor pool, amid the jungle of tropical foliage of the Patio Caribe, they incongruously discussed Gisikis Shipping affairs before moving on to what most preoccupied them both — Costas.

Talking to Charles was immensely unburdening

for George. He, like George, could make no sense of what he was told by Stelios from Athens, nor could he communicate with either of the twins, who refused to return his calls ever since he'd cancelled John's order with McLaren's in Park Lane.

He showed no surprise when George told him of his trip to Athens. It was something he'd considered himself, but he had to tread carefully.

'Unfortunately,' Charles confided, 'Helena has an outrageously large allowance and something of a free hand at squeezing a bit extra. She allows the twins to do as they wish with it. But she's sailing too close to the wind, and I assure you that the party won't last for ever.' He offered to accompany George to Greece, but George felt he should at least try to sort out this family crisis on his own. If John and Maria or Helena, for that matter, proved awkward and unco-operative, then he would have to deal with them as and when. He was not going to allow them to brow-beat him. It was insulting to Costas and made a fool of a defenceless old man on his sick-bed. They shouldn't under-estimate his power, or his anger. He loved his father, and no one would be permitted to walk all over him or harm him in any way.

Charles accompanied George to the Virgin check-in to confirm his economy seat on an airbus shuttle to Athens. It was vital that he arrived incognito in order to maintain that disturbing element of surprise.

Bright sunshine filtered through the window of the hotel near the Baltic into which Anthony had booked himself. He hadn't had enough sleep because he'd decided to take time out to explore Athens the previous night. His research had taken him to an assortment of bars and clubs, where he'd drunk a lot of ouzo and retsina, with Metaxa chasers. He could hold his drink but this was enough to make him sleep in the following morning.

The hotel was situated opposite the Baltic. Anthony had asked the taxi driver to take him to the hospital from the airport, and he'd spotted it en route. Its front rooms overlooked the entrance, so he felt that, for once, luck was on his side.

Anthony was a sophisticated man, not unused to international travel, but this trip was different, and he felt somewhat vulnerable and ill at ease. The Gisikis family had a lot of influence in this city, and he would have to pursue his inquiries with some care.

Clearly, the Greeks simply loved Costas. The taxi driver had spoken of him passionately. He described him as a great benefactor, who had donated generously to his people over the decades. No one spoke ill of him. Upright. Honest. Compassionate. If Anthony were pursuing a case against Gisikis Shipping, it was hard to reconcile his doubts about its financial integrity with the praise afforded the head of its tycoon owner. He was held in the highest regard, talked of with the greatest respect.

But still Anthony knew his instincts were correct. All he had to do now was to prove them so. He stood for a long time that morning just watching the traffic in and out of the Baltic. It was a busy hospital, with a constant flow of medical staff and visitors, of ambulances and taxis. He noted the change of shift times for the doctors and nurses. The hours most visitors favoured for visiting. Who and what used the timed parking zones. In the back of his mind, a plan began to take shape.

Among those Anthony saw arriving at the Baltic was the driver of a brand-new Porsche. Business was obviously booming in the health industry, he thought, as he watched him park up in one of the reserved bays.

Stelios had arrived for work late that day. He was getting into bad habits, out clubbing most nights, taking E and never going to bed alone. His nerves couldn't take it. But if he stayed at home and tried an early night, he just brooded and got nowhere. Either way, he was stymied.

Stelios was acutely conscious of the extra security at the Baltic. He didn't care for it. Somehow it wasn't appropriate in a hospital full of the ill and dying. But it was essential to release his own staff to get on with their duties. Still, it made him feel ill at ease, and he was worried that questions might be asked at the next meeting of the hospital executive.

He was taking advantage of a gap before afternoon surgery, doing some paperwork over a strong cup of black coffee when there was a loud knock at the door. Whoever it was didn't wait to be invited in. He was frowning at the interruption, preparing to berate the intruder but, when Maria and John burst in, he stopped himself. They were both so obviously agitated. Maria looked even more deranged than her twin, like a tightly coiled spring about to be released and fly sky-high out of orbit.

'We're in seriously deep shit,' she said without any of the usual introductory courtesies, hysteria edging her voice.

'Come on, Maria, it can't be as bad as all that. I know ...' Stelios began.

'No,' Maria interrupted fiercely, 'you know fuck all! And what you don't know and need to know is that we just took a call from our contact at airport security, Barbara and Jacques' man. He was routinely checking the passenger list, when he discovered something he thought might interest us.'

And she paused, as much to catch her breath and stop her words running panic-stricken into each other, as for dramatic effect.

'George,' she repeated her brother's name for emphasis and to remind herself that it was all true, 'George is on a Virgin flight from Heathrow due to land in one hour's time.

'It looks like baby brother's on to something. And we've got to stop him. He'll blow our cover. Him and his wretched integrity, his fucking honesty. Who does he fucking well think he is? That he can walk in here unannounced, when we're handling everything. He'll lose us our inheritance. Oh God! Just do something, for Christ's sake! I can't stand it any more.'

And she began to rant and rave uncontrollably as if by doing so she could bully the world into submission, as she'd done so successfully up to this point in her life.

'Maria,' John began to try and reason with his twin, 'there's not a lot we can do. George is sure to head straight for the hospital. And that will be the end of it. We're finished. I think the best thing for Stelios to do is to get the old man out of that contraption and make out he just died. Announce it to the Press.'

Stelios began to nod in agreement, resigning himself to what he was beginning to see as inevitable.

'Are you both fucking mad?' Maria interrupted, the colour rising in her cheeks in anger. 'We're well into this. We've started, so we'll finish. We just have to think of something, damned quick.'

Without waiting for either of them to reply, Maria reached over to Stelios's desk and picked up the phone to dial a number that she obviously knew by heart.

'Barbara,' she said, 'it's me, Maria. Listen. George is about to arrive at Ellinikon. Yes, in less than an hour, and I want a tail put on him the minute he crosses through Customs ... Sure, but be discreet. We don't want him to guess we're on to him ... No, no need to cramp his style as this point. Thanks! Keep me posted ... of course. Bye.'

When she put down the phone, John just looked at her, shaking his head and asking, in a flat, expressionless voice, as if he'd had all his life breath punched out of him, 'Why on earth did you do that? Why put those gorillas on to him? He's our brother when all's said and done. You never know what those maniacs will do.'

Maria stared through him and into space and didn't say anything for what seemed like a very long time.

'Our little brother is not as predictable as we thought. Who knows what he's up to?' she said finally. 'We'll need to know if anyone meets him at the airport, if he makes any calls and, more importantly, if he contacts the police.'

She pushed a few strands of hair from her face and sighed, sort of relieved, as if she'd expurgated something poisonous from her psyche. 'I'm not ordering Stelios to take the old man off the machine unless it's absolutely necessary. Is that clear, Stelios?' And she turned her attention on her hapless cousin, who simply shrugged.

'Whatever you say, boss,' Stelios replied, without a trace of irony.

CHAPTER ELEVEN

George's plan to slip into Athens unnoticed went smoothly until he approached passport control, when the immigration officer recognised him and offered to call the VIP representative to assist him. George was adamant that he could manage on his own. The plane had been packed with conference delegates, so there was a crowd for him to hide among. George found it useful to mingle among them while waiting to collect his suitcase, thereby concealing himself from any other solicitious member of the airport ground staff.

He cleared Customs quickly and moved swiftly to the head of the queue at the taxi rank. Lying back in the familiar battered upholstery of the cab's interior, he began to feel more at ease than he had for a while. But if George had known that the driver of the white Toyota that emerged from a side-street, cutting into the traffic to settle in behind his cab, was one Jacques Schotsmans, no doubt he would not have felt so comfortable.

Jacques was talking on his mobile phone, a state-of-the-art Nokia 9000, which combined a fax-modem and personalised computer. He wanted only the best for himself and that was what he usually got. The means he took to get there were inevitably alarming. His area of expertise was high-explosives, which was how he knew how to handle Barbara. They'd met two years earlier, just after she'd finished a long haul in a German high-security jail for working as a hit-man with a terrorist group under the codename 'Icewoman'. She was a mercenary at heart, though many doubted she had ever possessed one. Their alliance was an unholy mixture of business and pleasure or, more often, terror. For the hard man was like putty in Barbara's hands. And he enjoyed her domination.

'It appears that they're heading north, towards the hospital,' Jacques said.

'Fine,' Barbara replied, 'I'm on my way there myself. Just stay on his tail. Don't lose him, whatever you do.'

Jacques knew better than to deny Barbara anything she requested. He was bound to her. And she was as unemotional with him as she was about the lives she blew away on someone else's whim. She was well paid to kill. Each time she did so, she enjoyed it more. It gave her great pleasure to see fear in the eyes of her victims. She personified depravity. And something in Jacques liked her like that.

'George is about twenty minutes away, stuck in traffic,' Barbara announced, putting her phone back into the pocket of her padded jacket. She poured herself a glass of water and sat back down on Stelios' vast leather sofa.

'I have one of my men guarding the isolation wing. I'll introduce you so he knows you're the only people he should allow through.'

Standing by the window, Barbara took a long drink of her water and asked, 'So, what's the plan?'

It was Maria who replied. John said nothing, preoccupied by his misgivings about how events were beginning to unfold. He felt Maria had really overstepped the mark this time by bringing in Meier and Schotsmans. He vaguely heard his sister in the background, organising him, slotting him into her plans. God, Maria was always so determined when she felt the need.

'John and I will time it perfectly. We'll effect an accidental meeting with him just as he's approaching the isolation wing. We'll pretend we've just checked out the old man, and I'll be crying and stuff, and make out that it would be too distressing for George to go in to see him.

'We'll play on his closeness to Costas. Spin him the line on how dear George is to him, and that he must believe that the sight of our father now he's so sick would be too much for him to bear. Better for George to remember him as he was, not the shadow of the man he's become. You get the drift. Then we'll edge him out of the hospital and escort him back to the house.'

Barbara said nothing. Merely raised an eyebrow with slow disdain.

'I see,' she said. 'And what will you do if he doesn't fit in with your plan?'

'I don't know,' Maria replied glibly. 'We'll cross that bridge if and when we get to it.'

Barbara's mobile rang again. She slipped it briskly from her pocket. 'Yes,' she said impatiently. 'OK ... OK ... OK.'

She barked her orders to the rest of the room, like

a troop commander on military manoeuvres.

'Right!' she announced, 'He's here. Paying off the driver at the front entrance. John, Maria, let's get over to isolation. I'll introduce you to the guard. Then I'll come back and wait for you here. OK! Let's go.'

George took the service lift up to the top floor of the hospital and then made his way carefully down the back staircase until he was within sight of the isolation unit. He was about to push through the double swing doors that led him to its corridor, when John and Maria beat him to it, coming the other way.

Maria summoned up all her not inconsiderable skills as an actress to express her utmost surprise at George's presence there.

'Christ, George, what the hell are you doing? In Greece ... in Athens ... here! Stelios was just telling us that he'd only just spoken to you, well, recently.' With the agility of a seasoned performer, she abruptly dropped her astonishment to pick up distress, and fell into her younger brother's arms, sobbing.

'Oh, George, thank God you're here. But what the hell are we going to do? Papa looks so dreadful, I just can't think what's best any more.'

As Maria sobbed on to his shoulder, George felt himself stiffen emotionally and felt decidedly awkward at such an unaccustomed closeness to his sister. He felt himself freeze, not able to respond to her. John watched the scene with some admiration at his twin's astonishing and alarming aptitude for her new role. All he could manage himself was a rather disingenous, 'Nice to see you, George. Why didn't you let us know you were coming?'

Before George could reply to either of them, Maria was talking at him again, blowing her nose and wiping her tear-stained face with a convincing show of recovered spirits and renewed determination.

'We were just leaving,' she said, rather self-evidently. 'I don't think it's wise for you to go in now. It would break your heart to see Papa. Stelios is going to change his drugs, to improve things for him, make him more comfortable. You should wait. Papa is terribly changed. You would not recognise him, better to remember him as he was. So strong, so vital, so ...'

And Maria found herself unable to continue as she broke down in a fit of uncontrolled sobbing.

'Oh, Maria, I know what you're going through. Please don't distress yourself any further. But I've come all this way and I must see him, I must ...'

'No, no,' Maria screamed. 'Absolutely not. You can't, Georgy, you can't.' And she fell to the floor and hung on to him, anchoring him to the spot.

'Get up, Maria, for God's sake!' John said with an edge of disgust in his voice. She was really overdoing it now. Christ, didn't she ever know when to stop? He turned to his brother to explain that the nurse was changing Costas' sheets and medication drip and attending to various mundane hospital procedures from which visitors were routinely excluded.

But George was adamant and not to be dissuaded. He wrenched himself free of his sister.

'Where the hell is Stelios?' he yelled as he swung through the corridor door towards the isolation ward. 'And what on earth's got into you both? Why should you suddenly want to protect me for my own good, for God's sake? You've never given me a moment's thought before now.'

He now rushed along the corridor and towards the isolation ward and the glass partition through which he'd last seen his father. And when he got there, breathless from panic, from running and from his struggle with Maria, he just stood, for what seemed like an eternity, with his face pressed against the transparent wall of the isolation chamber.

Only two metres separated father and son, but it could have been that George saw him from across the universe, because there was no reaching him. Costas lay quite still and perfectly horizontal, suspended at eye level above the floor by thick cable wire in a transparent glass tube. There were none of the usual tubes up the nose and in the arm, no electro-cardiac monitor, no drip feed, no sheets even. He lay there naked and embalmed in a mist of dry ice.

And what was most remarkable was that he was totally motionless. George refocused on his father's face, but no, there was no flicker of expression, no movement. No life. Slowly, it dawned on George that his father was dead.

Anthony Burton kept vigil at his hotel window for the best part of two days. With his newspaper archive cuttings and photographs to assist him, he'd observed a lot of Gisikis activity in that time, and not an inconsiderable demonstration of their wealth and ostentation.

He watched the expensive, smart cars; the designer suits and couture dresses; the pampering by chauffeurs and doormen; the full, red-carpet treatment. And it disturbed him, that some people should set themselves so apart, so above, others. And it firmed his resolve to make them part with as much of their wealth as he could under the due process of law.

Anthony was not a malicious man. He liked to think of himself as fair. And what he observed was in no way that. Why did some people own the world and others be reduced to living on the street?

It was true that Anthony himself enjoyed the high life when it suited him. He bought his shirts in Jermyn Street and his suits in Savile Row. He took his wife to dine at Bibendum and The Ivy. His holidays were always abroad. He spent the odd weekend at Cliveden and the Manoir aux Quatre Saisons. He lived in Chelsea, just off Cheyne Walk, close by the river, and he belonged to the Chelsea Arts Club.

He was rich by most people's standards, with an income bolstered by his wife's earnings, which were far in excess of his own. Like Costas Gisikis, Anthony Burton had come a long way from his humble start in life. He didn't want to punish the very rich for their greed. Nor did he have a chip on his shoulder that linked back to his impoverished early life, as his colleagues often suspected. He'd never been really poor and never deprived of what really mattered in life — the love and support of those closest to him.

No, it was more a sense of fair play that motivated Anthony. He believed that one should render unto Caesar the things which are Caesar's; and unto God the things that are God's. And unto the poor that wealth that rightly belonged to them so that everyone had a decent stab at life, in a sort of universal karmic balance. Feeling exhausted after his hours on watch, Anthony decided to relax and take the rest of the day off. He headed into the centre of town and strolled for hours around the Acropolis. Its rocky, naturally fortified heights were the original city, where the kings lived with their courts. Its summit was nearly 100 metres above the general level of the modern city.

Life on the street preoccupied him, too. He liked its vibrancy and wanted to join in. To stroll around it like a tourist, absorbing its ancient culture and hectic modernity.

He found himself walking not far from the Palace of the exiled last king and then passed by the Benaki Museum. Inside, he learnt that Antoine Benaki had spent 35 years collecting objects from Europe and Asia. He arranged the collection in his family town house and presented it and its contents to the state. That's more like it, Anthony thought, as he scrutinised a gold bull's head from the 6th century BC. A bit of give and take.

George felt unsteady on his feet, and the short journey to Stelios' office, with the twins as escort, was a slow and painful one. Once inside the room, George sank down heavily into a deep armchair and leant his head back into its soft cushions, his face turned up towards the ceiling, his eyes shut. When he finally opened them, he stared fixedly at the ceiling, before asking, in a voice faint with emotion, 'How long?'

And then, more distinctly as he cleared his throat, nervous at his question, never mind the answer,

'How long ago did he die?'

Maria answered him with a plain matter-of-factness, as if he'd merely inquired about the weather.

'He died within 48 hours of his stroke. There was nothing we could have done to save him, or, believe me, we would have moved heaven and earth to do so.'

On the other side of the room, George was aware of Stelios talking into his intercom stating that he was in conference and must not be disturbed. But as the enormity of what had happened began to sink in, he became increasingly conscious of the other people in the room. Not only Stelios, Maria and John, and in a corner, Helena (who had been summoned with a cursory 'Tell her to get her arse over here immediately' from Maria), but also Barbara Meier. God, not her. What the hell was she doing there? And he asked her just that.

George had met Barbara once before, at the Gisikis mansion in Athens. He hadn't trusted her then, and he didn't trust her now. But that was hardly surprising. He'd found her so alarming on that first meeting that, knowing how she was employed as a security guard to members of his family, he'd run a security check on her.

When nothing came through the authorities in Greece, he'd moved his inquiries elsewhere. Barbara had a slight but nonetheless distinct German accent. It was, in fact, gained from her early years living in Hamburg with her mother, who'd gone there from northern Greece to find work in the 1960s. She had become pregnant with Barbara by the married owner of the restaurant where she worked as a waitress.

Barbara's arrival in the world was not to open arms. And, tragic as it was that her father had never acknowledged her, she'd been protesting about it ever since.

Through contacts in Germany, George was able to get the full story, involving her later imprisonment for terrorist activities. When George had passed the information on to Maria, she just laughed at him.

'Why do you think I feel so safe around her? Of course Barbara has the instinct of an untrained Rottweiler.'

Apparently, Maria was happy to use the services of a practised killer. The two women had even become friends, of a sort, and, from what George was beginning to piece together about the situation in which he now found himself, some of Barbara Meier's less attractive qualities were beginning to rub off on his insecure and impressionable sister.

In a voice thick with suppressed rage, George addressed everyone in the room when he said, 'As you're obviously all involved in this, perhaps one of you would care to explain to me exactly what's going on.'

It was John who spoke first.

'You are aware of the reasons why Papa returned to Greece. And we wanted to support his wish not to donate the major part of his estate to the UK tax authorities.'

'So you pretend he's still alive to the rest of the world, including me, perhaps the only person here who really loved him, and you're saying you did this because he would have wanted it. That you're carrying out his wishes. That it's on his instruction that you've tried to pull the wool over the eyes of the authorities and his business associates, as well as most of his friends and family, so that you can get your hands on your full share of the Gisikis empire's global assets.'

Maria picked up John's thread. Maybe, she thought, there's a way through this, of somehow getting him on our side.

'Frankly, Georgy,' she wheedled, using his pet name for the second time that day, 'Papa would turn in his grave if he knew that his hard-earned assets were largely handed over to the coffers of HM Government.' 'Turn in his grave?' George queried, his voice tiny and crazed with incredulity. 'Don't be so bloody ridiculous!' Anger was surging through his veins in a great rush of adrenalin.

'Now listen, and listen carefully!' he ordered, brooking no opposition. 'I want father removed from that contraption, whatever in God's name it is, and I want him placed in the hospital mortuary before we can arrange to give him the proper funeral he deserves and bury him next to Ariana. That's what he wanted for himself. Not this ... not this ... obscenely amoral fraudulent deception that you claim he would sanction. You damn yourselves twice for that.'

When no one moved, when no one spoke, when he realised that no was going to do anything, it just enraged him even more.

'You are all mad!' And he turned specifically on Helena. 'How, how could you let this happen? After all Costas has done for you over the years. You'd deny him the right to a decent burial.'

Helena looked shocked by his outburst, but said nothing as George turned his attention to the twins.

'You both disgust me! And I'm not going to let

any of you get away with this,' he said, addressing himself to the everyone in Stelios' office now. 'My father is to be buried now!' he repeated, 'and once he is laid to rest, I shall be contacting the authorities, the police, the taxmen, whoever needs to know. You all need to be either sectioned or locked up or fucking both.'

And with that George lunged forward to grab the phone from Stelios' desk. 'I'm calling Charles,' he announced naïvely, overlooking, in his panic and anger, the fact that this was the last thing they'd allow him to do. John snatched the receiver from his grasp.

'We have spent millions ...' he spat at his brother through clenched teeth, 'millions of pounds on this. And we are not stopping now. Screw your head on straight, little brother! You, Kimberley and your kid will profit from this just as much as we will.'

He lowered his voice to an almost menacing whisper. 'Just think about it, will you? And fast!'

Every muscle in George's body tensed and, without a word, he span round from John and began to walk towards the door. Just as his hand touched the handle, Maria's voice yelled out behind him, 'Don't move, George. Take your hand off the doorknob and turn round.'

A cold shiver like a bolt of lightning passed through George's body as he stopped at the touch of a cold metal object against his temple. Maria meant what she said, and to enforce it she had a gun pointed at his head. Barbara was heard to murmur her support from the other side of the room. George could see the shock in Helena's eyes that it had come to this.

'What are you going to do? Kill me?' George laughed in his sister's face, his own etched with hate for what she had become. He continued to stare at her fiercely, intensely, as he turned back to the door and started to open it.

George barely felt Barbara's highly trained fist chop the base of his skull, just behind his left ear, before he slumped unconscious to the ground. The single blow knocked him out cold. He had swayed for a split-second before dropping like stone on to the marble floor.

Maria leaned against the door, forcing it shut. Her hand shook nervously as she replaced the small hand-gun in her make-up bag. There was silence for a moment, and then Stelios stirred into action.

'I'll get a knock-out jab for him. If we can keep him unconscious, he won't be able to give us any more grief.'

Helena was sobbing quietly in the corner of the room. She wasn't so much upset for George as for herself. What was she going to do? She turned her head slightly towards Barbara as she began to plan their next move, but she could not bear to look the woman in the eye. She might take it the wrong way and attack her. She was a loose cannon, that at least was certain.

'That island your father bought, the one that's unoccupied now, where he used to be a shepherd?' She addressed her question to Maria.

'You mean Myra?' Maria suggested. Helena flinched at the mention of her island home. It was an innocent place. Was it now to have blood on its soil?

'The same. I'll helicopter George there. He won't be able to leave without a chopper or a boat, so we'll be able to mind him there until such time as you can announce Costas' death and claim your full inheritance.'

When Stelios came back into the room, Barbara had George bound and gagged. The surgeon couldn't bear the sight of his cousin's frightened, pleading eyes as he stuck the hypodermic into a swollen vein just above the rope tied tightly around his wrists.

Helena sat rocking back and forth, trying to comfort herself, persuade herself that it was only a bad dream. But when she heard the full extent of Barbara's evil proposal, she knew that it was truly a living nightmare.

'My services don't come cheap,' Barbara said. 'And you will thank me for coming up with a way to make George's family pay up for most of my fees.'

She stood next to George's roped and trussed body, resting a foot on his slumped form, as if he were a wild animal she'd just run to earth.

'I'm kidnapping George for a £10m ransom. I'll drag it out until such time as you are able to announce to the world that your father is dead and claim his fortune with impunity. I shall release him on payment of the ransom.'

She seemed pleased with her plan and continued to outline it with some confidence. 'When George is released and goes to the authorities with the story that you had put his father's corpse into an icy suspension to avoid payment of a global tax bill, there will be no evidence of it to back him up. You can always claim that the shock of imprisonment at terrorist hands has left him mentally unbalanced. And recommend psychiatric help to sort out his confused mind.'

Barbara finished what she had to say and released any accumulated tension in her body with a long, languorous stretch. She looked like a woman at the start of a new love affair, her face suddenly bright, beautiful and relaxed. It was an ingenious solution to an intractable problem. Maria was ecstatic with relief. John grudgingly accepted it. Stelios was resigned to its pragmatism. But Helena could not reconcile herself to her fate at all.

CHAPTER TWELVE

The lobby of the Baltic Private Hospital was packed with visitors, just as Anthony Burton had concluded it would be at that time of the evening. With a large bouquet of flowers in his arms, he strode purposefully past the reception desk unnoticed. Squeezing casually through the bustle, he made his way towards the lift at the furthest end of the entrance hall. He wanted to get into an empty lift and stop at every floor. But the odds were against that.

In the event, he shared the elevator with two nurses, who'd jumped in just as the doors were closing. They pressed the button for the eighth floor, which turned out to be the very top of the building. Oh well, he thought, at least he could start there and work his way down.

When the lift doors opened at their floor, Anthony stepped aside to allow the women to leave before him in a great display of chivalry. This appeared to amuse them, and they giggled and chattered between themselves, turning back to glance at him shyly. Anthony had a way with women, and they liked him.

His plan to recce the hospital floor by floor fell at the first fence. All the signs were in Greek. He stood there, looking around him helplessly, and noticed a security guard on duty at the end of a very long corridor. He couldn't make out what the sign above the door said, but the universal red-and-white symbol clearly indicated 'No Entry'. It would hardly be an operating theatre or intensive care. They didn't merit that kind of protection. Entry to specialist medical units was usually monitored more casually, by a harassed looking orderly or preoccupied nurse or, at most, by a coded, push-button or intercom system.

A few yards from where he'd left the lift, near the entrance to the corridor where the guard was standing, there were two washrooms. These he recognised as such from the pictograms on each door. He decided to move in their direction, using the flowers as a shield behind which to hide in his masquerade as an anxious relative.

As he made his way slowly towards the toilets, he took the opportunity to glance surreptitiously into all the rooms he passed en route. They were mostly full of patients in various states of illness, watching television. But an ancient woman, who lay asleep in a huge private room, attracted his attention. And he memorised her room number as he made his way into the men's room.

Anthony left the bouquet of flowers on a ledge beside the washbasins and took himself into a toilet cubicle. He closed the door and, lowering the toilet lid, sat down to search through his pockets. There he found a crumpled scrap of paper, wrote the old woman's room number on it in large figures, folded it and stuffed it back in his jacket pocket.

Anthony waited a moment or two before pulling the chain and returning through the cubicle door back into the public area of the washroom. There he gave himself a cursory once-over in the mirror — looking OK, under the circumstances, he decided, slicking down his fashionably cropped hair closer to his scalp and picking up the bouquet, he went back outside and along the corridor.

Summoning all his nerve, he went for it, heading straight towards the double swing-doors. The guard was coming to the end of his shift and was less awake than he might have been. He failed to notice Anthony's arrival until he'd managed to edge one of the doors slightly ajar. As soon as he did so, the guard was on full alert and grabbed him fiercely by the arm, yelling at him in Greek at the top of his voice.

Anthony didn't make any attempt to struggle and, instead, just reached awkwardly into his jacket pocket to find the piece of paper on which he'd written down the old lady's room number, apologising to him all the while in English and juggling the flowers and negotiating the guard's restraint as he did so. In the confusion the folded scrap of paper fluttered out of Anthony's grasp on to the floor, from where the guard retrieved it.

The hefty-looking man, who would have made Mike Tyson look small, was not someone of whom one would want to make an enemy. And it was fortunate when he read the note that a glimmer of understanding spread across his face in the form of a slight smile. At this, he nodded his huge bull head at Anthony and released his iron grip on his arm, guiding him more gently towards the old lady's room. But once inside and alone, sitting devoutly at the bedside of the ancient Greek matriarch, as if in prayer, his flowers laid across her like a floral shroud,

Anthony reflected on his extraordinary good fortune.

For what the guard had not prevented him from doing, when he'd barred his exit into the isolation area, was from seeing the armed guard that forbade entry to a room some doors further along the corridor. Now an armed guard. In a hospital. Well, that was something. And could surely mean only — he'd lay odds on it —that he'd located the place where Costas Gisikis was confined, either dead or alive. So near, yet so far. But he had to get through, past the gorillas with the guns, to establish that for himself.

It was mid-afternoon in New York, and Kimberley hadn't stopped since she'd arrived at her office in downtown Manhattan. The Homelessness Project had centres all over the city, in some of its roughest districts, but its headquarters were in the Financial District near Wall Street.

She buzzed her secretary for a sandwich — would she mind? She didn't like to ask, but she was really up against it today — and, as she put down the phone, it suddenly occurred to her that she hadn't heard yet that day from George.

Christ, he'd been gone for the best part of 24 hours, and he always rang in to touch base from wherever he was in the world, especially now that they were both so concerned about the situation in Greece. She dialled his mobile phone number. Not operational. He must have turned it off. How could she reach him? She couldn't call Athens, because he wasn't expected, and if, for any reason, he'd been held up, he wouldn't thank her for making an announcement in advance of his arrival.

Feeling increasingly panicky, she decided that the

one person she could call was Charles Bradley in London. But when she got through to him, he could tell her only that he'd seen George on to the plane to Athens at Heathrow. As far as the lawyer knew, his godson should have already arrived in Greece.

There was absolutely nothing Kimberley could do to track down her husband at that moment. She felt totally helpless and, for some reason that she could not explain, very anxious about him. As her stomach muscles tightened into a hard knot of worry, she knew intuitively that something terrible had happened.

When George regained consciousness, his body ached as if he'd been dragged along a track of boulders by wild horses. He was trussed up like a Thanksgiving turkey, but he had nothing to be thankful about. Nothing at all. And it was so dark behind his blindfold. Pitch-black, with no chink of light. His mouth was taped shut, so he couldn't talk, only groan. But he couldn't even find the strength to do that. It took him all his energy just to breathe.

Christ! he thought, as he recalled what had happened. What a fucking mess. The fact of his father's death came back to him with a tremendous jolt. A sledgehammer to his already fragile emotional state, it brought a lump to his throat and a dull, tight heaviness to his heart.

How could he grieve for the man who had brought him into the world, who had given him everything, when his own life was now in jeopardy? Costas had taught him everything he knew, had held his hand through the bad times, had rejoiced with him over the good times, had always been there for him. His father. The axis on which his world turned. Nothing would ever be the same again.

But he could consider none of this. Not while he was incarcerated alive in this — what was it? It smelt like a wooden crate. He was convinced his body was full of splinters from it. Christ! What were they going to do with him? Perhaps they'd just bury him alive. With the twins it was never safe to assume that blood ties meant damn all to them. Money was all that mattered to them, and he knew they were far enough gone now to kill for it.

The noise of a jet engine filtered through to him. No, he was mistaken. He felt the machine sway as it took off. That could only be the moment of lift-off in a helicopter. And the rhythm of the chopper established itself as it settled on course.

As George lay there in the dark, bound and helpless in a limbo between life and death, he started to feel suddenly very angry and determined, absolutely, that he would get out of this mess alive. His outrage swelled in him like a river in flood. He felt murderous with rage. Good God! Did they really think they could get away with it? They'd have to release him eventually, or die themselves in the attempt.

And his bravado carried him along on a wave of furious optimism. But the reality was that he was their prisoner, powerless and at their mercy with no chance of parole.

It was a bright, sunny morning in Athens, and for once Helena was up and about before midday. She'd never been any good first thing and, over the years, that had extended to include all the hours before noon.

She'd been feeling off colour for some weeks now, ever since the subterfuge over Costas had moved into a different gear. And her ability to sleep well had suffered. Normally, she just put her head on her pillow and went out like a light, sleeping through until mid-morning and dozing thereafter, until her maid came at noon to wake her with a coffee and the mail.

But although she got off to sleep easily now, she found herself habitually awake at 5.00am, and often not able to get back to sleep again. This morning was one of those. But she'd decided to deal with it by getting up and starting her exercise routine earlier than usual. She'd been for a swim in the heated blue waters of the marble pool and enjoyed a soak in the jacuzzi. But nothing improved her spirits. She still felt nervy and on edge.

After a couple of strong coffees, she went through into her study to make a few telephone calls to ask her masseuse to come by and fix up a lunch date with a girlfriend. The fax that had come through while she was in the bath did nothing to improve her state of mind, even though she'd been prepared for it. Barbara had warned her, and John, Maria and Stelios, that she'd be contacting them with her kidnap statement and ransom demand. But when Helena saw it in black-and-white, it filled her with dread and a foreboding of evil.

IF YOU WANT TO SEE GEORGE GISIKIS ALIVE AGAIN, FOLLOW OUR INSTRUCTIONS AND AWAIT THE NEXT TRANSMISSION. THE RANSOM IS 10 MILLION. ALL FORMS OF HIS

FAMILY'S ACTIVITIES AND BUSINESS
AND PRIVATE COMMUNICATIONS ARE
UNDER SURVEILLANCE. DO NOT
CONTACT THE POLICE OR GEORGE
GISIKIS' HEAD WILL BE DELIVERED
TO THE GROUNDS OF THE ATHENS
MANSION.

It was the starkness of the threat of her nephew's
mutilation that most alarmed Helena. Of course she
knew it was all a set-up, but with the Icewoman in
charge, God only knew what might happen. She
feared for her youngest nephew. And for herself.

But the hardest part was telling Kimberley.
Although Helena had never liked George's wife, she
nevertheless felt for her when she phoned her in New
York with the news. But she hardened her heart
against herself. After all, she had been blackmailing
one of the richest men in the world for the past 40
years, so she could manage a small-fry like Ms
Newark, New Jersey.

George had no idea how long he'd been airborne
when the helicopter bumped down on what could
only have been the rough ground of a makeshift
landing pad. He didn't know what day it was, never
mind where he was or how far they'd flown to get
there. His heart began to pump, his pulse to race,
when he realised from the sound of splintering wood
that the crate in which he'd been packed like a spare
part for an old car was being prised open.

Still roped in the foetal position, George was
hauled roughly from the crate and rolled out on to a
metal floor, along which he was shunted a couple of

times before being thrown to the ground from what felt like several feet. Not able to scream out because of the tape that sealed his mouth shut, he groaned in agony, which sapped all his remaining strength.

George could see nothing, but he could hear Barbara and her partner Jacques, it must be him, he strained, trying to get more clues from what they said. Someone untied the tape that bound together his hands and feet, and he was able, for the first time in too long, to uncurl his body. Doing so sent him into paroxysms of agony, as he struggled to straighten himself and his muscles started to cramp. He was rewarded with a sharp kick in the kidneys.

He could hear heavy footsteps thudding towards him, and Barbara laughing as she kicked him hard, this time on the leg. George flinched in agony again and tried to rub his bruised shin. But before he could do so, Barbara, George imagined it was her, from the brutal way it was done, picked him up by the arms and hauled him along a rough dirt track. George tried to keep his knees curled up towards his chest as well he could, for it was too painful to stretch out fully. But the speed at which he was dragged along made this almost impossible.

It was all proving intolerable — the pain, the unbearable physical torture into which this simple act of moving him from the helicopter presumably to a place of cover was turning. When his leg knocked into what felt like an iron post, George's body could take it no more and, mercifully, he passed out.

When George awoke, beams of sunlight were filtering through cracks in the cabin's log-built walls. It was obviously daytime, but whether it was morning or afternoon was not clear. George's throat was parched and dry. He was desperately thirsty and very hungry.

His hands and feet still tied, he pushed himself into an upright position. They'd removed his blindfold, and he was able to look around the place that was now his prison.

He knew instantly where he was. Myra. The island on which he'd spent so much happy time in his childhood, fishing, walking, working alongside the few remaining islanders. It was deserted there now. Everyone had either died or left for the mainland over the last decade. So there was no one there to help him, of that he was certain.

He sat with his back to the cabin wall and scanned his immediate surroundings. The hut was empty of furniture, and the two windows had both been boarded up. As he looked around him, he started to become aware of an acrid smell assailing his senses. Then he realised it was coming from him. He'd wet himself at some point and the crotch of his trousers was stiff with dried urine.

God, this was awful! He felt like retching with disgust. But that wouldn't be easy with the tight gag around his mouth. If only he could remove that he'd feel a whole lot better. He raised his wrists, red and swollen from their rope tie, towards his face, and tried with his fingernails to tug at the edges of the tape in order to remove it. This went on for some time, and he was just at the point when he'd managed to raise an edge of the tape, when the door flew open. It was Barbara.

'Naughty boy!' she chastised him. 'Here, let me help you.'

And she walked over to where he sat, by now

cowering against the cabin wall. She squatted down beside him and, grabbing him by the hair, wrenched his head forwards so as to reach the ends of the thick black sticky tape at the base of his skull. Breathing heavily, almost panting with pleasure, she then straddled him and with one brutal tug she removed it, together with a layer of George's skin and strands of his hair.

George howled in pain, but Barbara paid him no heed. She just laughed it off and ignored her captive who lay writhing in agony on the floor, his filthy hands cradling his bloodstained face. As she left the room, she barked out her orders to Jacques.

He came into the room some time later to give George water and a plate of food. Things were looking up, George thought. But the truth was that they weren't.

CHAPTER THIRTEEN

George had forgotten what it was like not to feel some degree of pain. It was no longer a question of what hurt because, in fact, everything hurt. It was more a matter of deciding what hurt least.

Apart from his physical distress, George found himself facing a moral dilemma. He had always considered himself a fair man, who, although not God-fearing, largely believed in the basic common sense of the Ten Commandments, most especially Thou Shalt Not Kill. And the one about not bearing false witness against thy neighbour, which he preferred to operate along the lines of love thy neighbour as thyself. So it was hard for George to reconcile all this with the fact that he felt murderously hateful towards Barbara Meier.

He thought that of her every time he licked his split and swollen lips, or felt the cuts on his face tighten painfully when he began to speak. Or experienced the dull, dull throb of pain from his splintered shoulder, which he was sure he'd fractured when he was dropped from the chopper late the previous night. He could not escape the ignominy or terror of his captivity, of how his life was now at someone else's command. His neck on the block. And he just wanted to kill the woman responsible, slowly, unpleasantly and with the maximum amount of suffering.

But that was his fantasy. It was as far from reality as Maria turning down a revamp of her wardrobe with the new spring collection from Karl Lagerfeld's Haute Couture Collection at Chanel, or John declining the services of the best whore in Phuket. In any case, Barbara had left Myra that morning.

George had heard the chopper taking off just moments after Jacques had brought the food and water she had ordered for him. He was 99 per cent certain that they had been the only three on the island, so it must have been her who had flown out.

George felt a slight sense of relief to be left alone with Barbara's accomplice, because, as cruel and intimidating as Jacques could be, he was a pussy cat in comparison with the Icewoman. With this thought to calm him momentarily, George finally collapsed into a deep and dreamless sleep.

In Athens, that same early morning, Anthony Burton woke from a nightmare in a fearful sweat. He had dreamt that he was searching for something in the freezer at home when he chanced upon Costas Gisikis' corpse, its eyes wide and staring, almost appealing.

Anthony lay beneath the thin hotel blanket for a few moments, staring at the ceiling, glad that he was back there in the small box of a room with the sounds of the city just outside in the streets of north Athens. The traffic noise was, for once, reassuring.

After a few minutes, Anthony felt calmer and

pushed back the bed covers impatiently. He would take a quick shower and get on. He had a lot to do that day.

His first task was to work on his plan to change his appearance. He wanted to get back unnoticed and unchallenged into the Baltic, and to do this he felt it was necessary to disguise himself. He left the hotel in a hurry, his shopping list for the news stand, the drugstore, a medical supplies shop and an optician's short and concise.

'Kimberley,' Helena pleaded, her voice shaking as if she were fighting back her tears, 'Oh, Kimberley, what can we do? I waited all day yesterday for another transmission. I never left my study or the fax machine. But nothing, not one more word, has come through from George's kidnappers.'

The bags under Helena's eyes indicated that she had not slept for a week. Her hair, however, was glamorously styled, with not a strand out of place. She looked as immaculate as ever, but the strain she was under was apparent in her face. And her figure, usually pencil thin, was becoming painfully so.

'I finally went to bed tired, but my nerves were too wired up to let me sleep. I locked the door to the study. I wanted to make sure that none of the staff should get to the fax machine before me. No one except us must know anything. Otherwise George might die at the hands of those lunatics.'

At this, a look of utter horror swept across Kimberley's face. Jet-lagged and already fearful for her husband, she could not bear to hear her speak like that.

'Oh, don't say that, Helena. We have to believe

that George will be OK. We'll just have to do what they ask. I still think that contacting the police might be our best option.'

'No!' Helena interjected, equally horrified. 'Absolutely not! Then they will murder him. Of that I am certain.'

And Helena started to sob hysterically. For although she knew the truth behind the charade in which she was playing a lead role, she was also aware that Barbara was quite capable of carrying out her threat on a violent impulse if they did not obey her plan to the letter.

'Here,' she said, handing Kimberley the envelope containing the original fax. 'See for yourself. We mustn't leave this lying around. No one must know about it. I feel so scared of everything and everyone. I just want my nephew back in one piece. That's all I ask.' And she started to weep again.

For a moment, Kimberley forgot her own distress and moved to comfort Helena.

'You need some rest,' she said kindly but firmly. 'This has all been too much for you. You must try to sleep for an hour or two. It must have been hard for you to cope with this all alone here.'

'No, no,' Helena gulped back her tears, 'the twins have been wonderfully supportive.'

Even in her greatest moments of unhappiness, Helena was prepared to jump to the defence of John and Maria, who had not deigned to show their faces downstairs that morning, sleeping off the excesses of the previous night, for them, for once, discreetly conducted. They knew that Kimberley had arrived from New York overnight, and Helena began to apologise for them.

'I'm sure they will be down soon. Poor darlings, first their father's stroke, now their brother's kidnap. They are being very brave, but I could see how upset they were, and I gave them both a sleeping pill last night. It must have made them oversleep this morning.'

Kimberley smiled wryly at her husband's aunt. Surely, this of all times was the moment for plain speaking.

'Helena, there's no need for you to make excuses for them,' she said, appealing straightforwardly to the older woman, on an occasion she felt was not the right one for pretence. But Helena was immovable, and unwilling to admit that the twins were simply indifferent to anyone's welfare other than their own.

Kimberley decided not to pursue her point and suggested instead that she should go to the hospital to sit with Costas. But Helena dismissed that, too, with a force that surprised Kimberley. Stelios would not know what to make of her sudden appearance in Athens, Helena said. He might become suspicious. He might wonder why George had not accompanied her. And ask why not. Or about where he was. They just couldn't risk it.

Helena was amazed at how easy it was for her to deceive her nephew's wife. But she had no qualms about it. She had never liked the woman and owed her nothing, though now she did feel sorry for her.

'We don't want to have to start lying to cover up what has happened to George. Stelios doesn't know his cousin has been kidnapped. We simply must not tell anyone. George's life depends on it.'

And Kimberley could not argue with that either. But she felt as trapped as George was feeling at that moment, not so very far away from where she stood, had she but known it. And she was not at all easy about putting all her trust in Helena's instincts. The woman had always been so self-serving. But, for the moment, she had no option but to row alongside her.

In front of the mirror, Anthony Burton put the finishing touches to his new look. He'd bleached and tinted his black hair brown, and toned down his eyebrows to match. He was dressed in white jeans and a blue shirt, which he covered with a long, white doctor's coat. He buttoned this up and jammed a stethoscope into his top pocket and a pair of thick-lensed, dark-framed spectacles on to the bridge of his nose.

From a brown paper bag on a table next to the TV he took out a magazine. This was no ordinary glossy lifestyle mag or specialist journal. Well, it was, of sorts. Hardcore porn had its own particular market, he supposed. From its pages he tore out an especially explicit image, a double-page spread —he laughed at the accuracy of this description — and rolled it up carefully before secreting it in an inside pocket of the white coat.

He took his camera from its place where it hung by a strap on the back of the door and tucked it into a large side-pocket of his new uniform. And, taking a final look at himself in the large wardrobe mirror, he picked up his hotel keys and left the room.

Outside the hotel, the tax collector crossed the street briskly and purposefully retraced his steps through the hospital entrance, into the lobby and up to the top floor via the lift. This time, he shared the elevator with a woman in a wheelchair, whom he gallantly helped out when they reached the top, glancing casually around him as he did so.

The guard from the previous day was there, large and threatening as before. Anthony's heart started to pound at the prospect of a run-in with him, and he suddenly felt an overwhelming desire to ditch the whole enterprise. But his in-built determination took over, and he made his way along the corridor towards the gents and the old Greek woman's private room, clutching his stethoscope as if he had some intention of using it.

Luck was on his side. The old lady was fast asleep again, but he took great care to move quietly around her room. He pulled her meal trolley over to straddle her bed at chin level. And then removed the page of the porn magazine from his pocket, propping it up in front of her and securing it in place with an alarm clock that he set to go off in five minutes' time.

As if he'd set the fuse on a time-bomb, he walked with speed from the room and made his way into the men's toilets, noticing as he did so that the security guard in front of the isolation wing had been joined by another man. Anthony recognised him as the armed officer who had been on duty the day before outside Costas Gisikis' ward unit.

In the gents, Anthony stood in the middle of the washroom area, staring fixedly at his watch. Believing himself alone there, he almost jumped out of his skin when he heard the sound of a cistern flushing in an adjacent toilet cubicle. Anthony darted into a urinal as someone emerged from the toilet. He hadn't reckoned on meeting anyone else. The other man was fortunately in too much of a hurry to upset his plans and rushed out without even washing his hands.

Anthony began to breathe more easily but still glanced constantly, nervously at his watch. Suddenly, he heard what he was waiting for — a shrill, frenzied scream. The sound of the alarm clock had obviously woken the old woman, possibly to her first brush with pornography. He waited just five seconds before investigating and, as he peered through a crack in the door, he watched the two security guards and a nurse rushing towards the old lady's private room.

At this, Anthony made a dash for the swing doors of the isolation wing and, camera at the ready, he raced to where he believed Costas Gisikis was lying. Sure enough, there he was, incredibly suspended in mid-air, in what could only be described as a transparent body pod. In a scene that resembled something out of Michael Crichton's sci-fi horror, he lay there horizontally, several feet above the ground, with nothing to hide his nakedness.

It took Anthony only seconds to aim his camera and shoot — once, twice, three times he photographed the bizarre scene before running back through the double door and into the relative safety of the men's toilets.

Shaking like a leaf, Anthony removed the film from the camera and stuffed it into his pants. The camera he returned to his outside coat pocket. He stood expectantly by the door into the corridor and, when he heard voices and the sound of laughter, he opened it slightly. It was all clear, and so he headed out and straight for the lifts without looking to either side of him. As he passed the old lady's room, however, he'd sensed the commotion he'd created there, but he couldn't afford to stop to take a look.

Back in his hotel room, he slammed the door shut behind him and fell exhausted but jubilant on to the bed. He rolled on his back and punched his fist into the air. He had fucking well done it! he congratulated himself. Now he had the proof he needed. There was no way that man was alive, lying there in the corpse position, his arms beside him, palms facing upward in that vast glass test tube. And when he'd calmed down a little, he put through a call to his wife to share his triumph with her.

'I think you should stay here and not put one foot outside the house!' John cautioned Kimberley, almost threateningly. She'd been keen to get some air, but the twins backed up Helena's reservations about Kimberley announcing her presence there in Greece. You just never knew when the Press would turn up, on some spurious tip, and then she'd find her photo splashed over the pages of the daily papers.

Time was passing so slowly for Kimberley, and she felt so helpless. But she did as they said and spent the day with them, reading or watching television, especially the news, glad that there was nothing about them or any of this among its headlines. Christ! That was all they needed.

Every time the phone rang, she jumped. Kimberley was impressed by how professionally Helena fielded the innumerable calls from George's office, making all manner of excuses. After all, he was the acting head of one of the world's largest shipping empires.

Kimberley was secretly disturbed, though, at how plausible a liar Helena was when the need arose. But Kimberley had no opportunity to assess Maria's skills at deception at this point. When anxiety had given way to hunger at around nine that night, they were all gathered silently around the table, eating without enthusiasm, when a maid came to summon Maria to the telephone.

'We have a problem, Maria,' Stelios announced ominously when she picked up the phone in her father's study.

'Now what?' Maria snapped at him gracelessly.

'There was an incident on your father's floor at the hospital. Chaos broke out when someone played a practical joke on a 90-year-old female patient in a room near to Costas' isolation wing. Somebody left a page from a porno mag on a bed trolley, right in front of the old girl while she was sleeping. When she opened her eyes, it was to the sight of the biggest dick in all Greece, right under her nose. The old bat started to scream blue murder.

'It was farcical really ... amusing as hell. But the downside is that the two security guards around Costas were distracted by the drama of it all. Guess they were just following their instincts for trouble.'

Maria started to laugh and was bent double in hysterics by the time John came into the room. He took the receiver from his sister, and Stelios explained everything briefly to him. But, unlike Maria, John was not amused. Not in the least.

As he stood there, tight-lipped and pale, Maria suddenly realised the full implications of what had happened. She felt mortified that she hadn't done so sooner, which made her even more angry. She snatched back the phone from her brother and hissed into the mouthpiece at Stelios.

'Idiots!' she spat. 'You mean the guards left

Costas' room unattended?'

'Yes, Maria,' Stelios replied. 'Maybe you should choose your security staff more carefully,' he added, not willing to take the blame for what had happened, although Maria seemed quite prepared to ascribe it to him.

'Listen,' he continued, satisfied that he'd made his point, 'there's no way anyone could have got to Costas in that short space of time without having been seen. Believe me, there's nothing sinister about this. The old woman's an absolute bitch who makes our lives hell here. She's demanding and damned rude — none of the staff can stand her. Even her own family refuse to visit.

'My guess is that a young ward orderly must have decided to get his own back. In my book he deserves a rise. But ...'

'I don't feel good about this, Stelios,' Maria interjected flatly. 'Father's body must be under constant guard. There has to be no doubt about that. Otherwise anything might happen.'

Stelios picked up on Maria's paranoia and was prepared to indulge her on this occasion.

'OK, I hear what you say,' he said abruptly. 'There's a security camera in the hallway of the isolation wing. If it will put your mind at rest, I'll get someone to check the tapes. As a matter of fact, one of your own people can do it. Perhaps Barbara. She's just called to say she's on her way over to rebrief the guards and check up generally on how things are going here security-wise.'

'Fine,' Maria said, heaving a huge sigh of relief at Barbara's timely arrival. 'I think it's important to scan those tapes. Tell Barbara I'll call her later tonight, when she's had time to study the videotape.'

Maria stood in Costas' study gnawing distractedly on her lips for a few minutes, gazing around the room, admiring its opulence. Her twin sat with his back to her, preoccupied by snorting a line of coke. At first she ignored him as he turned to hand her the rolled-up banknote he had just used to inhale the white crystal. This will be mine, she muttered to herself under her breath. Whatever it takes. She snatched the makeshift straw from her brother's outstretched hand and stuck it up her nose, inhaling deeply from one of several trails of powder laid out on a small hand-mirror on the antique hardwood escritoire.

CHAPTER FOURTEEN

John was relieved that Kimberley had opted for an early night because he didn't want her around when Maria put in her call to Barbara at 10.30pm. As it was, the day had been tortuous while they sat around waiting for news of George via the fax machine.

Nothing had come through. And at 9.00pm, Kimberley had taken herself off to the Gisikis family chapel in the grounds of the house to pray for her husband and her father-in-law. She could, of course, have saved any special pleading she might have made on Costas' behalf.

At 10.30pm sharp, Maria dialled Stelios' number at the Baltic. Barbara answered. Maria would have been surprised to know that her security guard was wearing only red-leather crotchless panties, her legs spread revealingly as she sat on the edge of Stelios' desk. Around her tiny waist was a wide, black-leather belt that accentuated its wonderful smallness in contrast to the large, firm peaks of her breasts. This was all that Stelios had eyes for as he lay bound and gagged beside her.

'Nothing untoward on the tapes so far,' Barbara said, although the truth of it was that she hadn't even looked. She'd been too involved with Stelios, who liked a bit of the rough stuff when the mood took him. As Barbara was talking, he lay strapped and spread-eagled across his desk, totally naked and at her mercy with his dick erect, huge and expectant and waiting for Barbara to put down the phone and finish what she'd started.

Maria began to complain to Barbara about Kimberley. Couldn't she, Barbara, fax something else over soon about George, some demand that would require her sister-in-law to return, pronto, to the US?

'I'll send something over later tonight or tomorrow morning,' Barbara guaranteed.

She would have promised Maria anything in order to get back to Stelios, who was behaving, she felt faint with excitement at the thought of it, most co-operatively. But before she put down the phone, she added, for good measure and to titillate Stelios unbearably, 'By the way, your little brother George has been a very good boy. I've treated him really special.'

At this, Barbara had to reach over to Stelios to adjust the gag that covered his mouth. She had to do something to prevent him from groaning too audibly with pleasure and pain, that enticing mix that was arousing his lust so wantonly. And, as she did so, her ample breasts brushed across his face, her nipples grazing his lips.

George had lost all track of time. He didn't know how long he'd been held captive. First the drugs. Then the journey. The beatings. And now the captivity. Had it been a day? A week? He at least knew where he was. That was a comfort to him.

George took solace from the fact that he was on Myra. He loved the place, its smells, its tranquillity, its isolation. It was certainly the latter that made it certain that, without a boat or helicopter at his disposal, he would not be able to leave the island. And as long as Jacques remained alert and on guard, as Barbara had ordered him — and who was he to gainsay her with the prospect of the sexual rewards he would reap if she were pleased with him? — he would have no opportunity to slip shorewards to signal at passing fishing boats or ferries.

George ate whatever food the shaven-headed thug brought him. That was how George saw Jacques, and it helped him to keep a check on his tongue. He kept wanting to put the man down. God knows, it was easy enough.

At first, it was difficult for George not only to open his cut and swollen mouth to bite, but also to chew and swallow whatever fruit, vegetables or bread he was given. He was almost past eating, but he knew that if he were to have any chance at all of escaping his remote island prison, he would have to persist and take whatever he got to regain his strength. With an adversary like Barbara to deal with, he would need all the help he could get — and the rest.

Anthony Burton was still high on adrenalin when he checked out of his Athens' hotel. Before he'd left his room, he'd caught sight of himself in the full-length wardrobe mirror, and he liked what he saw. Reflected in its glass was a man who had succeeded in his mission. His suspicions of a massive tax fraud perpetuated by the Gisikis clan were now vindicated by indisputable photographic evidence. He'd been proved right. But it wasn't that which pleased him as much as revealing the inherent corruption of the super-rich.

As his cab pulled away from the hotel, Anthony glanced up at the Baltic. Someone in there had co-operated with the Gisikis heirs, someone very high up, who was about to take a fall from which they would never recover. Well, that wasn't his problem. It mattered not who else was destroyed in this purge, only that the rot was stopped before it took on the proportions of an epidemic. At Ellinikon, Anthony did not hang about. He had no bags to check in, only a small hold-all, which he could take himself through Passport Control and on to the plane as hand luggage. In the bar of the departure lounge, he bought a large five-star Metaxa. Somehow, it always tasted better than the supposedly superior seven star, he mused as he downed it in one.

Anthony felt himself start to unwind as the brandy hit his empty stomach and worked its way up to his brain. He felt soothed. Calmer than he'd been for a while. It was then that he remembered his wife. He'd wanted to buy Margaret her favourite scent from Duty Free, Guerlain's Mitsouko.

In the queue at the perfume counter, Anthony began to feel edgy again. For some reason, the person standing beside him was staring at him. And the effect of the brandy was not enough to curb his paranoia.

Anthony turned away to look around him. Was there anything he needed from Duty Free while he was there? He forced his mind to wander, but when he faced the counter again to sign the Visa counterfoil, he felt those eyes boring into his side. His hand shook as he signed his name to authorise the purchase.

As Anthony waited for the completion of the sale, and for the Guerlain rep to add free samples to the bag containing his purchase, he couldn't stop himself from taking a surreptious look at the man next to him. His persecutor, as he had come to consider him, was tall, well built and of Mediterranean origin. His most distinctive feature was a thick, black moustache that dominated his face. His clothes were smart, a blue designer-label suit and brown suede brogues, probably Church's, but he carried an incongruous-looking sports bag, much like one that a professional footballer would use to carry his kit.

Anthony started to sweat profusely when he realised that he had seen the man somewhere before. But he calmed down when he remembered that it had only been at check-in. Christ! He was feeling jumpy. So near, yet so far. Almost to the finishing line, but not over it yet. He had to get that roll of film back to the UK and into the hands of the authorities. He could feel the canister pressing against his leg in his trouser pocket. The responsibility of it was too much. Fuck! What was he going to do! It would be hours before he could rest easy. He'd just have to bite the bullet. And quit moaning. But panic overwhelmed him.

Anthony turned away from the sales counter, beads of perspiration in a line along his brow and upper lip. He felt his under-arms break out into a sweat as though someone had turned on a tap in his armpit. His nerves on edge, he began to walk towards the exit, when a hand gripped his shoulder. His voice stuck in his larynx as he moved to protest, only to discover the Guerlain woman handing him the small package he had left beside the till.

What a fucking relief! God, the next few hours were going to prove a test of all his resources. Over at the Guerlain counter, he saw that man again. Still looking in his direction. He'd put his sports bag on the counter. What on earth was it about that bag? It just didn't fit. His mind raced. Perhaps he was carrying a gun. Surely not. The X-ray machine at the security gates would have picked that up.

Then, unnervingly, the man began to smile at him across the shop. Oh fuck! Anthony thought, what does that mean? What the hell does he want? Does he think he knows me or something?

A line of sweat trailed down Anthony's face from his temple to his jaw. He'd had it for now. What could he do? It was then he remembered he had a flight to catch, and without any further delay he headed straight for the departure gate that was flashing next to his flight details on the screen of the overhead monitors.

Anthony's relief was short-lived. In the lounge beside the boarding gate he was rummaging through his bag for his book, balancing it on his knee, when he glanced up and noticed that the chap from Duty Free had just turned up and was heading in his direction. With a smile of acknowledgement, the man came over and sat down in the seat next to Anthony's.

This was the final straw. Anthony finally lost his cool and decided to confront him. But before he could do so, his bag slipped off his lap and on to the floor, spilling its contents all over the place. His self-possession momentarily deserting him, he began to swear with frustration. At this point, his neighbour came to his rescue, offering his assistance in a tone of voice that could only be described as high camp.

'I better help you with this mess, love, or you'll end up missing your plane.' And he handed Anthony a shoe that had disappeared under his seat.

Anthony's relief was palpable. The last thing in the world he'd expected was to be picked up by a gay man at Athens airport. He'd been expecting one kind of trouble and got another. But this he could deal with, he decided. By the time the plane landed at Heathrow, the two men had discovered that they had at least one thing in common —a liking for Bloody Marys.

It was 6.00pm. Nearly 24 hours since Maria had last spoken to Barbara, but there was no fax, nothing, no communication at all from George's kidnappers.

Maria was going stir crazy cooped up in the house with Kimberley, having to maintain the pretence about her concern for her missing brother. She just wished that whore Barbara would contact them so that the American bitch would get back on a plane and disappear back to the States. But no such luck. Maria couldn't even indulge in her favourite alcoholic beverage. A glass of Cristal Roederer seemed too celebratory under the circumstances, so she had to settle for a medicinal brandy instead, albeit a fine Hine.

Stelios could tell that his cousin was feeling the strain when he phoned to say that Barbara had left a message with him advising Maria to meet her in a small café in Kolonaki Square.

'You'll have to hurry,' he advised her. 'You're meant to be there in half-an-hour.'

But all he got in reply was a mouthful of abuse for

having left it so late in the day to contact her.

When Maria got to Kolonaki, she found the fashionable coffee shop without difficulty and installed herself at a table by the window. An evening in late autumn was too cold to sit outside. 'Damned tourists,' she muttered to herself, as she dismissed all those still brave enough to give the outside terrace a chance. 'They don't have a shred of taste and always spoil the view.'

She had a point. Aspects of Greece had suffered from its tourist boom over the previous three decades. It was only in winter that the plastic cafés were transformed back into the local *ouzeri*, and the *bouzouki* replaced the electric guitar. But Maria was more concerned with how the volume of traffic in the tourist season made it harder for the stretch limo to get her around on time.

Maria sipped her coffee and watched the world go by, her temper becoming fouler by the minute. She stubbed out her Marlboro Light in the ashtray and lit up again almost immediately. Barbara was late. Where in God's name was she? She employed the woman — she should at least be punctual. She hunched, chain-smoking, over her coffee cup in a state of great agitation, the nicotine and caffeine only fuelling her impatience.

After a quarter-of-an-hour, Barbara had still not shown, and Maria's irritation was turning to aggression. When a waitress, only doing her job, made the mistake of asking her if she would like something — anything else? — Maria just snapped back at her, 'Fuck off!' The waitress backed off immediately, more surprised than angry, and didn't bother her again.

Maria was beginning to lose it, to feel that she'd explode if she stayed there a moment longer, when she spotted a young woman she recognised from somewhere, heading along the street toward the café. Oh, yeah, that was one of Barbara's girls. An athletic, natural-looking woman in her late teens, with her long hair tied back in a ponytail high on her head. Wearing casual DKNY. Only the best for Barbara and her team. Just the kind of over-confident kid Barbara liked to take on and wear down.

For the moment, the youngster had retained all of her charm and lost none of her confidence, all of which she needed to deal with Maria just then. But her message for the Gisikis heiress was simply that Barbara was indisposed. There'd been an emergency. She'd explain when she called her at home later that night. When Maria tried to get more out of the girl, she turned and walked off, ignoring the tirade of insults that Maria hurled after her, until she turned the corner and raised two fingers behind her.

Once through the Customs' Green Channel, Anthony left Heathrow Arrivals by one of the airport's courtesy buses to collect his red BMW from the long-stay car park. He felt in excellent spirits, full of life and optimism. Sitting at the back of the bus, he transferred the precious roll of film from his trouser pocket to his briefcase, worried that the heat of his body might affect it. Then he called Margaret on his mobile. He said he couldn't wait to see her.

'Wait up for me, darling. I'll see you in an hour or so. I love you,' he whispered.

At the compound, Anthony quickly located his car and brushed off a few specks of the dirt that had settled on its bonnet over the past few days. Once in the driving seat, he turned the key in the ignition and was pleased when the powerful German engine turned over at the first attempt. He appreciated his car. After Margaret it was his obsession. He'd wanted a BMW for years, and now he'd got one, just like most things in life. He felt he was on a roll. Things were going his way. And he began to sing tunelessly — more with relief than happiness.

He drove towards the exit barrier faster than he should have done. But he felt careless and abandoned. A sort of end-of-term feeling. He stopped at the toll gate and inserted his pre-paid voucher in the ticket machine. The barrier swung up and open, and Anthony revved up the engine for a fast getaway. Back home. Triumphant. Mission Impossible Achieved. He'd show that bastard Argent. That job-for-life merchant. Well, there wasn't room for people like that these days.

Anthony began to feel increasingly buoyant. Untenably so, much like a hyperactive adolescent on a first date. It really was a reaction to all the tension he'd been under, he reasoned. He'd taken on a lot. And alone. And he'd pulled through. Carried it off.

Braking hard at the junction of the car park and the main road, Anthony looked carefully both ways, pausing briefly to buckle his seat-belt before engaging his clutch and starting to move confidently into the main stream of traffic. Except there was none. Only him. He had the road to himself. Or so he thought. Because, suddenly, out of the corner of his eye, it seemed as if a street lamp flickered and blew.

Something cast its shadow over him, blocking his line of vision, and he suddenly faced the huge metal grille of a huge lorry, an impenetrable wall of chrome rose up in front of him. And there was no stopping. And no getting round it.

Anthony's 'No! For Christ's sake!' turned immediately to a high-pitched scream as the lorry crashed with great force into the supporting pillar of the arch above the exit to the car park. The collision destabilised a concrete reinforcing joist, which came thundering down on to his car. On to the roof. Through the roof. On to his head.

When the choking dust finally settled, the radiance of the street lamp shed its light on the carnage. The overhead light was in perfect working order after all. It was Anthony Burton whose lights had been punched out.

At midnight, the call came through to the Gisikis mansion. Barbara let Maria rail at her for several minutes, before she finally got a word in edgeways.

'I rang to tell you ... there was someone on the hospital security videotape. Right at the end. But we spotted him. And I've dealt with it. He won't be causing us any trouble. He's been taken care of. You can count on that.'

Maria wasn't listening, too intent on her having her say. Why hadn't she been informed earlier, instead of being kept in the dark, sentenced to comfort her vile sister-in-law with no idea of what was going on? But Barbara just cut her short.

'Get your dealer to change your drugs, Maria,' she said dismissively. 'The ones you're on don't suit you.'

And she put down the receiver before Maria could say another word. Barbara had heard enough of her client's drug-induced paranoia. The hysterics of a spoilt rich bitch and the culling of Anthony Burton were all in a day's work for a pro like her. Both were surplus to requirements.

CHAPTER FIFTEEN

The emergency services crew worked to free the driver of the red BMW. It was a fight they were struggling to win. His life was balanced on a knife edge between life and death as they raced against time to save him in the eerie blue glow cast by the flashing hazard lights.

It was just as the fire brigade arrived with their cutting equipment that the ambulance driver saw her, stepping out from behind the car, negotiating the tangle of metal and concrete and glass. He was puzzled for a moment. Where the hell had she appeared from? Had she got out of the car? Walked out of that pile-up? What the fuck was she doing there? And he began to shout at her. Warning her out of the way. Panicked that she might be hurt and concussed. That they hadn't noticed her. She might need their help.

But then he was distracted for a moment by the chaos of the scene. They were about to pull him out. It was touch and go. Pretty clear that there was little anyone could do to save him now. But someone asked for something — and fast — distracting him. When he looked again, she had gone, disappeared, like a figment of his imagination, out and into the night.

She'd been some woman, he mused. Amazonian. Not a cuddly, pint-size like his missus.

Barbara Meier stepped into the bright lights of the departure concourse at Heathrow Airport, where she put in another call to Maria in Athens. It was short and to the point.

'Make sure you have some cash for me tomorrow evening,' she said. 'My expenses are piling up, and I want some money up front.'

'How much?' Maria asked.

Barbara told her and did not wait to hear what she knew would be her outraged response.

With her mobile glued to her ear, fixing this, fixing that, Barbara strode confidently into Terminal Two and over to the Air France ticket desk. She paid cash for a one-way flight to Paris and gave what she thought was a sweet smile to the saleswoman. It was like being smiled at by a tiger, but the Air France rep acknowledged her with a curt 'Thank you, Madame Carrier. Enjoy your flight,' as she moved on to take care of her next client.

In the hospitality lounge of Air France, specially reserved for Club Class clients, Barbara — or Mme Francine Carrier as her passport falsely declared her — sat and pondered how she would pass the next 24 hours. Perhaps she'd stop off in Paris and spend the night at the Ritz. She wanted to keep a low profile for a day or two. Not too much toing and froing at Ellinikon. In any case, she needed a break. She'd had an exhausting few days. A suite at the luxury four-star hotel in the magnificent Place Vendome, at the expense of the Gisikis family, was just what she needed.

After Anthony had phoned from Heathrow, Margaret went down to the cellar to fish out a bottle of something bubbly to celebrate. Hunting around in the dank dark, she located a bottle of Moët. It wasn't the best champagne in the world, just what she pulled out first, but it would do.

Back upstairs, she put the bottle in the fridge to chill. They simply had to mark the occasion somehow. Anthony had done so well. With no support from Argent or any of that feeble lot he worked for. He was so shrewd and determined. It was partly these qualities for which she had married him. Well, those and his other, more erotic virtues. A meeting of minds and baser instincts.

As she walked around the house, lighting candles and turning down the dimmers to create a sultry atmosphere for the intimate evening ahead she was planning, Margaret caught sight of her reflection in the drawing-room mirror. She pushed her long blonde hair away from her face. Should she wear it up or down tonight? she wondered. She wanted to look stunning for her husband's arrival. No, it would have to be down. After all, the best place to drink champagne was in bed.

Margaret then decided to take a long, lingering bath, scenting it with exotic oils, and adding a special measure of the aphrodisiac ylang ylang. Afterwards, wrapped in a huge fleecy Descamps bath-towel, she examined the clothes in her wardrobe and selected from it something slinky, in this case a see-through, low-cut, black-lace Versace dress.

She left it hanging in her dressing-room while she slipped on some underwear — a black-lace Wonderbra and matching lace, G-string panties. The push-up design of the bra made her already large breasts appear double their size and pushed them into a wonderful deep V of a plunging clevage. Eat your heart out, Caprice Bourret, she thought, as she considered her own delicious curves and compared them favourably to those of the latest hottest Californian supermodel.

Anthony would appreciate her efforts, she knew. And she stood in front of the mirror and admired herself, assessing the impact of her skimpy lingerie. Maybe it would be sexier for her not to wear any panties at all? And she considered stepping out of them then and there. The thought of their lovemaking when Anthony arrived home excited her greatly. And she fed her suddenly aroused libido with a chilled glass of *grand cru* Chablis.

By midnight, Margaret had long finished the entire bottle of white burgundy and was toying with the idea of opening a second. She'd tried to contact Anthony on his mobile, but he'd switched it off. Perhaps he was waiting at the all-night photo lab in Soho for the film to be developed. He'd mentioned that he might try to get the photos tonight if he could. But it was unlike him not to tell her if he was held up for any reason.

Margaret could only speculate about what had happened to her husband. But one thing she knew for sure was that she was impatient for him to arrive. In anticipation of this, she had stepped in and out of her G-string several times, trying to decide whether she should play bold or a little more coy. She had decided not to wear the Versace. Instead, she'd pulled on a froth of a garment, one of an earlier season's floral see-throughs by Valentino that called out for an underslip. But she would wear it without.

Margaret relaxed on their large double bed, sinking into the soft luxury of the goose-down pillows and enjoying the silky seductiveness of the sheets. She had discarded all her clothes for the moment. She gazed absentmindedly at herself. Focusing for a moment on her body, her eye moved down to the tangled triangle of her pubic hair.

Anthony preferred it when she grew it long and bushy and, since before their Greek holiday, she had allowed her bikini line to grow wild and unkempt. She contemplated her unmanageable bush just long enough to want to tidy it up a little. Perhaps she'd have it shaved into the shape of a heart. She liked that idea. Anthony would, too. But she'd have to have it done professionally. For now, she'd just trim it up herself.

Feeling the effect of a whole bottle of fine Chablis, Margaret steered a slightly unsteady course into the en suite white marble bathroom and started to shave the outer edges of her pubic hair, trimming the rest of her fluff, but still leaving it long and entangled.

The doorbell went just as she was admiring the expertise of her styling. Good timing, Anthony, she thought. But he must have mislaid his keys. Oh well. She stopped only to step into her G-string and brassière and pushed her feet into a pair of Manolo Blahnik frippery, some barely there, skinny stilettos, to complete the effect. Thus attired, she rushed downstairs to fling open the front door and greet her errant husband. 'Welcome home, sexy!' she gushed, a bit drunk and over-excited. But she had absolutely no way of hiding her embarrassment at finding on her doorstep not her long-awaited husband, but two uniformed police officers.

When she answered the door again moments later, she was more suitably dressed in a heavy, opaque red-silk kimono and Chinese slippers. But apprehension had taken hold of her, drumming out her mellowness. There was no trace of her former friskiness. The thrill had gone. Where was Anthony? What were these jokers doing on her doorstep at this time of night? She soon found out.

Later, as the policemen helped Margaret into the police car that sat outside the Burtons' Chelsea home — she'd been requested to accompany them to identify the body — Margaret asked, apparently out of the blue, an oddly mundane question. What about her husband's camera? A Canon Sureshot? Had it been found?

The officers looked puzzled, reassuring her that all her husband's possessions were safely under lock and key in police custody. Why, they wondered, did the woman wanted to know about his bloody holiday snaps or family photos when he lay dead on a mortuary slab? Well, it was beyond them. But in all their years of dealing with this distressing aspect of their job, they had learnt never to be surprised at how grief took hold of a person.

Fred Argent was a creature of habit. He would buy *The Times* on his way to the railway station, take the underground from London Bridge to Borough and then walk the unprepossessing route to his office. His routine was always the same. As he left the tube station, he would discard his *Times* and buy a tabloid, usually the *Sun*, which he tucked immediately into his briefcase.

He was always the first to arrive at work. He'd take advantage of this, not to get through a mountain of paperwork by 9.30am or sort out how he might best delegate the current workload, but to make himself a cup of Nescafé — with so much added sugar that the spoon could almost stand up in it unaided — and then secrete himself in his office to pore over the pages of the *Sun*.

His staff were under the mistaken impression that he was in by 8.00am to keep ahead of the game. They saw him as hard working and respected his diligence. They would not have been so admiring if they had known the reality of his early-morning routine.

Reading the *Sun*, Argent felt, kept him in touch. He was right. It was the heartbeat of the street, and a perfect way of keeping his finger on the nation's pulse. He'd observed no end of human disgrace in its pages, the scams, scandals and sensational exposés. If the upper echelons of the IR might have been surprised at how he kept himself up to date, it would have paled in comparison with the response of his underlings. Especially if they'd caught sight of Argent's most careful consideration of page three.

But today, Argent had got more than he'd bargained for. The headline on the front page screamed out at him: HM QUEEN'S ATTEMPT TO SAVE BRIT BURIED IN CEMENT GRAVE AT HEATHROW. The picture that accompanied the report of the man's grisly death at London's major airport was none other than his erstwhile employee Anthony Burton, who had happened to die under a ton of rubble. The story really fixed on the fact that a member of the royal entourage had been the first on the scene. This was why it had made the front page. Not Anthony's absence, but royalty's presence. Apparently, the Queen's bodyguard had called for the ambulance on the royal mobile.

His heart pounded as he read the story, muttering to himself. 'You're not even fucking alive any more, Burton, and you nearly gave me a heart-attack.' And he reflected on how the younger man was no longer a threat to him now. Strange how life turned out sometimes.

But mingled with Argent's feelings of relief were those of anger and regret. He looked away from his desk and stared around his office and out the window. Momentarily, he covered his face with his hands. What a waste! he mused. What a bloody waste! Once he'd taken his early retirement, he'd been planning to hand over the reins to Burton. The man had integrity, a promising future, so much to live for.

Burton had irritated him. More than that, he'd been a thorn in his flesh. But he would miss his energy and enthusiasm, his campaigning spirit and zest for life. No one else in the department stood up to him. They were all too scared of becoming dispensable. With Anthony Burton gone there was no one else in the whole damn building who was fit to hold a candle to him.

He started to think about what had happened the last time he'd seen Burton. He'd been so certain that the Gisikis case was a candidate for Special Compliance. So clear that there was some kind of deal going on to defraud the UK tax authorities of their due share of the tycoon's estate. But Burton had booked himself a week's leave. And that wasn't up yet. He'd obviously come back early. Presumably because he'd found something.

Stelios Gisikis was a bag of nerves as he smuggled the security tape from the isolation unit down to the basement of the hospital. He didn't want anyone to intercept him while he had the incriminating tape in his possession. God forbid it should fall into the wrong hands. It was with some relief that he found the boiler room unoccupied, allowing him to fling the offending cassette into the flames of the hospital incinerator. He had no wish to know what had happened to the man who'd been seen gaining unauthorised access to Costas' solitary suite, who had even taken photos of the tycoon in his state of icy suspension. He'd viewed the tape with Barbara and observed her reaction to the intruder. What she'd planned to do with him was inhuman.

Stelios had had plenty of time to think recently. And he'd decided that all the extravagant spending in which he'd been indulging over the past few weeks was not worth it. If he could turn back the clock to the time before Costas' admittance to the Baltic, and his own involvement with the twins' attempt at deception, then he would do so without a moment's hesitation. He'd cancel his order for a £200,000 Aston Martin Vantage, give back his entire wardrobe of Armani suits and Gucci loafers and move out of his huge apartment in Kolonaki.

He'd cancel all his A-list social engagements, where he knew he'd rub shoulders with the rich and the famous. He'd relinquish his mooring for the Ariana among the super-yachts of Monaco for the Grand Prix and his proposed trip to the remotest islands of the Maldives. He'd surrender his pole position to get back his old, drab life.

I wish, I wish, he thought. He wished that he'd

resisted John and Maria's entreaties. That Costas Gisikis' death had been announced to the world as soon as he'd died and that the billionaire had been put to rest in the tiny private chapel on Myra beside his wife.

Stelios knew he looked awful. He'd been tanned and healthy just a few months earlier, when he was a respectable and respected surgeon and the esteemed director of the top private hospital in Athens. Stelios now had huge black stress pouches under his exhausted slits of eyes, his skin was drawn and pale. And now he was party to a large-scale tax fraud that involved a body on ice and a kidnap that might or might not end in making him an accessory to murder.

From that to this in such a short space of time. His road to hell had been paved with no good intentions. Stelios was aware that he'd ruined his life. And that there was not a lot he could do about it. He'd barely eaten during the past 48 hours and had taken up smoking two packs a day. His nerves were shot, and never more so than when, back in his suite of offices, the door to his inner sanctum burst open. It was Barbara.

'What's up?' she demanded, knowing full well that she had just frightened the life out of the man.

'Why can't you at least knock first instead of barging in like that?' Stelios asked, trembling now not with fear but with annoyance.

'That's no way to treat a friend who comes bearing gifts,' she cooed back at him. Barbara's attempts to be seductive irritated Stelios even further. But he stopped in his tracks when she took a small camera from her jacket pocket and handed it to Stelios.

'Is this what I think it is?' Stelios asked, alarmed,

putting it down on his desk immediately as if unwilling to touch it. He took her silence as a 'yes'. 'Christ, Barbara, you shouldn't be walking round with that. Get rid of it immediately.'

'Don't sound so horrified. I can't think what you're worried about,' Barbara countered with fake ingenuousness. 'You should be pleased.'

With a wild look in his eye, for a moment Stelios stared long and hard at Barbara. Had she lost it? he wondered. Or was she being serious?

'This is evidence against us, I'm sure you know,' he said finally. 'Proof that we had some connection with what happened to that poor bastard who was snooping about with it here. We have to dispose of it directly.'

With that in mind, Stelios picked up the camera, a Canon Sureshot, from where it lay among all the neglected paperwork and administrative muddle that Stelios' directorship of the Baltic had become, and walked towards the door to his office. Just as he was about to open it, John and Maria turned up, unannounced and in a state that could only be described as dishevelled.

Maria carried under her arm a large package, which she handed to Barbara without saying a word. Barbara just balanced it in her hands, feeling its weight and smiled. It was her interim fee, in used notes, for expenses. She wouldn't be keeping that under her mattress.

'I owe some of this to Hans,' she said for some reason, but certainly not to soften the blow of the sum involved. Barbara seemed to want to talk. To boast, even, about her former partner, by profession an international HGV driver, by trade one of the world's finest hit-men.

Why was she telling them this? To boost her profile? But she was tough, harder than nails, and everyone in that room knew it. No, she was building up to something. She never normally bothered to explain herself. Certainly not to them.

It was Hans who had driven the lorry that had been involved in that tragic traffic accident at Heathrow, she told them. Oh, of course, they wouldn't have heard about it. How silly of her! she rebuked herself gently. Not important enough for Reuters to pick up on and distribute to the Press worldwide. But it was nevertheless so unfortunate. So unlucky that he had collided with the BMW driven by that nice young tax inspector who had been snooping around the Baltic. So unlike Hans to drive so recklessly.

Barbara didn't bother to check out the effect her words had made on her clients. She continued regardless, dismissing the incident by saying, 'Well, now that's been taken care of, everything's fine and under control. Except my nails, that is.' And she started to examine the acrylic wraps that adorned her fingertips, painted with Chanel's Rouge Noir, the fashionable vamp colour.

'It's hard on my hands, this line of work. I must find myself a decent nail salon. I don't think Supernail has reached Athens yet, has it, Maria?'

But Maria was off somewhere else in her mind and took no notice of Barbara. It was from Stelios that she got a response.

'How can you say that everything's under control,' he said, almost shouting with frustration and pent-up emotion, 'when you create mayhem like that? And then you walk in here with that damn camera, a vital piece of incriminating evidence, which you swing around the place as if you were about to take a few shots for the family album.'

Still clutching Anthony Burton's camera, he waved it around, almost threateningly, like a weapon. 'I'm going downstairs to the incinerator to burn this. It's where everything seems to end up from here these days. Then I'm getting the hell out of here. I need a fucking break.'

'Silly you, doctor. Now you have your fingerprints all over the camera.' Which was hardly alarming given that Stelios was about to melt it down into an unrecognisable lump, but Stelios was not able to think straight any more. His automatic reflex was to drop the camera as if it were already a piece of hot, molten metal. It fell to the floor of his office and cracked open.

It was Maria who noticed it, the crash as it dropped to the ground, bringing her down to earth with a bump, from whichever planet her latest drug cocktail had taken her.

'There's no film in that camera. Where is it? That's the whole bloody point. Where's the film, for Christ's sake?' She was, for once, cold and rendered almost emotionless by the intensity of her feelings.

'Don't you worry your pretty little head about that, Maria. I have taken care of it. I am nothing if not thorough. You know that.'

'Did you destroy the roll of film, Barbara?' John asked, direct and to the point, spelling it out, leaving no room for ambiguity or doubt.

'I cannot tell a lie,' she replied. 'I did not. But the film is safe. Rest assured. That is all I have to say on the matter.'

It was then that Stelios finally lost what little control he had left of his emotions and collapsed in an exhausted and dejected state in a corner of the room, not caring any more about his dignity or comfort. He wished now only to save his life. It just came down to that. And to get out of this God-awful mess, never to clap eyes on any of these lunatics again. It was clear that Barbara Meier was unstoppable. She had stitched them up. And blackmail had no pleasant ring to it, however you said the word.

CHAPTER SIXTEEN

Fred Argent leafed through the BT Business Directory until he found the telephone number for the airport police at Heathrow. When he picked up the phone and dialled it, he was transferred immediately to the regional office that was dealing with the Burton case. And then to the investigating detective sergeant, who was at that moment in the interview room with Margaret Burton. When the phone rang, it made her jump. Her nerves were raw. She was understandably in deep shock and extremely distressed.

The detective sergeant took the call. He asked Argent to spell out his surname as he began to take down his details. Hearing the name of her former husband's boss in that unfamiliar environment made Margaret even more agitated.

'Let me speak to him, let me speak to him!' she insisted to the bemused police officer. 'I know him. He worked with Anthony.'

'Just a minute, Mrs Burton,' the detective sergeant began to say, but the woman was just so insistent. Speaking briefly to Argent to explain the situation, 'I have the deceased's widow here with me. She would like a word,' he handed the receiver to her. The policeman was relieved to let someone else take the heat for a moment. She was becoming quite hysterical. Claiming that her husband had been murdered when it looked like a straightforward road-traffic accident to him. There she was now, ranting at that poor unfortunate caller.

Oh well, he could handle her while he took a breather and worked out what to do for the best. Whatever, he wanted to get home to watch the football live on Sky. In which case, he'd have to wrap this up within the next half-hour. Or he'd be disappointed with himself and miss the game.

'They've killed him, Fred, you know that, don't you? The Greeks have murdered Anthony. When he called me, he told he'd got the photographic proof he needed from the hospital in Athens. He was coming back a couple of days early because he'd got what he went for. And now he's dead. And his camera's missing. Not among his personal effects. I know this because I asked.'

Margaret didn't pause to take breath. It all came tumbling out in a great unwieldy rush, a verbal vomiting that made Fred Argent feel sick, too. He'd imagined the same scenario, during an idle moment of reflection in his office that morning, but he'd never imagined for one minute that anyone would be able to prove that Argent had been intercepted and destroyed.

That was the stuff of Bond movies. Not of daily life at the Revenue. And he began to fear once more for his retirement pension and his dreams of a home sweet home. He took a long, deep breath as he considered how he would handle his ex-colleague's wife. Margaret Burton was clearly distraught. And Anthony's death was obviously making her unreasonable and unstable of mind.

She had moved from the shocked and tearful stage of grief to the angry, blaming phase, and he wanted to keep out of the firing line before she found her full voice in it. And started to point the finger at others. In this he feared for himself, which was why he went on publicly to dismiss her fears as the paranoid rantings of a grief-stricken widow. Of a person who would lash out at anyone or anything to avoid facing the cold, harsh, empty truth that her husband was dead and never coming back.

'Now, Margaret, I know this has come as a terrible shock. But you must accept the facts ...'

But she would not hear it and wouldn't let him finish, starting to tell him again of her suspicions.

'Anthony was a victim of cold-blooded murder,' she announced, almost coldly this time. 'And no one at all is prepared to listen to me.'

The detective sergeant turned his eyes heavenwards as he saw his chances of catching the match retreating. He hadn't bothered to set the video because he'd been so certain of getting back early that night. It was an open-and-shut case. But she wouldn't have it. His greatest concern was that she'd do anything to get herself heard, and if she started talking to the Press, God knows where it would all end.

Kimberley had fallen into a deep and dreamless sleep around dawn, after a long, dark night of her soul, in which she had mostly lain awake. But her rest was disturbed two hours later when she was pulled from its depths by a frantic knocking at her door. She sat bolt upright in bed, imagining the worst, disorientated and disadvantaged by being only half-conscious.

She stretched out beneath the sheets, willing herself out of her somnolent state, rubbing her eyes to help her see straight. When she finally managed to focus properly, it was on Maria, who was standing purposefully at the foot of her bed. She smelt great wafts of her perfume, the sultry Paloma, much too heavy for morning use. But then she'd probably been up all night. Kimberley wished to God she'd somehow managed to remain asleep.

'Good morning, Kimberley, I hope you had a good night,' Maria said civilly, not unlike an air stewardess might welcome a passenger on board. It was more an automatic courtesy than a real wish to show any true concern for Kimberley's well-being.

'I have not woken you unnecessarily,' she continued. 'But I thought you would like to know that we have received a fax. I shall tell you exactly what it says.' And Maria read out loud what was only the second brief statement from the kidnappers since George's capture.

GEORGE GISIKIS IS ALIVE AND WELL. IF YOU WISH FOR HIM TO REMAIN SO, FULFIL THE FOLLOWING INSTRUCTIONS AND ADHERE STRICTLY TO THE CONDITIONS HEREWITH.

1. DO NOT CONTACT THE POLICE OR ANY OTHER LAW-ENFORCEMENT AGENCY.

2. ORGANISE BEARER BONDS TO THE VALUE OF £10,000,000 DRAWN ON A

MAJOR EUROPEAN BANK.

3. WAIT FOR HANDOVER INSTRUCTIONS,
TO BE ADVISED WITHIN FIVE DAYS.

AWAIT OUR NEXT TRANSMISSION.
DO NOT FORGET THAT WE ARE
WATCHING YOU CONSTANTLY.

Thank God, thank God, Kimberley thought to herself.
Thank God he's not dead. And she lay staring blankly
at the ceiling, stunned with relief and aware that
Maria was talking to her, but taking in none of what
she said. Eventually she came to and heard Maria's
last few words as she left the room.

'You'd better get Charles Bradley to release some
money from the Gisikis estate to foot the bill. None of
us has any spare cash like that feathering our bank
accounts.'

What a nasty piece of work that woman was,
Kimberley reflected as she watched her leave, her
Vivienne Westwood bustle protruding insolently
behind her. There was really nothing anyone could
say in her favour. She had the sensitivity of a lump of
concrete. All she ever thought about was herself and
money.

Feeling marginally less distraught by receiving at
least some news of George, Kimberley began to
reflect on what had happened over the past few days.
George had boarded a plane for Athens from
Heathrow, where he was last seen by Charles. He had
travelled to Greece spontaneously, without any
advance warning, even to her. George didn't even
know his own plans virtually until he'd made them,

so how on earth had a bunch of kidnappers managed to be so well informed?

Kimberley's new found spirit of optimism almost foundered here. Christ! Who the fuck had taken him ransom? Of course, the entire Gisikis clan were all potential kidnap targets, much like the Gettys or any other fabulously wealthy family. But it was odd that he'd been abducted when he was somewhere away from the fairly regular routine of his life. If he'd gone while jogging in Central Park, or disappeared from his offices in Wall Street, it would have been more understandable.

On the face of it, George had been making an unscheduled visit to his sick father in hospital. But it was the place where no one in the family — not John, not Maria, not Helena, not even the surgeon Stelios — had encouraged them to go. In fact, they'd been actively discouraged from visiting and bundled back to the States believing that was the best for everyone, especially Costas. But George had been querying the appropriateness of his father's treatment just before he left. That was why he flew to Athens, for God's sake! And so, in her mind, although half-mad with worry and grief, Kimberley began to put two and two together and make four.

While Kimberley was lying on her bed in the Gisikis mansion in the mid-morning sun, George was using the fact that he'd seen it rise four times to calculate the number of days he'd been in captivity. That made it roughly five days, give or take a day or two when he was too drugged or battered to notice whether it was day or night.

Involuntarily, George started to yawn. But he

flinched as he did so when the damage inflicted to his face, now thankfully crusting over into scabs, caused him pain. God! That woman was completely crazy. Thank Christ she'd been away for most of the past few days. Jacques was like a guardian angel in comparison, nonetheless at the very bottom rung of the nine-fold celestial hierarchy.

Life had been relatively easy with Jacques. He was not in the least sociable, so there was no daily human interaction. But neither was he needlessly cruel or callous. And he gave George the freedom to wander around outside a little, albeit within close range of his captor.

When George had asked Jacques about the progress of the ransom demand, all the big man would tell him was that Kimberley had flown over to Athens as soon as Helena had contacted her. The information that his wife was not so distant from him was encouraging for George. And he knew that she would do all she could for him. Wherever she was in the world.

George was sitting in the shade of a stunted pine tree, soaking up the morning sun, which was bright but not hot. Of course, it was winter, so why should it be? But living in New York, George somehow always thought of Greece as the land of baking sun, where everything grew and everything was possible.

Costas had taught him that, imbued in him an enthusiasm for life, a zest for it, a belief in its vigour. The air was soothing and smelt so clean, unlike that of Athens or of Manhattan, for that matter. Oh, God! He'd loved these islands when he'd been a child. But now all he could think about was how to leave this one.

The cracking of dried twigs underfoot announced Jacques' arrival. And, although he should have got used to it by now, the sight of the barrel of a gun pointing down at him was something that made George's heart pound and his body break out in a cold sweat.

'Another fax has gone out to your family. I thought you should know.' That was it. All he said. The man had obviously never mastered the art of conversation. He began to walk off, the gun swinging away from its position in front of George's face as he did so.

'Well, thanks for telling me. But what happens next?' This was as close to controversial as George had dared to go in his dealings with Jacques. The man was a thug when all was said and done.

'I don't know,' said Jacques disconsolately. Then he just stared out to sea, as if he, too, were contemplating his departure. It was clear that he was also keen to return to the mainland and end his solitary duties. It wasn't exactly fun on his own. His prisoner was hardly a bundle of laughs. And he had to keep an eye on him constantly.

'Suppose you get your money,' George began, eager to talk as much as anything else, 'what do you plan to do with me then, given that I know much that I shouldn't?'

'Dunno, man,' Jacques replied. 'Listen, you ask too many damn questions. So just shut it, will you! I was never one for kidnapping you,' and he paused, before finishing his sentence and making his position clear, 'I was all for killing you then and there. Could have saved ourselves all this trouble. But Barbara has other ideas.'

At the mention of his partner's name, he stopped and gazed distractedly somewhere into the middle distance. George realised that the conversation was over.

Jacques suddenly decided it was time for George to return to the hut, something he indicated George should do by waving a gun in his face and then towards his prison. George felt the dread he always experienced when faced with any kind of confinement. He wondered sometimes if he were slightly claustrophobic. But this was a different sort of incarceration, and he certainly didn't respond well to it.

'I've left you some water and bread,' Jacques said, almost amiably, glad to get his prisoner off his hands for the rest of the day, or at least until he felt like giving him a bit of time out again. He had his own plans.

The truth of it was that Jacques was horny as hell. Barbara was due back any time soon. And he was anticipating her arrival with a great big hard-on. Well, sometimes it was harder than others. But whenever he thought of her, or talked of her, as he'd just done with George, it just got so that he felt as if his balls would burst.

Barbara had a voracious appetite for sex that matched his own. In this way they were suited. She was insatiable and knew how to arouse Jacques more than any other woman he'd enjoyed. What turned him on most was her preference for the pain end of the pain/pleasure spectrum. And she liked to cause the pain. She would whip him with her belt, hard, and groan with the enjoyment of it, which sent Jacques into spasms of lustful desire. He enjoyed her beatings as much as she liked carrying them out.

Knowing how hungry Barbara would be for sex when she returned made Jacques' cock throb until he could bear it no longer. His mouth felt dry and he poured himself a glass of water. As he did so, his hand shook and his breathing quickened. He went to sit in a corner of the room and touched the rise of his swelling erection through the denim of his Levis. He broke out into a light sweat as he pawed urgently at his wide leather belt — the very one used by Barbara, sometimes to beat him with, sometimes to tie him up — and unzipped his jeans, pulling them and his pants down to his knees.

Oh, the relief to have released his swollen cock from the restraint of his clothes. He held it lightly in his hand, and grabbed the shaft of his cock, gripping it tightly, massaging it in an up and down motion. His eyes glazed and lost their focus as he tried to muffle his groans of pleasure at the thought of Barbara on top of him, riding him mercilessly.

He made a big effort, and he was so very hard, not to climax, because he imagined Barbara's stern voice ordering him not to come yet or she would beat him again. Oh, God, yes, please! Please, please. Yes! The thought was enough to make Jacques totally lose control, and his body rocked with spasms of pleasure as his seed shot into the air above him like a milky geyser.

Weak from pleasure, he slumped on his side, his limbs relaxed like a rag doll, and heard only the sound of his own heavy panting before he fell into a blissfully deep sleep.

Kimberley's plan was going like clockwork. She had

called Charles Bradley in London to organise the transfer of funds. Then she had located Paul Mavros' address and telephone number in Costas' Roladex in his study. Scribbling it on a scrap of paper, she had handed it to her personal maid. Well, she'd had to trust someone, take that risk, and she had become friends with the woman in all the years she had been staying at the house in Athens.

The maid had come back on duty that morning and, as she helped dress Kimberley's hair into a sleek chignon, she gave her back the piece of paper on which Kimberley had scribbled Paul Mavros' number. Next to it was a brief message: Aphrodite's Hair and Body Salon, Maroussi, today at 5.00pm.

At breakfast, Kimberley announced that she simply had to do something to keep up her strength and make her feel better and more relaxed. Her maid had told her of a wonderful masseuse in Maroussi, and she wanted to go there for a treatment that day.

It was all organised, she protested, when Helena tried to dissuade her, suggesting she should try her own Swedish masseuse instead. He came to the house, brought his own table. He was wonderful, blissfully good. You couldn't do anything afterwards except sleep for hours.

But Kimberley couldn't be dissuaded and resisted Helena's suggestions. No, she'd made her mind up. In any case, it would do her good to get out of the house for a few hours. And she was used to a weekly massage in New York. George and she used the services of one of the city's best practitioners in Shiatsu.

'God knows what might happen to you up there! Maroussi's miles away,' Maria said, determined to get her word in and not at all keen that Kimberley should go out on her own. 'The best that can happen is that you'll just be followed, you know that, don't you? Couldn't you book an appointment with one of our people in town at least? It's humiliating that a member of our family might be noticed at some cheap salon in a suburban part of town.'

'You never counted me as part of your family before, Maria,' Kimberley replied, her eyes bright with anger, 'so you don't need to be anxious that I might let the side down now. Don't worry. I'll be fine. Although I'm sure that's not what you're concerned about at all.'

And with that, Kimberley made her excuses and abruptly left the room. She rested for a few hours, thinking, always thinking, trying to make sense of what had happened, planning her next move. At 4.00pm her maid knocked and came into her suite to advise her that Frank, the chauffeur, was ready to drive her to Maroussi, in one of the staff cars, so as to avoid any possible Press attention.

Kimberley was not surprised that they'd asked their puppet, the oily Frank, to take her. They would have primed him to watch her every move. And then there'd be the tail put on them by the kidnappers to consider. But they were unlikely to do anything direct at this stage. Not with a cool £10m at stake. They wouldn't put that at risk.

The drive to Maroussi was uncomplicated. They passed the Olympic Stadium, where Kimberley remembered seeing Bruce Springsteen play a few years earlier, and up into the fresher air of the suburbs to the north of Athens. There were more pine trees here, and in the summer the temperatures were cooler and more amenable than those in the centre of town. The garden city of Kiffisia, just a mile or so further north, was the place where many Athenians retreated in the often unbearable heat of July and August.

Maroussi was a kind of sanctuary for Kimberley at that moment. And once inside Aphrodite's, the receptionist accompanied her into a back room for her massage. But instead of starting to undress and preparing herself to be pummelled into a delightfully indolent state by a white-coated masseuse, she found instead Paul Mavros waiting for her. They had met several times over the 20 or so years that Kimberley and George had been together. And the warmth of feeling they had for each other was reflected in the long embrace on meeting. It had been perhaps five years since the last time. They couldn't believe so much time had elapsed. But it seemed like yesterday.

Sadly, it was not, in the sense that in the past George would have been with them. And then it took an initially angry and then tearful Kimberley a remarkably short time to summarise the living nightmare in which she now found herself. When she finished, she looked straight at her husband's oldest friend and said, 'I need your help.'

George listened intently to a sound that grew louder and louder, breaking the dense silence that eternally embraced the island. It was the churning engine and whirring blades of an approaching helicopter. Barbara was obviously returning, making use, he guessed, of the Robinson two-seater that John had recently persuaded Charles Bradley to purchase for somewhere in region of £100,000.

There was little else to hear in the deep calm of

those inaccessible Greek islands, miles from anywhere. These isolated lands had, in the past, been home to pirates and their slave markets. Now it was George who was captive there, and Jacques who was the slave to Barbara.

George felt himself tense at the thought of her. He feared for himself — she would show him no mercy — and for humanity, that it could produce such a female mutant, capable of such inhuman cruelty. He feared not the physical harm — though, of course, that concerned him — as much as her sick mind, her perverted view of life. Whatever made a person able to love, had, in Barbara, been poisoned, probably from when she was a child.

The helicopter landed. George could establish that at least by the calm that settled over the island once more. And he could hear voices, shouting, but only faintly, inaudibly. No doubt Jacques and Barbara were engaged in a touching reunion.

This was indeed what was happening in the cool of the winter afternoon. Jacques had run out to greet the helicopter, standing at the clearing where it would land, looking up at the sky, watching it increase in size as it approached. He shielded his eyes from the dust cloud it produced on landing.

But it was not only the helicopter that was now full size. Jacques' cock had risen in the air to greet his lover and was now straining at the fabric of his trousers. While the propeller blades turned more slowly, almost at a standstill as the engine died, Barbara leapt from the aircraft and ran over to where Jacques had positioned himself on the edge of the landing strip. She did not fail to notice the alluring bulge in his groin. It made her feel powerful. And horny.

Jacques was almost beside himself at the sight of Barbara's almost endlessly long legs, which he longed to have wrapped around his back, his cock deep inside her. Her full breasts bounced alluringly as she strode energetically toward him, mobilised by the strength of her sexual magnetism. And he let out a groan of pleasure when she caught up with him and placed her hand unambiguously on his bulging crotch.

'Is this big, hard cock a present for me, you bad boy?' And in no time at all she was heading him off into a pine glade, out of sight of the aircraft but still close enough to the helicopter crew to excite her voyeuristic tendencies.

Once behind a tree, Barbara quickly undid Jacques' belt and trousers sufficiently to see what he had waiting for her. She delved into his trousers to stroke the long thick rod of his dick and began to breathe fast, excitedly. She was aching for it. Christ! how she wanted him.

Her fingers explored his sex and searched now for the hard firm roundness of his balls. It was then that her lust turned abruptly to anger. And she squeezed hard on his balls. Jacques' legs buckled under him with pain, and he fell to his knees in front of her.

'I missed you,' he pleaded. 'I felt starved of you. Of your cunt, your breasts, the tangle of your bush, your long sensuous legs, the curve of your back. I lust after you. I am your slave. I love you, Barbara. I was thinking only of you when it happened,' he stopped, his excuses petering out as he realised he was getting nowhere.

Barbara was impervious to his pleas, livid that he had wanked himself off when he knew that she was due back soon. She didn't like the idea of Jacques cheating on her with himself. But she knew that people always wanted what they are told they cannot have, something she used all the time in her sexual power games, to spice up foreplay. And she was certain that Jacques would have spent hours fighting the desire to jerk himself off simply because she had told him that it was forbidden. In any case, she loved fucking with his head, almost as much as she enjoyed fucking his body.

'You belong to me. Every part of you. And you've started without me. Your balls are shrivelled up, deflated, empty. You disappoint me.' And with this she hit him hard across the face, splitting open his lip, instantly drawing blood, the sight of which enraged her even more. Engaged and excited her.

'You must be punished for this. Right now,' she ranted, just the way he liked. And she stormed on and on. Tearing off his clothes, she used his belt to whip his naked arse as he stood erect against a tree.

Their tryst lasted for hours. Just long enough to tie Jacques up and beat him again until he begged for mercy. And then for Barbara, her love juices sticky between her inner thighs, to sit on his face while he brought her to a loud climax.

After her orgasm, Barbara slept for half-an-hour, until she awoke to find Jacques still roped and bound. This aroused her once more, and she climbed back on top of him. This time choosing to position her pussy over his stiff dick rather than his wet mouth. In time they orgasmed noisily, violently together.

When the helicopter took off again some hours later, George was reassured to know that Barbara was inside it. The couple had been stacking supplies in the room next door, too near for comfort, when he'd heard Jacques complaining about the brevity of her visit, that he'd expected her at least to stay the night. They'd rowed about it. George was surprised. He hadn't realised how vulnerable Jacques was around the woman.

Thankfully, Barbara hadn't even bothered to grace George with a visit. George felt a sense of relief that Barbara had exhausted herself with Jacques, that for the time being she had satisfied herself with him. He had listened to the violence of the beating she gave Jacques, followed by the unmistakably sexual tones of a frenzy of lovemaking. Thank God she'd left him alone this time, he thought. George slumped to the floor, exhausted by the strain of having the bitch on the island, of worrying that he'd be next in line for the whip or worse. He was relieved that she hadn't come in to check on him, because he'd almost passed caring now. And he might have gone for her. Hit back. Which would have given her the perfect excuse to pump him full of lead.

He was really up against it now. Depression was beginning to take hold. And he distressed himself further by thinking about his family. His heart ached for them, knowing how distraught Kimberley would feel, how hard Oliver would find it to face the fact that he might never see his father again.

George was desperate to leave the island, to go home and comfort them, to tell them that everything was going to be all right. But in his own mind he knew that was not necessarily so, and he could offer himself no reassurance there either. He wanted more than anything to be back with his family, knew that he would never want anything so much ever again in his life. And he felt his hard-won composure begin to crumble as he tried unsuccessfully to fight back his tears.

He was a man, he shouldn't cry, he told himself. In the past, he would have despised himself for breaking down like this. But his sobs racked his body, as his tears rolled silently down his cheeks. He was no longer free or in charge of his destiny. He was trapped in a nightmare to which he could see no end. A prisoner in his own private hell.

The Gisikis family were taking their evening meal in the sumptuous formality of the dining-room. Half-way through the main course, Maria started her usual bitching, tactful as ever.

'Oh, well, Kimberley,' she said, 'at least you managed to achieve something today apart from just sitting around and crying your eyes out. And it couldn't have been easy for you when you called Charles and told him about the ransom demand. He's such an old woman. And he hates spending Papa's money. He must feel sick about handing so much of it over to the kidnappers. What a waste!'

Kimberley did not miss her opportunity, seizing it like the gift from the gods she knew it to be.

'Christ, Maria, how dare you say that, you spoilt, stupid bitch!' Kimberley had been practising her retaliation, but she surprised even herself at the force of it.

'How dare you consider the money when your own brother's life depends on it! You're unspeakably insensitive, indescribably selfish, and I'm not going to hang around here one moment longer to take any more shit from you.'

And, just as she'd agreed with Paul Mavros, who had stressed how vital it was that she should get out of the web of the Gisikis mansion and move into town, Kimberley announced that she'd be leaving then and there. She would keep in touch via Charles Bradley. The butler would book her a room at the Hotel Grande Bretagne in Sintagma Square. She wanted nothing more from them, but they could reach her at the hotel in central Athens if they had a civil word to say to her. And with that, she turned on her heel and left.

Barbara's visit had lasted barely four hours. Jacques had so wanted her to stay. And their argument over her too rapid departure had distracted him, and he'd forgotten to unload from the chopper all the supplies that she'd brought with her from the mainland. Most importantly, she'd flown off with the fresh batteries for his mobile phone.

Shit! he thought. Now he couldn't even communicate with anyone. Except his prisoner. But he had nothing to say to him. It was all Barbara's fault. She shouldn't have behaved so unreasonably. Anyway, now if she wanted to talk to him, needed something from him, well, she'd just have to bide her time. But patience was not something that Barbara had.

CHAPTER SEVENTEEN

Margaret Burton was turning Fred Argent's life into a living nightmare with her attempt to get him involved in setting up a murder inquiry into Anthony's death. She was telling everyone who'd listen — friends, family, the police, the Press — that he'd been killed because he was in the process of investigating one of the richest families in the world for fraud; that his death was the direct result of evidence that he'd found of the Gisikis family's attempts to defraud the UK tax authorities out of millions of pounds.

Press photographers and a reporter from the *Sun*, and two others from *The Times* and London's *Evening Standard*, remained camped outside his office day and night. Well, the scent of money always attracted the bloodhounds, Argent mused grimly.

What the hell if that Burton woman was right! Argent considered angrily. Anthony was dead now, and he, Fred Argent, just wanted a quiet life. But that was exactly what he had not had since the day Anthony Burton had been killed. He was harassed constantly by other people, finding it impossible to concentrate on anything. He lived in a constant state of panic.

What was worse was that his routine had gone haywire. He'd forgotten to buy his copy of *The Times* that morning. Apart from a brief look at the front page headlines and the sports section, he was missing his ritual of *The Times* crossword.

Once he got to Victoria he tried to buy his paper, but they'd run out at the W H Smith's on the station concourse and were awaiting a second delivery. On the tube, he'd been galled to notice the man opposite him reading his *Times*. It didn't exactly have his name on it, but he felt it should have been his. He was Murdoch's most loyal reader. Argent was furious. And, for a moment or two, his internal whingeing distracted him from the headline: GISIKIS TAX FRAUD LINKED TO HEATHROW MURDER.

When he finally focused in on it, Argent couldn't believe his eyes. He almost snatched the paper out of the other man's hands, so keen was he to read the story in full. But he needn't have worried about being ill-informed because when he got to his office and opened the *Sun*, it was no surprise for him to discover that they had an exclusive interview with Burton's widow.

Christ! What would she do next? But to make things worse his staff were all on to it. He gave them nothing to go on. He was handling the case himself, he announced. And they must not speak to the Press or put through to him their damned calls, or any from that stupid Burton bitch either. With that he closed the meeting and went into his management suite, slamming the door behind him.

In his office he put in a call himself to the detective sergeant handling the case.

'Fred Argent, here,' he barked down the phone at

the unfortunate man. 'Did you read the *Sun* this morning? That bloody Burton woman is mad! Completely mad!'

'Yes, I have. I agree with you, but we've got to sit tight,' the detective sergeant replied, already over preoccupied by the case. 'I've had my superiors on my back this morning myself. She's now accusing us and the tax authorities of negligence. But I'm taking it seriously because something like this can grow out of all proportion. And the last thing I want is an investigation that I don't consider worthy of valuable police time.'

'As far as I'm concerned, my office has nothing to do with the case,' Argent said quickly. 'Burton wasn't there on official tax business. He went on a whim without our backing. The poor bastard met with an unfortunate accident, and that's it. Nothing more and ...'

At this point, the investigating officer interrupted him. 'Excuse me, Mr Argent, could I please stop you there and ask you kindly to hold the line?'

'Of course,' Argent replied, 'but I'm busy this morning. Why don't you call me when you have some more news?'

And so it was left, until later that day, when Argent's secretary brought him a message from the detective sergeant. There was to be no further investigation of the Burton case. Margaret Burton had blown her credibility by talking to the *Sun* and being paid for the privilege. The police had decided there was absolutely no evidence of foul play. And the matter was now officially closed.

So Fred Argent was able to look forward to his pension, to relaxing after years of public responsibility. And who could blame him? He didn't expect a gold watch, but he did want peace of mind. He was not sure he would ever be able to have that.

Of course, Anthony Burton would never have his retirement to anticipate, nor indeed any other of life's pleasures. And his wife would never again feel the warmth of his presence beside her at night, or his daily words of love and encouragement.

No one believed her when she said that her husband had been murdered. Not her parents, who had never liked him. Not her friends, who felt she was half crazed by grief. Not the police, who could find no evidence to prove that it was ever anything other than a simple traffic accident. Nor Fred Argent who, for his own reasons, wanted nothing to do with any of it. But she knew in her heart, as she cried herself to sleep, that they were all mistaken.

In a simple ceremony in London, Anthony Burton was cremated. His wife flew to Greece with his ashes, which she scattered over the sea at Vouliagmeni. There, where they had been happy, she laid him to rest. What he knew about Costas Gisikis died with him.

Kimberley Gisikis was luxuriating in a long, hot bath in the wonderful en suite marble bathroom at the Grande Bretagne. She was enjoying the facilities of the luxury hotel. And, as a true American, was fascinated by its history. Originally, it had been a private house, built by Theophilus van Hansen in the mid-1800s, then used as an overspill for the Greek royal family who couldn't be accommodated in the Royal Palace nearby. Just over 100 years later, it had been enlarged and refaced in marble.

During the Second World War the Greek, German

and British forces in turn had used it as their operational headquarters. Winston Churchill spent Christmas 1944 there and was fortunate to escape a bomb, meant for him, that was planted in the sewers beneath.

Thankfully, the attempt was foiled, and the hotel was home now to many among the crowned heads of Europe when in Athens. And, of course, others, like Kimberley, who could afford its prices. She preferred it to the equally expensive Astir Palace directly across the square, which, as part of a luxury chain, did not, in her view, have the *cachet* of the established Grande Bretagne. Anywhere was better than the Gisikis mansion and being spied upon constantly by the ghastly twins and Helena, who was becoming weirder and more distant behind her heavy mask of face make-up and her couture body armour.

The older woman was seriously losing it. She'd started drinking heavily, from as soon as her day began, which admittedly only started around lunchtime. She had taken to sitting in the drawing-room for hours, a bottle of 60 per cent proof brandy or bourbon on the floor next to her. She drank it like water. And never seemed to get drunk. Until she stood up and fell over and had to be carried off to bed.

God, it was depressing. Though Helena was right. There wasn't much to life at the moment, with Costas half-dead and George God knows where, with Christ knew who. The only thing to which Kimberley had to look forward was the imminent arrival of Oliver. Seeing her son would give her the strength to fight on.

When John told Barbara over the phone that Kimberley had checked out of the house and into the

Grande Bretagne, she knew instinctively that something had gone wrong. When she said so, John's response was not repeatable. He'd had enough of being told what to do by the Icewoman. She was working for them, not the other way round. He was tired of her bullying, hectoring, interfering.

'For Christ's sake,' he said, 'you didn't have to live with her! Talk about a prig. She got up my nose with that snotty look on her face, disapproval written all over it, let me tell you. That is when she wasn't looking upset about our darling little bro. Christ! I couldn't stand it. Thank God she's gone. Tonight we're going to celebrate in a very big way.'

'I shouldn't, not if you know what's good for you,' Barbara cautioned fiercely. 'Don't you realise, you fool, that the safest place for her was right under your nose. At least you could keep tabs on what she was doing every minute of the day. That's much more vital to your well-being than throwing a fucking stupid party!'

At this point, Maria intervened, incensed at Barbara's incessant criticism, her patronising, Barbara-knows-best bullshit. She'd taken enough of her crap for a lifetime.

'You're becoming paranoid, Barbara. You haven't got a clue about our precious sister-in-law. She's just a hick from New Jersey who married well. Leap-frogged up on her husband's back. The woman has nothing between her ears. Trust me, Barbara, Kimberley is no danger to us at all.'

But Barbara wasn't convinced and backed down not at all.

'You're a pair of fucking amateurs,' she snapped. 'And you've given me more work to do. Well, it will cost you. Bugging a Grande Bretagne suite is damn difficult. There'll be a lot of baksheesh to pay. And my time, especially when it's wasted, doesn't come cheap.'

With that, she terminated the conversation, leaving John and Maria in a state of angry limbo.

'Come on, Maria,' John suggested in an effort to snap them out of it, 'let's go visit Kimberley and see how she's settling in. We can treat ourselves to a few Manhattans in the bar. And invite her to join us. It's the perfect cocktail for a girl from the sticks with blonde ambition.'

Kimberley had been out for most of the day, sightseeing, because she had always loved Athens, most especially the view of the city from the conical rock of Lykabettos. The hill had once been the north-eastern suburban limit of the city and was now an island in a sea of houses. The great plain of Attica had disappeared under the urban sprawl that was even beginning to inch its way into the foothills of the amphitheatre of mountains that surrounded it.

But the fact was that Kimberley needed to walk all day around the city in order to dissipate her anxiety about her husband. She felt helpless, yet so restless. She had done all she could. She had set the wheels in motion for the ransom money to come through from Charles. Paul Mavros had contacted him and confirmed to her that it would be with them soon. There was nothing else for her to do but wait. And this was the hardest part.

One of her favourite places in Athens was the Acropolis. Natural springs had encouraged people to live there for thousands of years. But she hadn't been for a while and found it disappointing. What was left of Pericles' grand scheme was slowly decaying. The Temple of Athena Nike was roped off, so she was denied sitting inside its ancient stones, which was what she enjoyed most. In any case, she consoled herself, the view from there of the Saronic Gulf was not what it used to be before the smog settled in over Athens.

She left the Acropolis through the ornamental groves of its western slopes and headed towards the Agora. It had been not only the market of ancient Athens but also the centre of its civic and social life. Here, the citizens of ancient Greece spent much of their day doing deals and debating, watching sport and street theatre. They would squabble and fight, plot and drink, behave lecherously and plot to kill each other. They were a scandalous, debauched lot on the whole. Nothing much had changed there, Kimberley thought. At least certain members of the Gisikis family seemed to have a direct line to their ancestors.

In fact, Barbara had not found it difficult to bug Kimberley's room at the Grande Bretagne. Disguised as a cleaner, she had managed to inveigle her way in. There had been plenty of time to install the state-of-the-art listening devices, after which she withdrew to her operations post in another room of the hotel.

She had almost given in to sleep when she picked up sounds that indicated Kimberley had returned from her tour of the city. One of her girls, the same one who had acted as her runner in the Kolonaki cafe with Maria, had tailed the American in Athens. In the event, it had been a long day for her. Kimberley had wandered so extensively around all its ancient hills and monuments that if her schooling with Barbara fell through, she would be able to take up employment with the Athens Tourist Board.

At first, Kimberley was on her own. She took a shower and then watched some TV. A short time later, room service arrived with her supper. She heard Kimberley protest that she hadn't ordered any. That there must be some mistake. It soon became clear to Barbara that the arrival of the meal had brought with it an unexpected visitor. Everything fell horribly into place after that. There had been no mistake at all. In fact, someone had been very thorough.

The man who had so considerately brought Kimberley's supper to her hotel room was not a member of the hotel's vast team of catering staff. He was called Paul. Barbara knew this because Kimberley kept referring to him as such during the brief conversation that followed. She didn't know exactly who this Paul was, but what was clear was that he was high up in the Greek police force. And Kimberley knew him and had contacted him to assist her. He was earning his keep. For a start, he had alerted Interpol just a few hours earlier. And made inroads with the rest. It was the CIA who'd given him the lead he needed, Barbara heard him say.

His contact there had told him that US satellite surveillance systems kept a close and regular watch over the Greek–Turkish border, especially the islands that fringed it in the Aegean and Samos seas. The boundary between the two nations in the eastern Aegean snaked untidily among the hundreds of large and small islands, making it difficult to monitor. Hurry up, you creep! Barbara muttered to herself. We don't want a lesson in political geography. Just get to the fucking point!

This Paul did. But the conclusion he reached did not please Barbara in the slightest. Apparently, she heard him say, the satellite had been scanning the region for any military or terrorist activity. With the uneasy peace brought about by the division in Cyprus between Greece and Turkey that threatened to flare up from time to time, they were specially vigilant. And their vigilance had paid off. But not in ways that they had expected. On a small, previously uninhabited island there was an unusual amount of localised activity.

When the satellite had honed in on the territory, it fed back pictures of an armed patrol of an area around a small building. Heat-detectors had picked up the presence of another person inside the cottage, whose movements appeared to be restricted.

Although originally not able to establish the identity of the interlopers, the one interesting fact that had emerged to excite Paul Mavros' imagination was that the island was logged as belonging to one Costas Gisikis. This, he decided, was a coincidence he had to follow up. And it was for this reason that they had been engaged in closer surveillance procedures. The result of this was to establish with total certainty that the man held prisoner on the island was none other than George. His captor, the well-known international terrorist Jacques Schotsmans.

But what appalled Barbara most as she sat hunched over the communications system that allowed her to eavesdrop on Kimberley and her tame cop was that a highly trained, combined crack force of the US Navy, the CIA and the Greek secret service were about to invade Myra.

For the first time in her life, Barbara panicked. What the fuck was she going to do? Well, call Jacques first, to warn him! And she picked up her mobile and punched in the number of his mobile. There was no reply except the infuriating message that ended with 'Please try later'. Later was no fucking good to her! she almost shouted in response to the disembodied voice. What on earth was going on with Jacques? And then she remembered. Oh, Christ! she thought, her spirits sinking, of course, he hadn't unloaded the batteries. She'd found them when they landed back in Athens.

Barbara sat with her head in her hands for a full five minutes, paralysed with shock. But, eventually, the panic and fear gave way to anger and hatred, feelings with which she was more comfortable and which she could deal with better. Now building herself into a peak of rage, she grabbed her gun and, taking the silencer from her capacious Gucci travelbag, screwed it on to the weapon. Her hands were shaking so much with fury that she dropped the gadget twice. She wanted to shoot a hole in that bitch, she railed. And that smug police fucker. Right then and there.

But when she went out into the corridor with the intention of doing just that, a group of people were lingering there, planning their night out, with all the indecision people on holiday in a strange group in a strange place always possess. Which restaurant in the Plaka should they sample that night? Where to drink retsina and play backgammon?

Christ! Barbara thought, bloody tourists at this time of the year. They get everywhere. You'd think those in a hotel like the Bretagne would have more up-market tastes than that. Despite her thuggish lifestyle, Barbara had a liking for the high life.

The distraction of the tourist group was enough to allow Barbara quickly to take stock. It wasn't necessary to deal with Kimberley and her friend then and there. That could wait. She'd always know where to find them. And find them she would. Later. Now her energies were better focused on getting to Myra. She had until dawn the next day. No more than six hours to foil the invasion.

Back in her room, Barbara gathered up all her bits and pieces of belongings into the one bag she allowed herself. She took great care not to leave a trace of herself behind. She wiped all the surfaces she might have touched in the course of her short time there, then hurriedly left the room to take the lift to the vast marble lobby from where she took a taxi to Athens heliport.

The call came through to Maria and John late that evening as they sat in a room thick with smoke from the strong black Turkish hashish they had bought from a dealer at the docks in Piraeus. To say they were stoned was an understatement, and the message from Barbara was short enough for them almost to believe that they may well have imagined it.

'You're a couple of dumb bastards. I was right about Kimberley. She's got busy. I'm taking the chopper to lift Jacques and my hostage off the island tonight. When I've dealt with that problem, I'll come looking for you. You're both dead meat already. But don't hang around to see if I change my mind.'

With that, the line went dead as she punched the

'Off' button on her mobile without waiting for any response. The atmosphere in the room, already dense with smoke, grew thick with the scent of fear. Barbara's words had managed to penetrate Maria's dope-fuddled brain. She felt now as if her head would burst with the confusion of her thoughts.

John sat beside her on the sofa. She grabbed hold of him for support and in hope of guidance, but she knew it was the blind leading the blind. Nevertheless, she tightened her grip on him as the adrenalin pumped through her nervous system, heightening the paranoia she often experienced when she'd smoked too much dope.

It was John who spoke first. And he did have something to offer her, for her to hang on to. Any port in a storm. He had everything worked out, he said. He'd been thinking about what they would do if something like this were to happen. Well, all they had to do was deny everything. It was that simple.

Who's to say that they'd employed Barbara? Only her. And she didn't count in the truth stakes. She was an international terrorist with no reputation to protect. She might well have a roll of film in her possession that showed the old man in a compromising position. But so what? There was nothing to prove they were linked to it. Stelios, if anyone, would take the rap for that.

In fact, they could let Stelios and Barbara take the blame for everything. He, Maria and Helena would claim that Stelios and Barbara had been working together. That Stelios had been counting on his share of the inheritance from the Gisikis fortune and just got greedy. After all they're not medically qualified. How could they possibly have known about their father's hospital treatment? They were taking their lead from their cousin, who was a specialist. How could they possibly know that he'd deceived them for his own ends?

And so John went on, obsessively embroidering his plan, deluded by the euphoric effects of the Turkish hash. Fantasy land sounded so logical and practical. And, for that night, Maria decided to go along with him. Because she couldn't at that point bear to engage in too close a scrutiny of her brother's plan, his glib solution to all that ailed them.

Maria took herself upstairs to deal with the latest crisis in what was turning into something worse than her worst nightmares. She did so in the way she had always done. She selected a cocktail of pills from an assortment of bottles and boxes on her dressing-room table. When she returned downstairs, it was to encourage her brother to lay out a line of the heroin that she had recently discovered was the best way to achieve forgetfulness. The warmest of warm blankets to her soul. In it, she could wrap up her troubles in one hit. There was, after all, no problem big enough that you couldn't run away from, she told herself.

Maria watched John chop and lay out the brown powder on the glass-topped coffee table in the living-room. As he was doing so, the antique wall clock in Costas' study nearby chimed midnight. Maria heard it with some dread. And she surprised herself by suddenly remembering a line of poetry she'd heard years earlier, from the days when she and John were schooled by the best tutors that the Gisikis money could buy. Not that it had done her any good, she laughed bitterly.

But still the verse went round and round her head.

Something about ... 'never ask for whom the bell tolls, it tolls for thee ...' But as the effect of the drug kicked in, it went totally from her mind, and she could remember nothing.

CHAPTER EIGHTEEN

It was just before dawn. The streets of Athens were empty. Everyone, Kimberley thought, weakened by her all night vigil, was sleeping, preparing themselves for the day ahead. Except her. She was excluded from its daily routine of getting up, going out, coming home, its highs and lows, its frustrations and triumphs. But always its enduring familiarity.

Kimberley had lost this. There was no longer anything she recognised in her world. All the usual markers had gone. Nothing, she reflected, would ever be the same, even if George were returned safely to her. She would never again take anything for granted. She'd seen a fragility to living that she hadn't noticed before, glimpsed the vulnerability of its blood and bones and vital organs beneath the skin.

It was mostly life's outer fabric that stayed the same. And in Syntagma Square below her hotel window, she could see much that was familiar and enduring. And it served to distract her for a while.

During the day and for much of the night the square was a busy, open space that teemed with life. To the west and below the level of Amalia Avenue, it bustled with cafés, hotels and air terminal buildings.

To the east, it was closed by the Royal Palace,

situated on rising ground, where the Greek constitution had been proclaimed from its balconies in the mid-1800s, and where tourists liked to watch the changing of the guard. For the past half-century, it had been the seat of the Greek parliament. In the paved, hollow square that fronted the Palace was the memorial to the Unknown Soldier.

To the south, along Amalia Avenue, were the National Gardens, designed for Queen Amalia for the Palace. The green and leafy space was a haven for Athenians from the summer heat with sub-tropical trees, peacocks, ducks and even, in the spring, nightingales.

Kimberley had visited Athens first when she was a student, taking time off in the summer to do Europe, like many American kids of her generation. She'd stayed then in a huge hostel, an old dormitory house, unbearably hot and airless in the boiling temperatures of a Greek summer. The building had probably been pulled down, but not before it had sheltered virtually every hippy who had followed the trail to the Greek islands.

Kimberley felt she knew it all intimately. She'd fetched up in Athens for a week when she'd run out of money, and had worked for a while as a flower-seller to raise the fare home.

Now married to George, she was an honorary Greek. She had visited Athens with him many times. And she had often waited for him in one of the many cafés that fringed Syntagma Square. Now she waited again. She shivered and turned away from the window.

Working along the lines of no news is good news, Dr

Stelios Gisikis had settled back into his old routine at the Baltic. He had heard nothing from Barbara for two days and was beginning to feel more relaxed. His fears about the blackmail had been shelved for the moment. He'd decided he couldn't worry about everything just in case it might happen. And he had his patients to consider. Even his staff had noticed that he was less highly strung than he'd been over the past few weeks. A few of them thought he'd started to date a new woman. Why else, they wondered, would he be sounding more cheerful all of a sudden? Whistling as he did during his ward rounds, even singing the latest popular tune to himself.

It could, of course, have been for lots of reasons, but was most likely connected to the new drug he'd prescribed himself, an idyllic mix of uppers and downers that kept him happily on an even keel. What he was failing to realise was that reality had a different horizon.

Maria had fallen into a heavy, drugged sleep around the time Kimberley was considering the approaching dawn over Syntagma Square. Her rest was short-lived, adrenalin pumping her awake two hours later. For a moment, she couldn't remember the root of her anxiety. But then it came to her like an encounter with concrete at 100mph. Christ! There was no way out this time. They were finished.

Downstairs, John had not given in to sleep at all. He'd just moved on to some of the finest cocaine Colombia could supply him. It never failed to lift his spirits, but he was getting through it at an alarming rate.

He began to suspect Maria of stealing his stash. Or

one of the household servants. Yes, that was more like it. Well, he'd just have to hide it better. And he spent the rest of the night looking for somewhere to conceal his drugs. When he finally fell asleep and woke some hours later, he spent much of the next day trying to remember where he'd hidden them.

Helena did not sleep much at all these nights. Her routine was simple. Drink all day. Blackout. Start drinking again. She wasn't a communicative drunk. She kept her own counsel. Yet you could see that she was troubled from the faraway look she had in her eyes. As if she were looking for something she had lost.

She had retreated into melancholia, anger laced with sentiment that was never expressed. Sometimes she would play music. They could hear it throughout the house. She was trying to say something through it that she couldn't express herself.

Glenn Miller and the 1940s big band sound meant she was feeling more spirited, though yearning for her youth. This was the happiest she got, after her first few drinks of the day.

Then it would be Dory Previn or Leonard Cohen, which meant she had moved on to the resentful, bellicose stage of drunkenness. No one went near her then. She was prone to throw things and lash out at anyone or anything, including herself.

But before too long, it would give in to the strains of Frank Sinatra or some Greek Zorba music. At this, if anyone were to interrupt her, put their head round the door to see if she wanted anything, the chances were they'd find her with tears pouring down her face, not just crying but releasing a lifetime of distress.

This was a two-stage part of the drunk's progress. And when she'd burned that out of her system, just before the comatose stage, she'd dance. One, two, three, kick, kick. Rarely displaying the flamboyant dignity of her island heritage, hers was a slow stumbling attempt at the traditional Greek dance pace. It led inevitably to her collapse in a stupor.

It was there, on the floor, that the household staff would increasingly find her at all hours of the day and night. They'd pick her up and sit her in a chair to recover. She would stay there, sometimes for an hour, like a puppet without strings. Still wearing her Chanel or Dior, only her face gave her away, her mascara and pan-stick having mingled in a messy palette around her eyes and cheeks. They thought she might be grieving for her brother-in-law. But, in truth, Helena was mourning the loss of herself.

Barbara scanned the surface of the ocean with her powerful binoculars as the helicopter approached the tiny island of Myra. Much to her relief, the deep turquoise sea was broken only by the trails of white foam left by the small fishing boats and private yachts that frequented its waters. She focused in on each of them in turn to make sure there was nothing amiss. She found nothing to alarm her, only fishermen trawling the deep and the odd early riser strolling the deck of a yacht.

They were almost on target, with just a few minutes to touch-down, when Barbara walked to the rear of the aircraft and unpacked a large leather bag she had with her. From it she removed two Uzis, two Kalashnikov AK47s, two machine-guns and four hand-grenades. She strapped one of the machine-guns

and an Uzi over each shoulder and dumped the
remainder of the arsenal on the floor. As the
helicopter descended gently, she pondered on how
best to use it. She wanted to get it to Jacques, but she
didn't want to hinder herself in the process.

She moved forwards to watch their descent. As
she did so, she failed to notice the two US submarines
that rose towards the surface of the ocean on opposite
sides of the island, each just 100 metres from the
shore. The submarine positioned in the sea facing the
hut side of the island rose just high enough to break
water. From its depths emerged Paul Mavros and 20
crack-shot commandos. They scrambled through the
exit shaft of the vessel, crouching on its deck before
they launched themselves into the assault boats that
had been inflated for the attack.

The thundering rotor blades of Barbara's
helicopter drowned out the gentle humming of the
small engines of the inflatables. She did not notice the
commandos as they crept stealthily ashore. Within
seconds, each one had taken advantage of the natural
cover of the island's dense brush.

Jacques had just allowed George out of the hut for his
early-morning slash when he had heard the distant
whirr of the helicopter's arrival. He had been
surprised by how readily George had returned indoors
at the mention of Barbara's imminent arrival. He had
even let himself back into the hut and waited for
Jacques to lock him in. Jacques turned the key to
secure his prisoner, but in his eagerness to get to
Barbara, he forgot to remove it from the keyhole.

Jacques headed off toward the helicopter's landing
pad. He was longing to see her, all too prepared to

forget their differences the last time they'd met. But Jacques' jubilance turned to consternation when he saw how weighed down she was with an arsenal of heavy weaponry. He moved forwards more warily, realising this lovers' reunion was not going to go as he'd imagined.

When Barbara saw Jacques, she waved at him impatiently. Get a move on. When he was in earshot, she yelled, 'We're under attack! Move it! Take some of this stuff. Hurry, for God's sake!' And then barked her instructions at the pilot to keep the engine running, prepared for take-off.

As Jacques got closer to Barbara, he could see she was seething with rage. She didn't stop to greet him, just kept on walking towards the cottage as she threw an Uzi and a machine-gun at him and handed him two hand-grenades, which he stuffed in the pockets of his filthy Levis.

'Let's just get that fucking hostage and try to lift off before the Navy arrive. They're on their way right now to rescue him,' she shouted at him, breaking into a run.

A massive explosion sent him and Barbara flying, then crashing to the ground in a cloud of earth and stones. Her prophecy had been fulfilled quicker than she'd possibly imagined. They lay there, winded but unhurt, and spat the dirt from their mouths, rotating on their stomachs to try to assess the situation.

To their horror, the helicopter had become a ball of flames. At its centre, the pilot was screaming in terror, unable to escape the inferno his aircraft had become. His face drained of all colour except for the blood that poured down it from a serious head wound, his mouth stretched open in the wide O of a silent scream. Nothing was audible above the noise and chaos of the explosion and fire.

The plight of their pilot and his craft was the last thing that Jacques and Barbara saw as they lay flattened, face-down, hugging the ground, their faces buried in the cradle of their folded arms. Then, as burning fragments of the helicopter fuselage thundered down around them, they covered their heads with their hands.

As they lay there, they could hear the remaining debris raining to the ground. An earthquake-like tremor shook them as the helicopter's entire tail section spun flaming into the air and thudded to earth to wedge itself in the dirt near their bodies, piercing it like a hot knife through butter.

In the odd silence of the aftermath, Barbara and Jacques got quickly to their feet and began to run once more in the direction of the cottage. But they flung themselves to the ground again almost immediately. There was gunfire and the sound of bullets. They lay prostrate and helpless in the scrub that surrounded the cottage for several minutes.

When the shooting stopped, the short silence that followed was quickly filled by a loud-hailer announcement: 'DROP YOUR WEAPONS AND GIVE YOURSELVES UP. YOU ARE SURROUNDED.'

Barbara and Jacques lay motionless in the dirt, not daring even to peer in the direction from which the order had come. Thirty seconds later, when they had not moved to surrender, the message was repeated across the island again, splitting the dawn silence. This time in Greek, then Turkish and finally in English. Again they did nothing. And an ominous silence followed.

'We should do as they say, my love,' Jacques whispered to Barbara at last, resigning himself to defeat as he said it.

From where she lay, Barbara could see Jacques' pupils were dilated with fear, his eyes like saucers. When she followed his gaze, she saw, in a copse just a hundred yards away, a line of guns pointing directly at them from among the trees.

'We haven't got a chance,' Jacques said, his voice matter-of-fact and accepting, not in the least hysterical. Slowly, he began to raise one of his arms in the air in surrender, pushing his weapons aside with the other.

'What the hell do you think you're doing?' Barbara screamed at him. 'What are you made of, for God's sake? You are nothing but a woman!'

'Barbara,' he said, trying to reason with her, 'your way is suicide. They will just blow us away. Think about it, will you?' he went on, suddenly more forceful. 'We haven't killed anyone they can pin on us. Our hostage is still alive. If we give ourselves up we will serve our time in jail, and eventually be released to enjoy our freedom once again. To be together. I want to share my life with you. And I'm not ready to die.'

'How can you accept defeat?' Barbara spat at him, disgusted. 'It is better to die than to give in. Than to crawl to them like cowards and put ourselves at their mercy, our lives in their hands.'

'Right now, a coward's life seems more attractive than a fool's death,' Jacques replied as he pushed another of his guns away from him and out of reach. He moved to lever himself up slowly from the ground. Turning to face the line of weaponry that was directed at them, he shouted his surrender into the Greek dawn.

'I love you, Barbara,' he said as he waved his arms above his head and started to walk towards the trees, 'and I want you to come with me. Please, Barbara, now. Please. Before it's too late.'

And he continued to move forward slowly. But there was no confidence in his steps. And he stopped for a moment, to resume his appeal to his lover, sounding desperate now.

'I want you to come and live with me. Some day, years from now, we can be together again. I can't be with you if all you want is to end up dead and in a grave. I don't want to be by your side then.'

When he heard her call his name, he thought he had succeeded in winning her over. Yes, she was coming. He could tell from the soft, wheedling quality of her voice.

'Jacques, please wait.' Yes, he'd wait. Of course, he'd wait. He'd wait for her for ever. But as he turned slowly to look at her, to encourage her on with him, he was met with her fury, not her compliance. All he could see was that her eyes were full of hate.

'You disappoint me, Jacques,' she said coldly as she pointed the Uzi at his heart. 'And you know how much I hate disappointment.' Jacques look aghast, and his eyes widened with horror as he heard her release the safety catch of the Uzi. He was appalled to see the beginnings of a smile spread across Barbara's face at the sight of his obvious fear.

'Oh, Jacques,' she said, feeling the familiar surge of sexual excitement, the sense of her own power that other people's terror always aroused in her, 'you do know how to make a girl happy.' Jacques tried to dive for cover as she pressed the trigger of the Uzi. But there was nothing to hide behind, and he was obviously not able to move fast enough to outmanoeuvre the bullets. One of them just tore a hole in his chest, his body flung backwards with the impact.

From the distant line of trees, the watery sun glinted on the metal of the guns and a voice rang out over the loud hailer. 'DROP YOUR WEAPONS. DROP YOUR WEAPONS.'

Barbara did as she was told, knowing full well that she had a hand-gun concealed beneath her clothing. She would take out as many of those bastards as she could before they killed her. She heard the sound of the loud hailer once more, instructing her to put her arms in the air and stand up slowly. But then she was distracted by Jacques. She heard him moaning in pain, clutching at his chest as his blood pumped from the wound in his body.

Then there was the voice from the trees again. And she turned to look in that direction. Not sure which way to turn but determined not to lose out totally. She did as they'd requested. Stood, her arms above her head. And then she stared hard and long in a gesture of defiance, fixing her gaze all the time in the direction of the copse that sheltered the enemy.

She had just made out something, some movement behind the trees. But what she failed to notice nearer to her, not 20 yards to the front and left of her, was Jacques. Despite the severity of the injury he'd sustained, he was reaching into his pocket and removing one of the hand-grenades that Barbara had given him. Now he was pulling the pin with his teeth.

Now with all the force that remained in his body, he was throwing it determinedly in the direction of his lover.

The last that Jacques saw before the pain overwhelmed him and slipped him mercifully into unconsciousness was the grenade hit its target. As he died, he did so knowing that he had not turned the other cheek. That he had taken Barbara's life just as surely as she had taken his.

George had been watching the rescue attempt through a crack in the wooden wall timbers of the cottage. And he was becoming increasingly confident that it would succeed. And he'd realised that Jacques had left the key in the lock from the absence of the beam of light that usually streaked through the keyhole and across his bed at this time of day.

The way out was via the door, why don't you use it? was how the old Chinese proverb went in its comment on man's tendency to over-complicate life. Well, he would — once he had managed to tease that key from the other side of the door on to the floor and within range of his outstretched fingers.

George was in the process of doing this when there was another loud explosion, just outside the cottage this time. Terrified, he cowered by the door as it ripped a hole in one of the walls. It was the wall through which he had been until recently observing the operations outside. He was more than a little thankful that his preoccupations on the other side of the room had moved him out of range of the immediate impact.

But George did not know what perils awaited him as he edged towards the gaping hole that permitted his exit. He had every desire to find out, but no time in which to do so. The timbers of the roof had caught fire and the room was beginning to fill with smoke.

Once outside, George rolled and rolled himself along the ground in an attempt to extinguish the flames that had started to make a fire of his clothes. He was just coming to his senses, keeping close to the ground, when a voice over the loud hailer addressed him.

'George, stay down,' it ordered in a familiar voice, caring yet edgy with urgency. Christ! George thought. Who was that? That person sounded familiar. But he couldn't think.

His musings were curtailed by a further instruction. This time from someone else, whom he immediately recognised. It was Barbara. She was lying not yards from him, apparently in an attitude of surrender. All she said was his name. But it sounded like an order for his attention. George turned to look at her. For a brief moment, the two of them lay there, their eyes locked in a look of mutual hatred.

Barbara had succeeded in picking up and throwing away the grenade that Jacques had intended for her. In her panic and haste, she had not thought where she was throwing it, as long as it was away. Out of range of herself. But she had not meant it to land by the cottage. The building could have provided her the shelter she needed to continue her hostage-taking. Now her best hope was to take George Gisikis hostage once more and use him to bargain with. For her life this time. As she lay prone in her position of surrender on the ground, she reached carefully, slowly, almost imperceptibly into the inside pocket of her jacket, from where she began to pull out her hand-gun.

From the copse the commandos were advancing now. Among them, Paul Mavros, who, as they got nearer, called out to his old friend, encouraging him. The sound of his voice, which George now recognised, released him momentarily from Barbara's icy glare. But it was only for a moment. And just long enough for her to point the gun in his direction and pull the trigger. It happened so quickly. So fast, in fact, that George was lucky not even to hear his skull split open nor feel any pain as the bullet from Barbara's gun made contact with his head.

CHAPTER NINETEEN

The story preoccupied the press for days. An SAS-assisted rescue mission had gone wrong on the Greek island of Myra. George Gisikis, youngest son of shipping billionaire Costas Gisikis, had been shot by his kidnapper, Barbara Meier, recently released from jail for terrorist activities. It was a tragedy compounded by further tragedy, for the tycoon himself still lay in a coma in an Athens' private hospital.

And then the sister-in-law who had brought up his children was admitted to a private sanatorium, in Switzerland, some said. Mental instability, others said. But the clinic was run along the lines of the Betty Ford in the States, so people made what they would of that.

Not long afterwards, John Gisikis was found knowingly consorting with prostitutes. He'd been discovered in an Athens' back street receiving a blow-job from a hooker at 3.00am. The arresting officer had found a drugstore in his pockets. So that was more trouble.

When it didn't seem like it could get any worse, Maria was caught shoplifting in Kolonaki.

Stelios was alone for once and counting his blessings. He couldn't believe his luck. He'd heard the news first from John, but the conversation was so garbled and labyrinthine. Christ alive! John and his persecution complex. His paranoia was verging on the certifiable. Stelios was convinced he'd started freebasing crack cocaine.

He'd got the full picture from the newspapers the following day. His relief was immeasurable, the vast weight of his problems suddenly lifted from him. He felt more light-hearted than he'd done in months.

Stelios had decided to reward himself with a few days well-earned rest and relaxation on board the Ariana. The winter sun was bright but not hot as he lay on the deck, a cashmere sweater from N Peal in London's Burlington Arcade slung casually around his shoulders. His trousers were his favourite chocolate-brown suede ones from Dolce & Gabbana, his shoes a pair of Patrick Cox's Wannabees in fake snake.

The purser, immaculate in white-and-blue trimmed with gold, came out on deck to see if there were anything sir needed. Why, yes, Stelios said. He was feeling a little chilly, needed something to warm him up. Had the head steward heard of the classic winter warmer that he'd discovered when he'd attended the Breeders' Cup at Belmont, New York? A Horse's Neck. That was what he wanted — three parts bourbon, Rebel Yell, if they had it, otherwise Wild Turkey would do, and two parts ginger liqueur.

He was surprised when the head steward came back to tell him they had the high-proof bourbon in the ship's bar. That would do the trick.

But even with the bourbon inside him and now wearing his cashmere sweater, Stelios still felt incredibly cold. He'd better go into the sun lounge and order breakfast there. Maybe he was sickening for something. Not surprising if he were, he told himself, it had all been such an intolerable strain.

Charles Bradley took one last look at himself in the mirror of the gents before he left his offices near St Paul's to take a cab to Heathrow and the Gisikis Shipping business in New York. Christ! he seemed to have aged ten years in the past few months.

Despite his work as one of the City's top lawyers, earning his living from life's injustices, he nevertheless felt that there was a natural justice to the world. Rules that operated below its surface. In the end, he felt, people tended to get what they deserved. But now, when he considered the fate that had befallen the Gisikis family, that belief, which was as close he'd got to having a religion, began to waver.

Charles studied his reflection long and hard in the square of glass above the washbasins. He could almost see Costas beside him, rinsing his hands and smoothing what was left of his once magnificent head of hair. Costas had had such presence and faith in life. He was an eternal optimist. He would never give in like this to depression and doubt.

'Now, Charles,' he could hear his friend say, 'the clouds may look black and full of foreboding, but remember there is sunshine behind them.'

Well, fine. So much for the homespun philosophy. Sometimes Costas could be so infuriatingly trite. And the fact was that there wasn't much daylight where Costas lay in his isolation ward, struggling in the twilight world between life and death.

But Charles decided nevertheless to take some comfort from the memory of his friend. And the despair at life's injustice that was etched in his face softened a little. He hoped that Costas was right to believe all was for the best in the best of all possible worlds.

Well, perhaps Charles wouldn't go that far. But, though it seemed impossible at that moment, the world might one day turn on a different axis. And the curse that now appeared to afflict the Gisikis family would be revoked.

Paul Mavros accompanied Kimberley and Oliver back to New York on board a US military flight. The media had laid siege to the house in Athens and then the Grande Bretagne when the Press discovered that key members of the family were staying there. They were hounded by them, followed wherever they went, the paparazzi snapping endlessly at the Gisikis grief to add colour to the column inches.

Kimberley, not unnaturally, was emotionally shattered. A state not helped in any way by the media circus in which she found herself the star attraction. She had nothing to say to any of them. There was nothing to add. No one could compensate her for the moment when Paul Mavros came through the door of her suite at the Grande Bretagne without her husband.

He'd told her what had happened. How the

military had been under orders not to shoot to kill because Barbara was a vital witness. So, in that sense, the evil bitch had been protected. She was known to be for hire, so no one doubted that she was under orders, though she always did things her way.

But she'd clearly been out of control and would have proved an unreliable witness. In cold blood, she'd killed her own accomplice, who was known to be her lover. So she'd had no hesitation in shooting a complete stranger at point-blank range. The bitch had blown a hole in George's head.

Paul Mavros' voice tailed off at the vehemence of his words. After a couple of minutes he started to talk again, his throat tight with emotion.

'I asked the troops to leave,' he said, fidgeting for a moment with his watch strap. 'At first they didn't move. Then their commander ordered his men to the shore front and instructed them to face the sea.'

He looked up towards the ceiling and muttered something to himself before returning his attention to Kimberley.

'I looked back to where George had been lying. He'd been moved already. There was only a drying pool of his blood on the earth, that was slowly soaking into it. Soon, no one would even have known he'd lain there.'

Paul pursed his lips and then continued, 'I pointed my gun at Barbara Meier, and all she did was laugh at me, contemptuously. She said that I might as well get it over with. Why didn't I do it for her? Because she'd just find a way of killing herself once she was in jail.

'I've never hit a woman in my life, but she just got to me. I punched her so hard she almost lost consciousness. Then I grabbed her arm and took hold of her hand, holding it in front of her face. I blew it off at the wrist.

'She didn't expect that. It was me who laughed contemptuously then. So I took her other arm and blew that hand off at the wrist too. Right in front of her eyes. She must have been made of something other than flesh because she didn't black out from the pain like you'd expect of anyone else.

'I told her ...' he said, hesitating but with a grim look of satisfaction on his face, as if he were building up the nerve to go on, 'I told her she'd have a hard time killing herself without any hands. Then I moved in on her again.

'It must have been the first time a hard bitch like her ever experienced fear in her life. The woman looked terrified. Before long she was screaming and squealing like a stuck pig, kicking at me frantically to keep me away from her.'

Paul looked at Kimberley questioningly. Should he continue? he asked apologetically. It was something that would give him nightmares for the rest of his life. He'd never forget.

He hung down his head and stared dejectedly at the fists he'd made of his hands. He'd become tense and angry at the memory of it. Oh, yes, how well he remembered. How clearly he recalled how his dearest friend had suffered at the hands of that evil bitch.

But Kimberley wanted to know everything. She'd decide, she told him, if it were too much for her. Would he please continue? In a strange way, she added, it helped her to accept what had happened.

'I can't believe I did it ... any of it,' he said, almost despairingly. 'I haven't stopped asking God to forgive me from that moment to this.'

Tears of frustration and rage came to his eyes. It was obvious to Kimberley that Paul Mavros felt confused and disappointed at his own cruelty. He ran his fingers through his hair nervously as he spoke again.

'I told Barbara I wouldn't let her get away. I trod hard on her leg and heard a bone crack. When she screamed in pain I aimed my gun at her and shot away her foot.'

Kimberley shuddered at this. Then nodded for Paul to continue. This time he looked at the floor as he spoke.

'I let her squirm, beg and plead for mercy for what felt like an eternity. Then I remembered why I was there. I'd show her as much mercy as she had shown George.'

He just shook his head at the very thought of it and said, 'She found some bravado from somewhere. She said I wasn't man enough to kill her. She would tell the world that George was behind his own kidnap. She had it all worked out, the bitch.

'I couldn't let her do that,' Paul said, looking straight into Kimberley's eyes.

'I couldn't let her harm George's good name. I couldn't allow her to cast a shadow over the Gisikis family. I couldn't let her hurt him any more.'

Paul stopped, put his hands in his jacket pockets and walked over to look out of the window at the view of Syntagma Square. He didn't turn round to face Kimberley as he continued.

'She was lying on the ground in a bloody heap, spitting out foul comments about George. He was my childhood friend, for God's sake. I had to shut her up.

'So I hit her hard in the face with the butt of my gun, knocking out a few of her teeth. She couldn't say anything more if she didn't have a mouth through which to speak, I reasoned. I was going crazy. But I knew I had to finish it.

'I took the grenade that she'd surrendered in her arsenal, and I put it next to her. I pulled the pin and walked away.'

The silence that followed was deafening and acute.

'It was wrong, I know,' Paul said quietly, 'God knows I shouldn't have done it. I don't know that I'll ever be able to forgive myself. Or whether God will ever do so for me.'

And he stared wildly from the window as if searching for some reassurance out there, for something, anything, that might help him.

Kimberley sat very still for a long time without replying. Then she walked over to where he stood. This time she saw the square bustling with energy and life. She took his hand and held it tight.

In the street below, the traffic was gridlocked. Drivers leant on their horns and out of their car windows, their faces a mixture of anger and resignation. Pedestrians walked by, glad of their own freedom to move more freely. The late afternoon sun lit the scene.

'Everyone's pain passes eventually. Time will

heal us all,' was all Kimberley could find to say.

They left Greece the following day from the military airport at Actium for the relative peace of New York. Well, that was the idea. The reality was somewhat different.

CHAPTER TWENTY

'*Shipping magnate Costas Gisikis died in Athens today after a long illness. The philanthropic tycoon, known as the Golden Greek, leaves an estate expected to be in the region of £6bn. He is survived by his three children.*'

Described in the Press not only as one of the world's richest men but also as one of its most loved and respected, the announcement of his death brought in sympathetic tributes and messages of consolation to the New York offices of Gisikis Shipping and the Athens' mansion from all over the world.

News reports covered every aspect of Costas' death for the best part of the week until the funeral. He was to be buried on Myra, the island of his birth, with a memorial service at the Greek Orthodox Cathedral in Athens one month later, at which the great and the good who wished to pay their respects would be welcome. His coffin, it was reported, would be made from the pine trees that covered Myra. Already, the wood had been transported to carpenters' workshops in Athens by private jet. On it there was to be a simple brass plaque, which would read: 'COSTAS GEORGIOS GISIKIS.' He was 74 years old when he died. But no one had been at his side when, according to Dr Stelios Gisikis, he'd slipped away quietly during a snowstorm.

Shock and grief were etched into Kimberley's face as she descended the aircraft steps at Ellinikon on her return to Athens for what she hoped would be the last time. Her father-in-law's death had come as no surprise, but its reality was no less distressing for that. Oliver was to join her later but, for now, she was on her own.

She had received support from Charles Bradley, who had spent some weeks with her in New York shortly after her return from Greece at the end of that first year. And, of course, from Paul Mavros, from whom she had heard regularly since the abortive rescue mission on Myra.

But there had been no contact from Helena, John or Maria for over two years, though she knew exactly what they were up to from the reports of them that appeared all the time in the tabloids and *Hello*! magazine. Christ! they really knew how to drag down the family name.

But that didn't concern Kimberley so much. She just wanted to get on with her life. With that in mind, she was staying once more at the Grande Bretagne in Syntagma Square. No one had even bothered to send the chauffeur to collect her from the airport, so she made her way there by cab.

That evening she was to dine with Paul Mavros. Normally, she loved the simple sophistication of Greek food, but for the moment she had no appetite. There was, nevertheless, much to discuss. She would make the effort.

The Gisikis mansion was humming with life and

energy. It was the day before Costas' funeral and Maria had a team of stylists, beauticians and dressers waiting on her hand and foot. She had to look her best. The world's attention would be focused on them tomorrow, and she hadn't got a thing to wear.

The outfit she had ordered from Valentino nearly three years ago especially for the occasion she no longer liked. She had never worn it. So she had asked Paris to fly over its best from the couture houses, and she was now trying to choose between Alexander McQueen at Givenchy or Stella McCartney at Chloe. Both were woefully inappropriate. Even Galliano at Dior was too outrageous for what was, after all, a sober occasion.

Oh, God! it was all too much for her. Until she had decided on her outfit, she couldn't choose her shoes, though there she was already decided on Manolo Blahnik or possibly Jimmy Choo. But then there was her make-up and the colour of her nail varnish, which had to be Chanel, though which shade to choose was so hard to decide. Well, it would just have to match her dress. She started to feel hysterical. Christ! she needed a holiday to cope with it all. How odd, she thought to herself as she took to her room, that now all she desired was almost within reach. She felt breathless at the thought of it.

It was time perhaps, she thought, for another one of those black bombers, the amphetamines she liked so much. The only problem was that she couldn't sleep at night after taking them late in the morning. She'd be up for days at a stretch. So if she wanted to rest, she had to knock herself out with sleepers.

Well, staying up all night wasn't such a bad idea, she reflected. The flight to Rhodes to board the

Ariana to Myra for the funeral was very early the following morning, she might as well stay awake until then. Why on earth had the old man wanted to have himself buried on that God-forsaken island in the middle of the ocean? It was just so inconvenient. And what was there once you got there. Fuck all! she thought.

Then there was her sister-in-law to deal with. But not for much longer. Once this was over there'd be no reason to see her, apart from at the reading of Costas' Will. After that, she could just crawl back to her New Jersey roots and take her witless brat with her.

Oh, well, she had a wonderful time in Europe to look forward to as her reward. She had to spend her inheritance somehow. Even for her that would take some doing. A third of £6bn, give or take a few million, was really rather a lot of money.

The small chapel on the tiny island of Myra was hastily refurbished for Costas' funeral. For all the preparation that went into it, the heavy scent of flowers in the air, the simple beauty of the place, the service itself was a short but moving one. After it, each mourner kissed an icon placed on the coffin before it was buried in the cemetery. At last, the great ship-owner lay at rest beside his beloved Ariana.

A tribute to him later in the day was held on board the yacht moored at anchor nearby. Costas had left instructions for what he wanted. No sobbing or chest-beating, no wake, but a party to celebrate his departure for better things. He requested that his family and friends should let him go with more spirit than sorrow. And he requested that everything the guests would eat and drink at his funeral party should be native to Greece.

So the champagne was from Rhodes, the wines from Santorini and Samos, the wild goat and rice and potatoes, the classic Greek peasant feast. Because that was how he saw himself, unerringly, over the years. He had come from the land. And he would return there.

The Gisikis shipping fleet had grown from half-a-dozen ferry boats to tankers and bulk carriers that dominated the world's shipping lanes. It was said his wealth was so immense that he had once purchased one million ounces of gold, and certainly there were innumerable antiques and works of art as silent witness to his status. In his heart, though, he remained that young man who had herded goats on an island in the Aegean. A Greek boy who grew up rich because he knew how to count.

Helena had known him then. And her return to Myra to say goodbye to him had not been easy for her. She had not been back there since she had left as a young woman to join her sister Ariana and her husband Costas in Athens. All those years ago.

The island was fragrant with the smell of citrus and oregano then. There were deep blue coves for swimming. Lush groves of almond and mandarin trees in which to stroll. Bread was baked in outdoor ovens, and traditional costume was worn. But Helena had hated it all. She'd longed to escape. She felt confined. A prisoner. She yearned for the bright lights of the mainland.

These she had found. But they had blinded her. Now she had no plans but to return to her clinic and learn how to live again.

John and Maria had none of Helena's doubts, nor had they inherited a grain of their father's modesty. This was apparent when they arrived in London at the Bradley & Bennett offices near St Paul's for the reading of the Will.

They thought it an unnecessary formality, given that they had seen the last Will their father had written. They had considered asking Charles to fax them over a copy but decided against it. The lawyer was a stickler for propriety, and this was the way things were done in the legal world. Properly. Besides which, the trip to London kept them in the public eye. The paparazzi would no doubt be out in force.

Maria was still upset about what had happened at Costas' funeral. The Press coverage had concentrated mostly on Kimberley and the question mark that hung over the continued funding of the Homelessness Project now that Costas Gisikis was dead. Would she or would she not stay on as director? Would the charity even be able to stay afloat?

Christ! thought Maria, exasperated, who cared? If she had her way, she'd cut off the money supply to it immediately. And so she was less than best pleased when she found herself neglected by the media and searched in vain for her photo in all reports of the funeral and its aftermath.

Today she had really pushed the boat out in her best, most expensive purchases at the couture shows in Paris. There was the shock value of Versace. Elizabeth Hurley had demonstrated that when she'd hit the headlines in that dress held together by safety pins. Well, if they didn't notice her, it wasn't from lack of trying.

But what was she worried about? Silly me! she

gently chastised herself, suddenly smiling and pleased again with life. Money to the media was like honey to the bee. Once she had her inheritance under her belt, they'd be swarming all over her. She'd be taking legal action to keep them away, for God's sake! Her face would be everywhere. She let out a huge sigh of contentment. But it was a Faustian deal she'd made with herself.

Helena had made a special effort to pull herself together for the occasion and appeared to be back on her old form for the moment. John and Maria could hardly believe the change in their aunt. She had taken up God in a big way. And talked of the temptations of the Devil. The latter were, of course, what kept the twins going. That and their dealer. No, they were one and the same.

Helena had discharged herself on a whim from the Swiss sanatorium, or clinic, as they are called these days. She wasn't sure what she was going to do, but she vaguely thought she might go and work with Mother Teresa's charity in Calcutta. Well, put it this way. She had smart friends in the city she hadn't seen for years, and she would go and stay with them. They had a big house with lots of room and relatives all over India whom she could visit.

If she found time to fit in some good works, then fine. Otherwise she'd just explore the Indian sub-continent and talk about what she'd seen there when she got back, as if she'd developed a liberal outlook and was on the verge of doing something to help out. Present herself as part of the solution instead of what she really was, part of the problem.

Helena's hands were shaking as she sat around the

boardroom table in Charles Bradley's office, waiting for him, as executor of Costas' estate, to read the Will. She had just had a run-in with John. He'd really behaved disgracefully and let the side down. What could he have been thinking of by lashing out at Charles like that? The lawyer was only doing his job. It was a tense time for them all, and important for everyone to behave like adults. Helena overlooked the fact that this was part of John's education she had left out.

John had left the room after his outburst, closely followed by Maria. She'd sort him out. That girl was alarmingly tough. The way she'd put Barbara Meier on to George, like releasing him into a cage of hungry tigers. After all, he was her brother when all was said and done. But Maria had never been one to let sentiment get in the way of her ambition. Underneath it all she was immensely self-centred and single-minded.

Helena was aware of Maria's drug intake, but she felt her niece could handle it. Frankly she had no idea at all of whether or not she could, but she didn't like to think about the possible implications of failure.

When the twins returned to the boardroom five minutes later, it was clear that they'd both topped up the level of chemicals in their bodies. Their mood had altered remarkably from panic to serenity. Now that everyone was present, Charles was about to start the meeting formally. As required by Greek law, Costas had written his Will in his own hand.

I, Costas Georgios Gisikis, wishing to settle my estate after my death and being of sound mind, am proceeding with the present

*handwritten will containing my last wishes
and order as follows:*

Charles stopped at this point. There was nothing like
it to gain a captive audience, he thought. The Gisikis
twins had never listened to anyone else in their lives,
but now they were totally rapt. The tension in the
room was high as he continued with Article 1.

> *As I write this will, at the age of 71, I ask for
> one-third of my estate to be invested in the
> Gisikis Shipping Foundation's Homelessness
> Project. If Kimberley Gisikis wishes to take
> up the position, I should like to appoint her
> President of the Gisikis Shelters Worldwide
> Foundation with a salary commensurate to
> her position.*

Boring, Maria yawned to herself. And so predictable
that her father would put his charitable works first.
Why he suffered from such a guilty conscience and
always wanted to help people who should learn to
help themselves, she'd never know. Why try to build
a better society when you could invest it in high
society? Diamonds are a girl's best friend, after all.

At this point she began to shuffle in her seat and
only stopped when she realised the lawyer was
watching her with displeasure.

God, how it dragged on! Charles Bradley would
remain acting head of the Gisikis Shipping Empire
until his youngest son, George Gisikis, chose to
expand his New York operational base worldwide. If
Charles were to take early retirement, his interim
successor, until George were able to assume control,

would be at Charles' discretion.

Charles then reached the part that had the twins and Helena sitting on the edge of their seats.

> *My assets that remain, bar five per cent, should be split equally among my three children. Of the five per cent, one-fifth shall be placed in trust for Oliver Gisikis, the remaining four-fifths settled immediately upon Helena Kokas, Kimberley Gisikis, Stelios Gisikis and Charles Bradley.*

'Yo, yo, yo!' John yelled, punching his fist into the air above his head in a victory salute. He reached over to take his sister in a flamboyant embrace. Two-thirds of their father's estate was an immense inheritance. Why should they sit there wasting any more valuable time? They were rich and powerful now, they didn't need to answer to anyone, least of all the lawyer. It was Maria who spoke first, interrupting Charles in mid-flow.

'Well, Charles, it looks like you still have a job thanks to Papa. John and I were actually going to sack you,' she went on with her usual degree of tact, 'but it looks like we can't. Just make sure you work hard to keep the money rolling in. I think I'll go now. I need some peace and quiet to consider which of the homes and jewellery I want to keep.'

Maria picked up her little Gucci handbag and prepared to leave. She was really not prepared at all for what happened next.

'Sit down, Maria!' Charles ordered her from across the room. 'I haven't finished yet.'

The unaccustomed ferocity of his tone stopped Maria in her tracks. But she pretended not to be phased by it.

'All right, Charles, but make it quick. I'm a busy woman. Places to go, people to see, deals to make.' With this last comment she winked energetically at her twin.

'There is an Addendum to the Will,' the lawyer announced ominously, observing the effect of his words on his clients, for once with some ill-disguised satisfaction.

'Stop fucking about, Charles!' John snapped, suddenly restored to his aggressive ill humour. 'Just tell us what we've got so I can get the hell out of here!'

'Very well, if that's how you want to play it,' the lawyer snapped back, 'I'll tell you precisely what you've got. Nothing! Or as good as! Is that the kind of language you understand?'

The silence that immediately descended on the room was followed almost at once by an hysterical appeal by Maria.

'You can't be serious! For Christ's sake explain yourself! What do you mean?'

'What I mean is precisely that.'

Once more, he began to read directly from Costas' script, on a fresh scroll of paper that he had just extracted from a buff-coloured folder in front of him.

Should I survive past my 74th birthday, the terms of my Will change. The five per cent of the estate that I assign to Oliver Gisikis, Kimberley Gisikis, Stelios Gisikis, Helena Kokas and Charles Bradley in equal measure remains. The share for the Homelessness Foundation also. Charles Bradley's arrangements as head of Gisikis Shipping too. The rest is invalid and revised as follows:

Unless Maria and John Gisikis, my two eldest children, are on the payroll as full-time employees of Gisikis Shipping or any of its subsidiaries or charitable foundations by the time of my 74th birthday, they shall not be entitled to profit from any of its activities.
I leave them only the 500 acres of Myra, the island on which I was born. They inherit it under the condition that it can never be sold, developed, or given away for unspecified profit. They can only benefit from its natural resources that require the farming of its lands and the fishing of its waters.
Should they refuse to accept the gift, Myra reverts as an asset to my total estate and will be redistributed accordingly.

Costas had been 74 when he died. The long and the short of it was that George had got everything. Which meant, as they saw it, Kimberley and Oliver stood to inherit the bulk of the £6bn estate.

'Was that fast enough for you, Maria?' Charles asked, leaning across the table to where she sat, for once lost for words.

'You will be hearing from us, Charles,' John said eventually.

'Oh, I don't think so, John,' Charles replied. 'All bequests will be declared null and void should anyone see fit to contest the Will. I have been urged, as executor, to fight any changes through all legal means.

'Believe me, John,' he added, 'we have the resources to use the best lawyers in the business. So I suggest you shouldn't waste your money on expensive law suits. Before it gets to that, you'll only be advised that your father has done everything legally possible to ensure that his Will can't be overturned. Why don't you gracefully accept that fact and be grateful for what you've got?'

John said nothing in reply. Shaking with rage, he gathered up the few personal effects he had on the table in front of him and turned instead to his twin, announcing that it was time to go.

Maria just glared at him, beside herself. Then, unexpectedly, she stood up and put on her fur coat over her flimsy ruby-red shift dress. She lifted her cup of barely-drunk coffee and flung it across the room at Charles Bradley. Her fur flying behind her, she ran towards the door, stumbling on the thin pivot of her high stilletos as she did so. Her parting gesture was to spit in the face of her sister-in-law as she passed.

For her, it was as dignified an exit as anybody could have hoped for.

When the twins had left, Helena wasn't far behind them. She could barely believe how her life had changed in the space of half-an-hour. The effect of the sedatives she'd taken were making her feel drowsy, and she was unsteady on her feet as she got up to leave.

But she was clear enough in her mind to know that greed had got no one anywhere. Paying UK inheritance tax was nothing in comparison to what John and Maria had lost. Helena touched her earrings. Diamonds. Yes, sometimes love was an eight-letter word. She'd get something for them, and certainly over the years she had been supported by Costas she had established a fine collection of jewels.

Between them and her inheritance she would be able to scrape by. She had little choice really. No man would look twice at her now. She had lost the allure of youth and had insufficient wealth to redress the balance to make her any sort of a catch. She'd just have to survive as best she could.

The twins were in no position to help her. Not that they would ever have done so. She had devoted her life to them. She had lived and breathed for them. But she had reared a couple of monsters, who'd stepped beyond what even she considered acceptable human behaviour. They were her cross to bear. And now they'd gone she had no one. Though that was in truth how it had always been for her.

Kimberley walked over to Charles and hugged him. She was in a state of shock. Not because of Maria's behaviour; she'd sort of expected something like that from her. No, it was her astonishment at the news of her inheritance. She was now an extremely rich woman.

'You deserve it, my dear,' Charles said, smiling at her benevolently.

'And so do you, Charles,' Kimberley beamed back at him, delighted for him by the considerable boost to his personal fortune.

'Possibly I do,' Charles replied, 'but I won't be keeping the money. I'm already rich in my own right. I have no immediate family to inherit. So I have no real use for the money Costas has left me. No, no,' he stopped her as she began to protest, 'it's true. In any case, you need to know this. These are not just the ramblings of an eccentric old man. I shall be donating my share of the Gisikis estate to your Homelessness Project. I insist.'

Kimberley was obviously moved by his words and his generosity and began to thank him. But once more he stopped her.

'Costas was my friend. That was what mattered to me most. All I shall keep of his is a personal letter he once wrote me, and a small gift he left me that I shall treasure for ever. To me, these are the things that money can't buy. They are also those that I value the most.'

With that, he turned away from Kimberley, too overcome by emotion to face her. He knew full well that she understood what he was saying. Some things in life were beyond price. And no amount of money could bring them back.

Outside the offices of Bradley & Bennett, John and Maria stood looking around for the white stretch limo that had chauffeured them to the City from Hampstead. But it was nowhere in sight. All too present were the paparazzi who had greeted their arrival. Now they felt like vultures at the feast, though they tried their best to smile through gritted teeth.

'Damn!' John said, irritated. 'We'll have to get a cab. And fast. I can't stand this much longer.'

Fortunately, a black taxi turned up on cue with its yellow 'For Hire' sign illuminated. They got in and asked to be taken to Hampstead. The driver set off west, heading for Fleet Street and the Strand. It was just as they reached the Strand's west end, near Trafalgar Square, that John noticed the sloping glass front of Coutts bank in the centre of an old piece of Nash architecture.

Hell! He didn't have any money to pay for the damn taxi. And he could be almost certain that Maria wasn't carrying any. Like the royalty she thought she was, she never did. Her Gucci purse would contain her cocaine stash and her Chanel lipstick — and little else.

'Pull over, please,' John said to the driver, yanking back the glass partition. 'I just want to get some cash from the machine over there.'

Maria was lost in a world of her own and didn't appear to notice that the cab had stopped, never mind the fact that John had got out and crossed the road. She did a few moments later, though, when he reappeared and dragged her from it, apologising to the cabbie. 'The bastards have cut off my money supply. I can't get any money out of my account. They've frozen it.'

Maria, at first disbelieving, surprised John by producing her own card from her tiny imitation crocodile bag. 'Refer to Bank' was all she got. And so they found themselves marooned.

As they walked back along the Strand in the direction of Aldwych, in search of public transport, it was no comfort at all to see Kimberley and Charles swing into the extraordinary forecourt of the Savoy, where its sword-bearing chrome warrior stood guard over the awning. Ensconced in the Rolls, no doubt they were on their way to celebrate with cocktails in the American bar.

When they finally got back to Hampstead, there was no welcome for them there. But when John asked, politely for once, if he could use the telephone, they were allowed in to make the one call he requested.

John had it in his mind to call Stelios. When he got through to him at the hospital, he quickly realised he'd get no change out of him. Nothing at all from the £3m he'd received from them as his pay-off.

EPILOGUE

'Shall I wait?' Victor Aspinall asked Kimberley as she stepped from the comfort of the leather-trimmed interior of the Gisikis Rolls-Royce. He'd pulled up round the corner from the busy Marylebone Road in Harley Street, just outside the London Clinic, one of the best-known private hospitals in the city.

'No, thank you, Victor,' Kimberley answered. 'As usual, I'll be staying for some time. Go home and rest up. I'll call you at the house when I'm ready to come back.'

Victor touched the peak of his cap in a gesture of respect as he returned to the car for the drive back to Hampstead. He enjoyed the young American woman. She was always courteous and appreciative. A distraction from his loss. He missed his former employer, even after all this time. Costas had treated him well, and his death had affected him badly.

Inside the Clinic, the receptionist greeted Kimberley by name. She made her way over to the lift and pressed the button for the top floor. Once there, she was received by an armed guard. But she was used to their presence so it held no surprise for her to be greeted by the barrel of a gun.

In fact, it was a source of comfort to her these days. Ever since George's kidnap, they had employed the services of two of the most highly-trained bodyguards, ex-SAS, who stayed at the hospital day and night. No one had claimed responsibility for the hostage-taking so it was assumed that the Gisikis family might still be on a terrorist hit-list somewhere. The guard would continue until it was established that Barbara Meier had been working alone, with only her lover as her accomplice.

Once at his bedside, Kimberley smiled warmly at George's nurse when she commented, 'Something seems different about him today. I can't see any marked improvement on any of the scanners, but it's just a feeling I have. What do you think? Can you see it, too?'

Kimberley leant over her husband's sleeping form to kiss him gently on his cheek. She had been praying for this. But as she watched him, she could not, in all honesty, see any visible change in his condition.

'He looks just the way I remember him when he was well,' she replied at last, her face tender with emotion, her eyes close to tears. 'So handsome and fine. Just like the man I married, aren't you, honey?'

She talked on and on to her husband in this way for some time. Holding his hand, running her fingers lightly through his hair. From time to time she massaged his arms, his legs, his feet. Talking to him constantly. The doctors had said it might help.

No one, in all honesty, knew what George could or could not hear since he had failed to come round after the major surgery required to mend the damage inflicted upon him by Barbara Meier's hand-gun. The bullet had not penetrated George's brain, merely skimmed its surface. But that was bad enough, and the neuro-surgeons had no real idea of how much harm had been done until George recovered consciousness.

Specialists were certain that he had an excellent chance of making a full recovery, but they wouldn't know for certain until he woke. For this, Kimberley had been hoping and praying ever since.

She had been horrified at her initial sight of her husband when his head had been stabilised in a metal grille, like something out of a horror movie. But this protective device had recently been removed, along with the endless drip-feed tubes that decorated him like a macabre Christmas tree.

The horrendous damage inflicted during the kidnap to his entire body, especially his face, had healed so well that he no longer showed any signs of the terrible wounds he'd suffered on Myra. Kimberley took it in turn with the nurses to clean and shave her husband every day. As she did so today, she began to think that the nurse was right. Maybe he did look better. Something was different. Perhaps it was his colour or possibly that his hair had started to grow back.

Every day, Kimberley sat and read one of his favourite books to him for half-an-hour or so — an Iain Banks or Dick Francis, sometimes Roald Dhal or Gerald Durrell. He'd also liked the 1950s American comedy shows like Lucille Ball in *I Love Lucy*. *Bewitched* was really his favourite. And so she found them for him on video. Kimberley felt she knew the scripts off by heart now. She'd sit next to George mouthing the lines along with the actors.

After a TV session, Kimberley would look over at

him expectantly. But he never woke up. She had to face it. The same was true today. It was no different from any other day. Who was she trying to kid? George was never going to recover consciousness. Kimberley's eyes glazed over with the sadness of defeat.

She slipped her hand into George's and sat there for a long time, his fingers limp in her palm. She sat there feeling no reciprocal squeeze of encouragement, like the one he used to give her when they held hands in the cinema and the film turned scary. Like in *Silence of the Lambs* or *Reservoir Dogs*.

Then, apparently from nowhere, Kimberley began to feel very angry. It came over her all of a sudden. The fact that he was not there to share her life any more. That she had no one to confide in or laugh or dance with. And she had Oliver to consider. Their son. He was doing his final years of growing up now without a father. She didn't want that.

And before she knew it, she was taking her anger out on George. All the tension and strain, the anguish and grief of the past months came pouring out in a powerful and unstoppable torrent of rage. A monsoon flood of emotion after an eternal dry season. She'd lived in the Tropics as a child and, when the rains came, she liked to run outside naked and race round and round the garden in the rain. Round and round the garden, like a teddy bear, one step, two step and tickly under there.

She picked up George's hand again and began to play that kid's game with his hand. She did it once, twice, three times. Each time more menacing than the last. She was not a child any longer. This was not a game. When she tickled him it was more pain than pleasure. That eternally fine line.

She built up slowly into her crescendo of rage. She was tired of being the dutiful wife who turns up each day at the hospital, hoping beyond hope that he would wake up like Sleeping Beauty or Rip Van Winkle. Kids' stories again. Why did she keep on coming back to them? Well, maybe, just maybe, she didn't want to be adult all the time. Perhaps sometimes she wanted her husband back to help her out. Not an unreasonable request.

In sickness and in health. Those damn marriage vows! What the fuck did they know about any of this endless waiting for the sickness to end and the health to return? Nothing. Nothing at all.

Kimberley was surprised to hear someone shouting, yelling even. Not something that happened very often in a hospital. Surprising, really, because they were places where people came when they were in pain. But the pain was always contained there. In the end, the pain either overcame them and they died from it, or they picked themselves up out of their goddamn beds and walked. Well, yes, she was looking for a miracle. That's what she damn well wanted!

'Wake up! Fucking wake up, will you? I'm tired, worn out by this madness, and all you do is damn well sleep. Wake up! I can't take this any more!'

Kimberley realised it was her who was shouting. Now shaking George. Trying to make him wake up.

'Please, please, please,' she heard herself pleading. 'Please, I can't stand this much longer. Wake up, damn it! Just wake up!'

Now the nurses had appeared in the doorway and moved over to the bed to restrain her. But their presence instantly brought her down to earth, and she stopped. She stopped and took up her post at George's bedside once more, quietly holding his hand as if nothing had happened.

But something had happened. Undeniably, something had changed. Kimberley's humiliation at her outburst turned slowly to shock and disbelief and then, ever more curiously, to a cautious happiness. Through the blur of the tears that poured silently down her face, Kimberley Gisikis looked closely at her husband. Because as she had sat there in the calm after her storm, she felt the unmistakable squeeze of her hand by George's fingers.